Nancy Eckenbeck

FRECKLES COMES HOME

FRECKLES COMES HOME

BY

JEANNETTE STRATTON-PORTER

GROSSET & DUNLAP
PUBLISHERS NEW YORK

By arrangement with Doubleday, Doran & Co., Inc.

TO

HARRY PAYNE BURTON,

WHO SUGGESTED WRITING IT,
THIS BOOK IS DEDICATED
WITH AFFECTION AND
ADMIRATION.

THE CHARACTERS

LORD TERENCE MAXWELL O'MORE, "*Freckles*," *a home-sick boy in a foreign land.*

THE SWAMP ANGEL, *the girl of his dreams in far-away America.*

MISS KATHLEEN STRATHERN, *who loves him too.*

BARLOW, *his faithful valet.*

LORD AND LADY O'MORE, *with whom he lives.*

THE MAN OF AFFAIRS, *the Swamp Angel's father.*

THE BIRD WOMAN, *with whom he falls in love.*

JAMES ROSS MCLEAN, *who leases the Swamp.*

RICHARD SUMMERFIELD, *who loves the Angel too.*

FRED MASON, *bookkeeper at the bank.*

BILL DILLON, TOM RYDER, AND BUD JORDAN, *his friends.*

MR. AND MRS DUNCAN, *who live on the edge of the Limberlost.*

AND RAGS, *of whom there is only one in the world!*

FRECKLES COMES HOME

CHAPTER I

Wherein a Second Feather Falls, and a Soul Is Awakened

"COME along, Rags, let's go for a walk through the broad and beautiful estates of my respected and congenial Uncle Maxwell."

Rags, being only a dog, and a common cur at that, missed the sarcastic note in his master's voice. He opened one eye and lifted an inquiring ear.

"Now don't high-hat me at this late date—you and I are the only two commoners around here, don't forget that, old man—so, shake a leg!"

His Lordship, Terence Maxwell O'More, of Dunderry House, County Clare, Ireland, watched Rags rise lazily, yawn, and stretch himself. Rags was a careless breed of dog, built after the general plan of an airedale, but with variations. His long shaggy hair, done in different shades of brown, was inclined to be curly; his whiskers, nothing short of bristles, were sparse and unevenly divided, and his ears stood at a sort of half-cocked angle, one higher than the other, so that the two sides of his face did not look as if they were mates. His especial distinguishing feature, however, was his tail. Long, heavy, and unwieldy as it was, it would not have been so formidable had it been allowed to remain in repose, or even had it been modestly wagged, as most self-respecting dogs manipulate their tails. But Rags' tail was peculiar to himself, as was most of his physical anatomy, and he insisted upon swishing it around violently in a perfect circle, upon the slightest provocation. There were times when dozens of such rapidly described circles became alarming, and if said appendage was wet and muddy, it became distinctly annoying. But even in its cleanest and most perfectly brushed condition, if any innocent individual unsuspectingly came within the bounds of this swiftly rotating object —he felt it.

Rags paddled about flat-footedly, carrying his sixty pounds with all the lumbering grace of a huge elephant; yet, like the elephant, when he did run, it was amazing the speed he made. He had a marvellous disposition; otherwise, he could not have accepted so amiably all the insults his looks and actions occasioned. His one redeeming feature was his eyes. When he looked at you with those large, appealing brown orbs, as if apologizing for something for which he was not responsible, it was just as impossible to keep from feeling sorry for him as it was to keep from laughing at him. All things considered, a more ungraceful, unbeautiful creature it would be difficult to imagine.

Watching him, Terence's thoughts strayed back to the time several years before, when he had asked his Uncle Maxwell for a dog.

"Quite all right," he had answered brusquely. "A great idea—I'll have some kennels built and get several thoroughbred dogs—the grooms can take care of them —might be interesting to have around."

But that was just what the lonely boy did not want. He wanted just one dog all his own; to care for himself; to be his pal; to love as only a boy can love a dog. He did not want kennels filled with perfectly trained and immaculately kept ornaments, to look at through wires, or over the tops of runways. However, this was always the difficulty with Uncle Maxwell. Nothing could be done simply or unostentatiously; everything must be done faultlessly, elaborately, and according to his own ideas, or not at all. As a result, the atmosphere of the entire estate was artificial; nothing looked natural; and when things are not natural they are not artistic, not to mention comfortable.

So the hungry heart of the boy cried out in protest, although he merely said: "Oh, that's too much trouble, Uncle Maxwell. Never mind—some other time will do."

And Uncle Maxwell never did understand the boy's sudden change of mind. Not even a few weeks later when Terence came into the house carrying a miserable, mud-caked, sore-eyed pup, picked from a gutter in the city. Aunt Ellen had shrieked in disgust, and ordered him to take it out of the house at once. Uncle Maxwell, furious himself, had tried to discourage the boy.

"Do not alarm yourself, Ellen. Undoubtedly the creature belongs to someone, and Terence will have to return him."

Terence smiled.

"No, I wouldn't say he belonged to anyone—he certainly doesn't look the part of a well-kept, pampered pet."

"I am afraid for once Terence is right. If looks are any criterion, the creature has had no attention for weeks." And Aunt Ellen left the room.

"Well, he's going to get a lot of attention now,

aren't you, pup?" Terence called out to his valet. "Barlow—Barlow——"

"Yes, sir."

"Barlow, I've brought home a trifle in the way of a dog. I'm afraid he needs a bit of washing."

Even Barlow was somewhat shocked at the filthy, wriggling mass. But he saw the expressions on the faces of Lord and Lady O'More. So that was it—the boy wanted the dog and they were objecting. Well, he was on the boy's side, every time.

"I will bathe him, sir. He has nice eyes, sir."

"Nice eyes!" snorted Uncle Maxwell. "But that isn't all he has!"

"Fortunately, it isn't."

"What is his name, sir?"

"Name? I hadn't thought of that—I don't suppose he has one. I think I'll call him Rags—seems appropriate."

"Rags!" exploded Uncle Maxwell. "Rags! Why not *Mop*—it would be just as suitable."

"And equally as aristocratic—but I think I'll stick to Rags. Let's take him to the stables to remove the first layer, Barlow." And he added, to his uncle's departing back, "I'll endeavour to see that Rags does not shock the delicate sensibilities of Lady Bird, and the other thoroughbred mares."

Barlow's masklike face cracked into a grin as Uncle Maxwell banged the door behind him.

After much soaking, scrubbing, and brushing, there emerged from the débris a ridiculous ball of coarse curling hair, which jumped and kicked and licked them indiscriminately with all the ardour of a grateful puppy heart.

"He's *ours*, Barlow, and he's going to stay with us all the time. No one can take him away from us," exulted Terence.

Barlow might have said that he did not think anyone would *want* to take him away, but being a well-trained servant, and being very fond of his young master, he only said: "Yes, sir, I'm very pleased, sir."

Then the boy saw the older man bringing a basket and blankets for a bed.

"Rags is going to sleep beside my bed, Barlow."

But, as a matter of fact, that was just an excuse to get the pup into his room at night, for when Barlow had put up the windows, turned out the lights, and shut the door, a long, lean arm would reach over the edge of the bed, and five slender, sensitive fingers would grasp a bunch of hair: there would be a struggle and a scramble: Rags and Terence would go to sleep, their heads on the same pillow, not a foot apart.

Uncle Maxwell had stormed and stamped in vain. He said the "common cur was a disgrace," and that he "was ashamed to have it seen around with any member of his family," and that he "could not see why Terence wanted him."

"I'm sorry you don't like him, Uncle Maxwell, but that's just too bad. One reason I want him is because he is the only living thing around here that makes me laugh."

So Rags stayed. Now he was a full-grown dog, and curiously enough, his beauty had not improved with age. He was over-fed and consequently too fat; as his legs grew longer, his feet grew larger; he looked more and more ungainly. But he had a loyal heart, and was a faithful and devoted pal, and that was all that counted with Terence.

Now the two took the little side path which led to the lower end of the gardens. Rags immediately began his favourite sport, chasing bees.

"Rags, I wish you'd stop that. Bees are the only things Uncle Maxwell hasn't chased out of this garden —I guess that's because they can sting!"

Rags paid no attention. He lunged and leaped at every bee he saw, and, strangely, the bees were afraid of him. He made their honey-gathering extremely unpleasant, sometimes even dangerous, for he had been known to kill bees, and he never had been stung.

At the end of the grounds they came upon Barlow, pacing slowly back and forth, reading a book. When he saw his master, he closed the book and started toward the house.

"Don't go, Barlow."

Terence sat down stiffly on a cold, uncomfortable marble bench. Preferably, he would have stretched himself on the grass, under a tree, but there was no grass—only gravel, and walks laid out with geometrical precision, bordered with stones.

"What are you reading, Barlow?"

"A—a love story, sir." Barlow blushed and looked apologetic.

"Well, if one found love anywhere around here, it would have to be in a book."

Terence gazed resentfully at the house: gray walls, small windows, towers, and cupolas—all a part of a design for effect, not for cheerfulness or homelikeness. If you formed this opinion from the exterior, the interior gave you no cause to alter your decision. Huge, high-ceilinged rooms, with dull, drab draperies and upholstering: no colour—no life—no music—no laughter—no song. Nothing to break the everlasting silence but the footfalls of Lord and Lady O'More, Terence and the servants. Even Rags had to be trained not to bark.

True, they entertained their friends in a formal, old-fashioned way. Only rarely were younger people asked for dancing and supper afterward: the friends of Lord and Lady O'More had nothing in common with their young nephew.

"Barlow, I'm very lonely here. As long as I was studying it wasn't so bad, although tutoring is no way to educate a boy. Now that my education is finished so far as school books and tutors are concerned, I'm afraid I cannot stand the pressure here much longer."

"It is lonely, sir."

"I'm fast becoming the world's worst grouch."

"I would not say that, sir."

"I know you wouldn't, but I would, and it's the truth. I never see my uncle and aunt excepting at meals, and then all Aunt Ellen and I do is listen to Uncle Maxwell storm, either at us, or someone else. It's a great life if you don't weaken, but I tell you now, I'm weakening."

"I'm sorry, sir, I've tried——"

"It's not your fault—you've always been great. If I couldn't talk to you, there would be only Rags—poor fellow—he endures a lot of my sour moods now without talking back!"

Rags, hearing his name, came up and laid his head on Terence's knee.

"Thank you, sir. I enjoy serving you, if I may say so, sir."

"You can say anything you like to me, even though

I know Uncle Maxwell does not approve of us talking together."

"Very well, sir. Is there no one among the young gentlemen of the countryside you like, sir?"

"Oh, they're all good enough fellows in their way, I guess. But they are all so idle, so lazy, so damnably useless. They have nothing to do, and all the time in the world to do it. The worst of it is, they have no ambition—they just drift. A job would scare them to death. I can't understand being so utterly satisfied with nothing."

"They think they have a great deal, sir."

"Sure they do—same thing that's been hammered into me: wealth, social position, education, and all that rot. Education is all right, if it's used for a foundation on which to build. If it's to be used only as a background for social stunts, then it's more or less a total loss so far as real purpose is concerned. Why, Barlow, there's nothing genuine about those chaps; even their laughter has no real mirth in it; they must smile to show their teeth!"

"Terence—oh, Terence——"

"That's Lady O'More. I will be going, sir."

"All right, Barlow. You might tell Her Ladyship I'm down here; I think I won't come in for a while."

Very soon he saw Aunt Ellen coming down the walk. She was a gentle, sweet soul, quiet and refined, with slender, quick hands and troubled eyes. "The only sort of woman that could live with Uncle Maxwell," thought Terence, as he watched her stepping daintily, and holding her heavy black skirt away from the shrubbery. She always wore black, Uncle Maxwell insisted upon it, but she did relieve the sombreness of it a little by creamy lace at her wrists and throat. Her white hair was parted in the middle and drawn back over her ears to a simple knot on the back of her neck. But the severity of it was lessened by a few stray curls which crept out and lay along her forehead and cheeks, as if in defiance of Uncle Maxwell's request that she do her hair "in a plain and dignified manner, as befits a woman of your age and position." Although she pretended to ignore them, Terence knew that she lived in constant terror of Uncle Maxwell's outbursts. Not that he ever struck her; he never forgot himself to that extent; but his tongue lashed everything and everybody. No one was ever right but him, and having his way did not make him happy. As Aunt Ellen had meekly remarked to him once, "I never did see why you always insist on your own way, Maxwell; you never seem to enjoy it when you get it." The few retorts of that kind she had made to him had stopped him for the moment, but they had had no permanent effect. So his ravings continued to insult her inborn gentility, and after each tirade she was forced to admit to herself that she was ashamed of him, and that she had lost considerable of her respect for him. Terence saw it, and felt sorry for her; he was fast losing his own respect for Uncle Maxwell. "She is just the kind," mused Terence, "who would be happy sitting on the grass under a tree, romping with a bunch of noisy grandchildren." But there were no grandchildren. Her only child, a son, had been killed in an accident. The only ornament Aunt Ellen ever wore was a miniature of him, pinned in the lace at her throat. "It's a darn shame, too," Terence had said to Barlow. "A few modern kids would bend that stiff backbone of Uncle Maxwell's in a hurry."

"Good-afternoon, my dear."

Terence rose and went to meet her.

"Good-afternoon, Aunt Ellen. Did you want me? I heard you calling and I should have come to you—I apologize—but it's so nice out here."

"That's quite all right, dear. I'm sure it is more pleasant out here than in the house. I came to tell you that I am going to try something new to-day; I am going to serve tea outside—beside the pool where the benches are."

"That's a great idea. Does Uncle Maxwell approve?"

"He—he has not been informed as yet. When tea is announced, it is just going to *be* in the garden."

Terence laughed.

"Better be careful, jumping over the traces like that!"

"What do you mean?"

"That's just another American expression—means jumping out of a rut. Traces are part of a horse's harness; if he jumped over them he would get tangled up in the harness and get himself into trouble."

Aunt Ellen smiled.

"Your expressions are so quaint."

It was Terence's turn to smile—he was thinking of a considerable number that were not so "quaint."

"Anyway, the change will do you both good. You don't get out in the sunshine enough. Wouldn't you like to get all tanned, and have a few freckles on your nose?"

"I think I might like it, but Maxwell——"

"Oh, bother Uncle Maxwell! Would you come riding with me some day?"

"I have not ridden since I was a girl, but I am sure

I would like it. I would need a habit. I—I will think about it."

"Well, do your own thinking. Don't let anyone do it for you."

"Thank you for asking me, dear. I'll expect you at tea time." Aunt Ellen started back to the house.

"What a sport she would be, if she had a chance! That might be a good job for me."

Terence walked back to the marble bench.

"Gee!" he muttered. "How I'd love to park the body on my old moss-covered log back in the Limberlost. I'd even accept with thanks a few mosquito bites for atmosphere!"

That set him thinking. He looked around the gardens, but their formality only irritated him. He let his gaze wander higher. The sun was playing hide-and-seek with a few stray clouds. His hand reached for Rags' head.

"Rags, old man, once, a long time ago, a feather fell at my feet from out of nowhere. It was a long, shining black feather from a bird flying out of sight among the clouds. It made me think, and it brought wonderful things into my life: joy—sorrow—pain—laughter—ambition—suffering—and—and love."

As Terence talked he closed his eyes, and before him swept visions of a far-away country—America. He saw acres and acres of his loved Limberlost Swamp, thousands of miles away—the trails he had blazed through it, the wild things that were his friends, the sounds and silences that taught lessons never to be forgotten. He saw the glory of it in the fall when it was ablaze with autumn colouring; when the frosts turned the brilliant greens of the foliage into gaudy masses of rich reds, yellows, and browns, and gave the last rosy touch to the red haws; when the nuts fell rattling through the branches to the ground, only to be snatched greedily by the provident squirrels, and hidden away in a hollow tree with their winter supply of food.

He saw the white radiance of it in winter, when everything was sparkling with snow; when he had to carry food to his bird friends, and crack the ice in the puddles so that they could drink. He could hear the snow creaking under his feet, and feel its feathery fluffiness as it closed over them when he waded through the drifts.

He saw the miracle of spring, when everything grew alive and beautiful under the warm coaxing of the sun and gentle rains; when the air was full of perfume from the bursting buds of dogwood and red bud and a hundred varieties of tiny flowers with which Mother Nature bedecks her most secret places; when tiny birds burst from their shells, cried for food, and sat uncertainly on the edges of their nests.

He saw it in summer, the gracious fulfillment of all the promises of spring; the more deeply coloured full-blown blossoms with gorgeously tinted butterflies drinking of their sweets; the wavering birdlings, grown strong, singing and chirping about their business of living; the air full of all the music of wild life.

Then through the mists and haze of the Swamp a face took shape—the face of an Angel; a face with all the rosy lights of dawn, seeing life through eyes of the sky's blue, and framed by hair not less golden than God's own sunshine. He thought of the day, years before, when he had walked down one of the paths through the Swamp; of the feather that fell at his feet;

of examining it, and determining to learn about the bird that dropped it, and how it lived. He would get books and study—and then—the bushes parted, and the face of the Angel looked through! How real she seemed! How he suffered when he opened his eyes and found she was only a dream!

As he opened his eyes now they fastened on a speck in the sky. A bird, he thought, but he seemed unable to take his eyes off it. No, it was not steady enough for a bird—it was something falling! Fascinated, he watched it, and Rags whined as the grasp on his head tightened.

"Rags," he whispered, "it *is*—it's another feather." Slowly it continued its wavering flight, Terence's eager eyes never leaving it. And then it fell, as that other feather years ago had fallen—at his feet. Terence reached for it. There was not much superstition left in his Irish soul, but there *was* a little.

"What does it mean, boy?" he asked Rags. "It must have been meant for me; it came right to me. That other feather set me thinking and made me study and learn things. I wonder if this one was meant to set me thinking now."

Terence examined it closely. It was not so long, or so large, or so black as that other feather; but it was a feather from out of nowhere—and it had fallen at his feet.

Terence stood up. He was trembling slightly.

"Let's go, Rags. Things don't happen if you just sit still and wait for them. I've got to let off some steam, so I think I'll go forth in search of adventure."

He carried the feather carefully, and when he reached his suite on the second floor, he took the feather to his desk and stuck it in the little jar of shot that held his pens, just beside that other feather that had fallen at his feet six years before. He looked at them silently for a few minutes. One had opened secret places for him to explore; the study it had inspired revealed to the lonely boy delights he had never dreamed existed. But had he made the most of them? What had he done with his life? He frowned. Was this last feather, from the infinite spaces above, a reproach? Was it a reminder that he had not lived up to the best that was in him? Was he a failure, and were his friends disappointed in him? Terence wondered.

"Barlow, will you order the horses while I change?"

"Excuse me, sir, but I laid out your suit for tea——"

"We will cut out the tea for to-day and see what happens. I feel like a ride before dinner."

He took a last long look at the feathers as he went out the door. "I'll try to figure out what you mean," he whispered.

CHAPTER II

Wherein the Homely Hero Rescues a Beautiful Lady

TERENCE was still thoughtful as he swung himself into his saddle and started down toward the road, Barlow and Rags following; a sort of bodyguard, those two. As they reached the end of the drive Terence called to Rags: "You'd better go back, old man. I feel like a good brisk pace to-day, and that's not your favourite speed." But Rags followed.

"Come on, Lady Bird, pick 'em up! Let's try a little canter!"

They rode in silence for a time, and then Terrence saw Rags struggling to catch them; so he pulled up and waited.

"Barlow, why do they build these high walls along the roads? One can't see the country—they shut off the breeze, too," and Terence choked on a mouthful of dust as he looked ruefully at the walls, with the row of little daisies blooming valiantly on top.

"I couldn't say, sir."

Terence rode over, and standing in his stirrups, plucked a tiny blossom and stuck it in his coat.

"Brave little things! It must require a lot of earnest effort to grow and bloom in such an unfavourable spot."

Terence frowned.

"I like to ride where I can look across the country.

I like to see trees, birds, lakes, rivers, flowers, and all the interesting things that are a part of any landscape."

"Yes, sir, that would be more pleasant, sir."

"I don't wish Ireland any bad luck, but I don't care how soon these walls tumble in a heap."

Rags caught up with them, and they walked their horses to the end of the wall.

"This country depresses me, Barlow. It looks old and dried up; it needs new blood in its veins."

"Yes, sir."

He patted Lady Bird's neck affectionately. "You're terribly restless to-day, old girl. What's the matter? Guess you must feel in the same mood I do. . . . The farms are so small; the men work so hard, with so few tools and machines; they know so little of modern methods of farming, and have no conveniences in their houses for their wives and families."

"Quite so, sir."

"They should have——" He paused. Down the road ahead of them they saw a heavy cloud of dust. Barlow shaded his eyes with one hand and squinted, trying to penetrate the thick masses of dust rolling steadily toward them. It was only a few seconds until they could hear the hoofs of a horse, beating the road in a thunderous gallop.

"A horse is running away, sir!"

"Yes," answered Terence laconically. "I suspected as much."

"If you will just pull up at one side, sir, I will stop it."

That was the last straw.

"I'll do nothing of the kind. I'll stop it myself. Damn this idea everyone has that I can't do anything! Stay here, and keep out of my way."

As the runaway came closer, they could see that the mount was a girl. She had lost control of her horse completely, and the other riders in her party were racing behind her, vainly trying to catch her. Terence glanced quickly at the girl. She had a cold, proud face—she would resent any interference unless it was absolutely necessary; so he pulled over, swung Lady Bird around, and as the frightened animal came up beside him, he touched Lady Bird with his spurs and kept pace with the runaway.

Her horse, a beautiful jet-black animal, was running easily, in long, even strides, with no evidence of slackening his pace. He looked as if he might keep it up indefinitely. Terence glanced at the girl again. He had met a number of girls, and he knew from observing those who came to the O'More house how to tell when a young lady was dressed properly and in good taste. Her black habit was of beautiful cloth, and perfectly tailored; her boots were black and shining, and he noticed that her spurs and the handle of her crop, which protruded from the top of her boot, were of silver. The saddle and bridle were silver-mounted and set to the horse as if they were part of him. The young lady's nose was thin, and her full red lips were parted over even white teeth. Terence decided that she was a very attractive girl, of good family, and faultlessly dressed; and from all appearances, refined and well educated. She had lost her hat and her long dark hair was blowing behind her. She was very pale, evidently frightened, but Terence scored one for her: at least, she had not screamed. Her arms were taut, and she was pulling with all the strength she could muster, but her efforts were not making the least impression on the racing animal. Terence watched until he saw her arms begin to relax. The horse, feeling the tension on the reins loosen, began to rear and plunge. Now was the time. Quickly he leaned over and shouted in her ear: "Slide your hands well back on your reins, and put them together. Did you understand me?"

She nodded.

It was a peculiar request, under the circumstances, but the girl had no time to ask questions—she knew she could not regain control of her animal by herself, so she did as she was told. Terence fastened his reins to his saddle with a specially made device, and with his left hand he grasped the girl's reins, just in front of her hands. A few strong tugs, and the animal realized he was mastered; he stopped, panting and snorting.

The girl looked at Terence gratefully, and for the first time he saw her eyes as they met his squarely. They were large and round, and as they looked into his with a sort of baby stare, he could see that they were a peculiar shade of blue shot with flecks of green and brown. They were the most peculiar eyes he ever had seen, and he could not make up his mind whether he liked them or not. They looked misty, as if he were seeing them through water.

A bit of the haughtiness was gone from her face as she said:

"My name is Kathleen Strathern. Thanks a lot. Black Prince is rather restless to-day."

Terence bowed as he handed the reins to her. "It was nothing at all, Miss Strathern. I am happy to have been of service. My name is Terence O'More."

Kathleen's shrewd eyes appraised the boy coolly: the thick shock of rebellious orange-red hair, gleaming in the sun and disarranged by the wind (he never wore a hat, much to Uncle Maxwell's disgust); the high forehead; the lean, tanned face, generously sprinkled with freckles; the broad shoulders. No, she decided as she looked away, he was not handsome, but there was something—something compelling in the insolence of the steely gray eyes that made her turn toward him and look again. She met his glance for an instant, and then her gaze lowered, and stopped—fascinated.

Terence's jaws set, and his lips tightened to a thin line. It was the same old thing he endured with everyone at a first meeting, for he knew that the girl was seeing his right arm—the arm that ended in an empty sleeve. Usually it was tucked carefully into his coat pocket, but the hard ride had loosened it, and it was hanging—just hanging. Terence caught it and tucked it quickly into his pocket.

The girl blinked and looked again, as if she thought she must be mistaken. That was the reason he had asked her to keep the reins together—so that he could grasp them quickly with one hand. And to do it, he must have let go of his own reins, leaving his horse without any control: he had taken a chance on it, staying beside the runaway; had it slackened its pace, or veered away, it would have meant a terrible fall for the young man. He must have a lot of courage, that boy.

And then the thing happened that Terence knew would happen; the thing that he always found himself instinctively waiting for; the thing he hated most in all the world. That look of *pity* crept into her eyes—that same old look of pity that inevitably did creep into eyes that noticed his deformity: the pity that made all women want to mother him, and all men want to be considerate of him. Pity! He did not want their pity! How he hated it—and, hating it, he suspected all kindness and friendship among casual acquaintances, because he suspected that only pity was at the bottom. "They are only being nice to me because they feel sorry for me," he thought. Was no one sincere or genuine?

Terence ran his hand through his tousled hair, and then dexterously unsnapped his reins from the metal ring fastened on the front of his saddle. By this time the others were riding up, and in the confusion of questions and explanations Terence slipped away. He saw Barlow and the panting Rags at the side of the road. Kathleen Strathern was too amazed to speak. She was accustomed to having a fuss made over her, to being admired and petted; but this man was indifferent. Here was a new manner of man. She watched him in silence as he turned and rode away.

"We'll take it easy, Barlow, to give Rags a chance to catch his breath. He's puffing like a steam engine. I guess in the excitement he's forgotten that he is built more like a covered wagon than a whippet."

He looked again at the noisy crowd gathered around the girl. They seemed to have forgotten his existence. He smiled bitterly.

"Let's beat it now. I don't need to be Exhibit A for her friends, anyway."

Barlow ignored the bitterness in his voice, and looked admiringly at the boy.

"That was great, sir! She might have been killed, sir."

"Oh, rubbish! Don't be like all the others—trying to make a hero out of me over nothing. That is just what any man would have done, yet *you* didn't want me to do it."

"I was afraid you would be hurt, sir."

"And you would be blamed for not 'taking proper care' of me. Well, I wasn't hurt, and if I had been I would have gotten over it like any other man."

"Very good, sir." But Barlow looked so hurt that Terence softened a little.

"Oh, I know it isn't your fault—I know you are hired to take care of me, as much as to wait on me; but I'm a man, not a baby, and my nerves get a bit on edge at times."

"I understand, sir."

"Yes, I think you *do*—better than either Uncle Maxwell or Aunt Ellen—and I'll try not to be nasty again. But please remember one thing: next time I want to do something, don't interfere, and *don't* try to stop me. I'll see that you are not blamed for it, if anything happens."

"Yes, sir. Very well, sir."

"Barlow, I wish you would talk to me. I really *need* someone to talk to me. No man has lived as long as you have without forming opinions on many things. Express yourself—give me the benefit of your experience and advice. I'm young: it would do me a lot of good. I'm so everlastingly fed up on 'Yes, sir,' and 'No, sir,' and 'Very well, sir.' Sometimes I think if you say those things to me again I'll fire something at your head."

"It's the way I was trained, sir. My answers were to be 'short, polite, and to the point.' It is the same way with all well-trained servants, sir."

"Yes, I know that. But I think it is ridiculous rot for a healthy, full-grown man like me to have a valet to wait on him. I suppose you know that I should not think of keeping you, or anyone else, if it were not for —for—my missing hand."

"You are like that, sir. You are very kind to me, and I have grown very fond of you, sir. You see, I've never had a son—and—and it's a damnable shame about—about your hand, if you'll excuse me saying so, sir. I don't blame you for being irritated and vexed sometimes, and I'll take no offense whenever you feel like throwing things, sir."

That was a long speech for Barlow, and he looked a bit frightened, as if he were afraid he had committed a grave error and was about to be reprimanded for it. But it was all right. Terence was smiling.

"You need not be afraid to talk to me, Barlow. I think we understand each other. A youngster like me needs to get things off his chest."

"Off his chest, sir?"

"That's just more of my plebeian American slang—means I need to blow off steam."

"Blow off steam, sir?"

Terence laughed, "Well, it means I get worried and need to talk."

"Oh, I see, sir," Barlow looked relieved. "But what about Lord O'More, sir?"

"We can talk when we're alone; then we won't shock Uncle Maxwell's delicate sense of propriety. I wish he was as particular about his own conversation as he is about mine."

"Very good, sir."

"There you go again! I guess there's no hope; it must be force of habit. Can't you just forget the 'sir'?"

"I wouldn't dare leave it out, s— s—— Excuse me, I might forget it at just the wrong time."

"All right. Just forget I mentioned it. There's no use of your getting balled out just because of my selfish notions."

"Balled out, sir?"

"That means reprimanded—how's that for a good word? I guess you are beginning to see why the English don't understand American."

They both smiled as they turned into the drive.

"Barlow, did you know that young lady?"

"I never saw her before, sir, but I know the horse. He is Black Prince, owned by Lord Aridulane, an old friend of Lord O'More's. But he is not a horse for a lady to ride, and Lord Aridulane's grooms know it."

"Hm-m-m. She must be a courageous young lady. I noticed she did not get panicky or hysterical."

As Barlow watched his young master he wondered if he could be at all interested in the young lady. He knew that he paid no attention to any ladies of his acquaintance, although Lady O'More had tried to interest him in several of the daughters of her friends. "Well," the old man thought, "it would be a good thing for him—it would take his mind off himself. He thinks too much about himself, as is always the case when people have nothing else to do. It is not good for anyone."

Terence swung himself down from Lady Bird and handed the reins to the waiting groom. Lady Bird began sniffing about his coat.

"Well, which pocket is it in to-day, old girl?"

Lady Bird whinnied when she came to his upper right coat pocket.

"Can't fool you, can I? I put it in a different pocket every time, too."

Terence extracted several lumps of sugar, and patted Lady Bird's neck as she munched them. Rags began to jump and bark.

"Oh, you want some, too, do you? Well, sit up and speak."

Rags "spoke," but the sitting up was not so easy. He could not balance himself, and he kept pawing the air with his front feet, like a drowning man fighting the water. But he got the sugar, which, after all, was the most important thing.

As Terence entered the garden, he could hear his uncle's voice. Those tones meant only one thing: Uncle Maxwell was irritated, and was bellowing at his wife. Immediately Terence was mad. Rags, running ahead of him, collided with Uncle Maxwell just as he came around a hedge. Unfortunately, Rags was not a dainty eater. Part of the sugar had escaped his mouth, and he was drooling nice, sirupy slobbers, which caught Uncle Maxwell just at the crease in his perfectly pressed trousers.

"Damnation!" he yelled, momentarily forgetting Aunt Ellen as he lifted his foot, aiming a kick at Rags.

Terence saw it and quickly stepped in front of Uncle Maxwell.

"I'm sorry, Uncle Maxwell, but you can't kick my dog."

"What are you going to do about it?"

"I'm not going to do anything about it—I'm just not going to let you do it. Rags, go to Barlow."

Rags lumbered off toward the stables, and Uncle Maxwell, seeing the dog leave, turned his attention again to Aunt Ellen. Terence saw that the maids and the butler were gathering the tea things in the garden.

The guests evidently had gone. So that was the cause of the present outburst. He had not liked his tea in the garden. No, he had not. In fact, he was most emphatic and disagreeable about it. Immediately Terence was sorry he had not stayed. Maybe his presence would have made things easier for Aunt Ellen. At least, he would see what he could do now.

"I tell you, Ellen, I don't like my tea in the garden. I've never heard of such a thing before——"

"Is that the reason you don't like it?" sweetly inquired Terence.

"I can't see that it's any of your affair *why* I don't like my tea in the garden. If I don't, why should I have it there?"

"Just at random, I should say because Aunt Ellen might like hers there."

"Rubbish! It's just an idea. She does not care where she has her tea, just so she has it!"

"How do you know? You never take the trouble to find out what anyone else wants or likes. Only what you want counts."

"Ridiculous! Tea in the garden! Insects! Ants! And a beastly bird——"

Aunt Ellen escaped into the house, and Terence roared.

"What's the matter, Uncle Maxwell? Did it decorate your manly bosom, or your cake?"

Terence did not wait for an answer. He whistled for Rags, and they went into the house. He had gotten himself into a fairly decent mood on the way home, but he had allowed Uncle Maxwell to upset him again. Why did the man insist upon taking little things so seriously? He never got any sympathy; and mostly he only made himself ridiculous. But he never saw that. He thought he was very masterful and awe-inspiring. He never dreamed that people either inwardly cursed his lack of self-control, or laughed at him. He seemed to think that it was a compliment to have the servants afraid of him. But it was not. The servants obeyed him because they must; not because they liked him and wanted to please him. However, that slight difference had not come to Uncle Maxwell's attention. So as he grew older, he grew worse instead of better. It is usually the case when one starts wrong.

Terence stamped upstairs to his suite, entered his library, slammed the door with a resounding bang, and flung himself into a huge chair before the window. Terence's suite was really the only livable place in the house. And that was because he had more windows cut in his rooms, took out all the old furniture, and bought new drapes and furnishings. The library was not large, but it got plenty of air and sun. There were a small fireplace, two bookcases, quite a large desk, a comfortable divan with several cushions, and two large armchairs with small magazine tables beside them.

Rags sensed something wrong with his master. He followed dejectedly, laid his head on Terence's knees, and looked at him reprovingly.

"Yes, Rags, I'm in about as rotten a temper as they're made."

But Rags did not mind. He tried to scramble up on Terence's lap, but Rags was not made to fit a lap—his long hind legs hung over one side, and his head and front legs hung over the other. He looked like a bag of meal that had been hastily slung across the back of a horse. Terence smiled.

"Can't *you* forget you're not a Pomeranian, old man?"

But he edged over and pulled the lanky legs into the chair beside him, while Rags snuggled down and laid his head confidentially across Terence's right arm—the arm that ended in the empty sleeve.

"You *would* do that, Rags, old boy. You're the only one who doesn't miss that hand. I guess you'd still love me if there was nothing left of me but my freckles and red hair!"

Rags cuddled closer, happy to have his master talk to him; and the man's face softened a bit as his hand strayed to the dog's shaggy head.

"You see, Rags, it's like this: I'm tired of books, and of being educated to be a gentleman; I'm sick of dignified tutors, exclusive clothes, perfect etiquette, and stuffy houses filled with handsome, uncomfortable furniture where you are afraid to sit down for fear you'll rub off some of the gilt. I always have a feeling that those spindle-legged chairs are going to crumble under me. I don't want to be told whether every move I I make, and every word I speak, is right or wrong—and as for society, I fervently pray kind heaven to deliver me from teas, receptions, and dinners. Even you would have to laugh at the teas, old boy. A lot of idle, lazy women, who don't *want* to do anything, talk about how sorry they are for themselves because they haven't anything to do. I can't stick 'em. I want——"

There was a discreet tap at the door. Terence scowled.

"Now it's time for me to do something, I suppose. Gosh, Rags, I can't even have a little visit with you in peace!"

Another tap, and the door opened.

"What's the next item on the programme, Barlow? I'd sure disrupt the routine of this household, if I didn't have you to keep tabs on me."

"Tabs, sir?"

"A little more American—means that you always know where I am, and what I'm to do next."

"Thank you, sir. Your bath is ready. Her Ladyship is having dinner at eight. There are guests."

"How surprising! Well, I don't want to take a bath, and I don't want to dress, and I don't want to go to dinner at eight, and I don't want to meet her Ladyship's guests, and I don't want to go through a lot of beautiful social gestures that don't mean a darn thing! Now what do you think of that?"

"I think you are a most unusual young man, sir."

"Do you really think I should do all this silly stuff, Barlow? Come on now, *tell* me."

"It is a matter of custom, sir. The O'Mores are an old family, and they have always lived like this—I dare say for generations past, sir."

"I hate it, Barlow. This rigid, frigid business gets my goat—now don't ask me what that means. I've explained it to you before."

"Yes, sir. But your social position demands——"

"Oh, bother my social position! I tell you, Barlow, it's an empty life for a man with any red blood in his veins. No work—no purpose in life—no interest in anything—ambitions stifled by conventions—not getting anywhere—and knowing that to-morrow and to-morrow and to-morrow will be just like to-day. It's like the child who wanted to know when yesterday would come. Yesterday might just as well come as to-morrow, for all the difference there would be."

"It is monotonous, sir."

"After four years of studying, I should be good for something. I've only one hand, but I know I could be of some use in the world if I were permitted a chance to try. But they throw a fit every time I mention work, and every time I do the most trivial thing. Why, the other day I was pulling a few weeds, and Uncle Maxwell saw me and sent a gardener out to do it so I wouldn't get my hand dirty. Let's see you tie that one!"

"Tie it, sir?"

"Match it—beat it—tell me an incident equally as asinine."

"I see, sir. But it irritates your Uncle Maxwell to see you work."

"He ought to see how some American fathers get 'irritated' if their sons *don't* want to work! He isn't a patch on them. When those boys ask 'dear old Dad' for money, they get blown sky high—and it's just a toss up whether they get it or not."

"It's a difference in the viewpoint, sir."

Barlow really thought Terence was right, but it was no good saying so. If he agreed with the boy, and encouraged his independent ideas, it would only make the situation more difficult. All he could do was ease him along, and try to keep him calm. After all, it is rather a task to convince anyone he is wrong, when you believe, way down deep, that he is right. The boy had tremendous energy, and it was being wasted. Not only that, but his disposition was being ruined, and the gnawing discontent was eating into his soul. Barlow thought of the laughing boy who had come to them four years before. There was nothing left of that boy but the red hair and freckles—even his expression and the look in his eyes had changed. Barlow's honest heart ached for the boy, but at the moment he seemed helpless. He looked so troubled that Terence began to feel guilty for all his fault finding.

"A penny for your thoughts, Barlow! I guess after these years of my increasingly turbulent disposition I owe you an explanation. You've borne the brunt of it more than anyone else. I'll tell you a little story, briefly. Sit down."

Barlow remained standing.

"But, sir——"

"Oh, for heaven's sake, let's drop the formality for a few minutes and talk like two men! *Sit down.*"

Barlow sat down.

"Pipe in your pocket?"

"Yes, sir, but——"

"Light it."

Barlow lit it.

CHAPTER III

Wherein Lord Terence Maxwell O'More Tells a Story

A LONG time ago, over in America, in a state called Indiana, I was a nameless waif in an orphan asylum. It seemed easy for the other kids to be adopted, but no one wanted me, because of my missing hand. Besides, I was not blessed with any fatal beauty—I was just as homely then as I am now. The asylum did the best it could by me for a long time; they kept me until I was sixteen, which is past the legal age for children in an orphans' home. Then they had to do something, so they apprenticed me to a farmer. They forgot to tell him the interesting fact that I was a hand shy, and when he saw me he beat me, took my clothes for his son, dressed me in the son's rags, and turned me out. At least, they always kept us clean in the Home, and I had never had to wear filthy, torn clothing before. I had no money or friends, and I looked so disreputable no one would give me work. I batted around about the country for two years, just managing to earn enough to keep from freezing or starving.

"Then one evening, when I was worn out from tramping twenty miles, soul-sick from hearing that everlasting refrain, 'only one hand,' weak from hunger, clothes dusty and in rags, and my feet in blisters from having no stockings, I came to a lumber camp."

Terence paused and looked out the window where the shadows were lengthening on the grass. Barlow lighted the fire as Terence continued.

"I'll never forget that sight. A huge, crackling camp fire, with sparks dancing through the smoke; cheery voices; softly neighing horses; the rattle of dishes; odours from cooking food; friendly sights and sounds everywhere—it seemed a paradise to me. Several men were sitting on a stack of logs, singing to the accompaniment of a banjo. I asked one of them where the Boss was, and instead of telling me, he said: 'Want a job, I s'pose. Well, he can't use you—you ain't got but one hand.'

"He was a Dutchman, named Wessener; we hated each other from that minute. I told him I'd like to give the Boss a chance to do his own talking, so grudgingly he took me to him, but before I had time to say a word, he again offered his choice tid-bit of information: 'Here's a kid wants a job, but you can't use him—he ain't got but one hand.' And what do you think, Barlow? That man never even raised his eyes to look. He went right on with his figuring and said curtly: 'That will do, Wessener. I'll interview my man in a minute!' Yes, Barlow, he said '*my man*' and he never even *looked!*

"You can see why I think James Ross McLean is the world's finest man. He was a tall, handsome Scotsman, about forty, with much of the milk of human kindness in his heart; all his men and horses were well fed, well housed, and fairly treated. He gave me a job guarding valuable trees in the Limberlost Swamp—a piece of virgin swamp and forest that lay just as it had lain from the beginning of time. I had to walk or ride a bicycle around the trail surrounding his land several times each day, to see that the wires were not down, and that no one trespassed. I'll never forget how frightened I was those first weeks, but I would have died before I would have failed Mr. McLean. The crackling of dead branches, the calls of the owls, and the croaking of the frogs frightened me—and the wind whistling through a hollow tree scared me stiff. Mr. McLean bought me suitable clothing and two revolvers, which he taught me to use. He said no one knew *what* was in the old Swamp, but he knew there were rattlesnakes and animals, and that it was a hiding place for criminals of all sorts.

"I lived with the head teamster, a giant Scotsman, Duncan by name, his wife Sarah, and their three kiddies. Sarah Duncan was the only mother I ever knew. She understood. When I was afraid and discouraged, she cheered me; when I was sick in body or soul, she doctored me; she packed all the things I liked best in my lunch box; she knitted my socks and mended my clothes; she knitted a heavy mitten for my hand, and a sort of armlet to keep the stump of my other arm warm. Only a knowing woman would have thought of that. She really loved me—she was the only mother I ever knew. They don't make women any finer than Sarah Duncan."

Terence's eyes softened, and he smiled as his thoughts strayed back to his old friends.

"Gradually, I came to love the Swamp. Its shadows held no terrors for me. The Duncans were kindness itself and I grew to love the Boss as I would have loved my own father. Then a woman we all knew as the Bird Woman began coming to the Swamp to take a series of pictures of the nest and babies of a pair of black vultures. She made nature studies to illustrate magazine articles and books, which she wrote herself. She made pictures with cameras, not sketches, and her patience was appalling. She is a very clever woman. Do you see those feathers on my desk?"

"Yes, sir."

"Did it ever strike you funny that a man of my age should keep two feathers on his desk?"

"Yes, sir."

Terence laughed.

"Well, the big one fell at my feet one day as I was walking the trail. I wanted to find the bird's nest, for I thought it must be huge. It was only when I discovered the nest in a hollow log, lying on the ground, that I realized how ignorant I was, because I had wasted a week looking for it among the tree tops. I decided right then I would send for books so I could learn about everything in the Swamp, and I did. I showed the nest to the Boss, and he took the word to the Bird Woman. That opened a new world to me, for when she came to photograph the birds, she brought with her——"

Terence hesitated, and the observing Barlow saw a light come into the boy's eyes that he had never seen there before.

"Were you ever in love, Barlow?"

"Yes, sir. Long ago."

"Did you marry her?"

"No, sir. She—she died."

Terence held out his hand.

"I'd like to shake hands with you, Barlow. I'd like to be friends instead of master and servant."

Barlow wiped away a tear and shook hands.

"The Bird Woman brought with her the loveliest bit of girlhood I've ever seen—all blue sky and sunshine, sparkling and radiant—only sixteen. I adored her. I adore her now—more than anything on earth. Her voice was music, and every move she made was poetry. She is the daughter of the village banker; her mother has been dead for many years. Her father sent her out with the Bird Woman to learn natural history. The Bird Woman mothered her, chaperoned her parties, and all that sort of thing. Her name is Dorothy Kingsley, known to all her friends as Dot; but she looked like an Angel to me the first time I ever saw her, so I named her the Swamp Angel, and the name clung to her among her family. And she called me Freckles, with such a teasing lilt in her voice, it used to send the blood racing through me like a torrent. How I long to hear it now, sometimes—no one here ever calls me Freckles!

"Well, Wessener came to the Swamp one day and tried to bribe me to stay on *one* side of the trail for a day while he and three more of McLean's men stole a tree from the other side. All the demons of hell seemed to let loose in me. I don't know yet just how I did it, but I licked that Dutchman within an inch of his life. McLean saw part of the fight, and it was then that he told me he loved me as much as if I were his own son. He gave me his name, and told me that the next year I was to go to his mother, and go to a grand school.

"Soon after, timber thieves came and caught me unawares. They bound and gagged me. The Angel and the Bird Woman saved my life. Then the Angel got in the way of a falling tree; I caught her and threw her out of the way, unhurt; but the top of it got me and crushed my chest. The Angel managed everything: a special train to Chicago, the nearest big city; doctors; nurses; surgeons; hospital rooms. But I tried to die. I loved the Angel, but I couldn't ask her to marry me without a name to offer her; and of course she knew that, although the Boss had given me his name, I was not the son of a bachelor Scotsman whom her father had known for years. Even then I had red hair and freckles and a bit of an Irish accent that has been fairly well eliminated, thanks to the united and determined efforts of Uncle Maxwell and various tutors.

"Nothing was too big a job for the Angel to tackle, and she finally located my people. It developed that my father was Uncle Maxwell's brother; my grandfather disinherited him and drove him from home when he married my mother, because he said she was not of sufficiently 'good' family. He must have had a temper something like Uncle Maxwell's."

Barlow smiled, and Terence went on:

"My parents went to America and lived in Chicago. Father failed in business, and the money began to run short just about the time I came along. Grandfather knew he was wrong, but he would never have anything to do with either my mother or father. They say it killed my grandmother—pleasant people, these O'More men.

"My mother had a beautiful voice, and she began to sing evenings, to earn money, hiring one of the neighbours to stay with me. One night while I was sleeping there was a terrible fire, while the woman left me to do an errand. She returned and carried me out, but a falling timber had crushed and burned my right hand so badly that it had to be amputated. My parents, returning together and not knowing I was safe, ran into the house after me. The house crashed on both of them—the only persons in the world who loved me. The neighbours were poor, and they had to take me to an orphanage."

Terence rose, allowing Rags to slide to the floor, and walked over to the fireplace.

"And the Angel, sir?"

"They operated on my chest, and the Angel was superb. She overheard a conversation between the surgeon and Mr. McLean in which the surgeon said I was dying because I was not trying to live; that I evidently wanted something I could not have; that if he loved me as much as he said he did, all he had to do was find out what I wanted, and give it to me. She heard my dear Boss answer him that it was she I wanted; that I loved her with all my heart and soul, but that he was powerless; that I could not tell her because I had no name, nor proof of honourable parentage. So she rushed into my room, and told me that she loved me. She told me about all the things I had to live for, and about how brave I was when I risked my life to save her. She told me I ought to be ashamed of myself. Then she said that if I insisted upon a name and people she would find them; and she did. She located my people in Chicago, hunting for me. You've guessed by this time—they were Lord and Lady O'More, Uncle Maxwell and Aunt Ellen—and here I am, in their house, where I have been for four years, and I am *Lord* Terence O'More!"

Terence sneered.

"We were engaged. The Angel had an alibi for every objection I could offer—that is, *before* she discovered

I was a 'Lord.' My Uncle would not consent—said we were only kids—excuse me, children. He said I must come back to Ireland with them and be trained and educated to be a 'gentleman' so that I could take my father's title and assume my 'rightful station in life.'

"The way I was educated was all wrong for a boy. I wanted to go to public schools—I used to pass them and hear the happy shouts of laughter as the children played in the school yards; and then I'd see them starting home after school, arm in arm, their heads together, discussing, no doubt, any one of the hundreds of weighty problems of youth. To me that was ideal, but Uncle Maxwell would not hear of it.

"'An O'More in an American free school—no, indeed!' He couldn't have been much more vehement about it if I had wanted to poke out someone's right eye. So I've had dull, stupid tutors—no youthful companionship, and no *interesting* instruction. Well, here I am: I've assumed and digested and assimilated all they had to offer, and look at me now!"

"A very fine specimen of a man *and* a gentleman, sir, if I may say so, sir!"

"The long and short of it was that McLean and the Angel's father agreed with my uncle and aunt. I believe that they loved me, as I love them, and that they hated to see me go; but they really came to believe that they would be depriving me of my birthright and my right to happiness if they permitted me to remain under their care. McLean was the only father I ever knew, and in desperation I said I would do whatever he thought was best. It's too bad for me that I didn't know Uncle Maxwell better. Had I been acquainted with the gentleman, I never would have come. But that doesn't help matters now. Post mortems are always painful. I thought I could depend on the Angel to side with me, but she must have been awed by the title, too—she agreed with them, and said I must go with them. She said she had to finish her education, too, and that by the time both of us were out of college, I would be 'sure to know what I wanted to do.' Sure to know what I wanted to do! As if I haven't known what I wanted to do from the minute I first saw her. God! how crazy I get to see her!"

Terence groaned as he faced Barlow. Barlow came over and laid a hand affectionately on the boy's shoulder.

"I wouldn't worry, sir. I'm sure she is waiting for you—that kind of a girl would be, sir. It's confidence in yourself you need, sir."

"We have written regularly, but I have grown up, and so has she. You see, that was four years ago—I am twenty-four now, and she is twenty. The agreement was that I was to finish my education, and decide what I wanted to make my life work, and then I was to go to her. But I can't go to her like this. I want to *do* something on my own—I've some pride, and I will not go back there with nothing definite accomplished."

"I understand how you feel, sir. I wish I could help you, sir."

"So behold me! I'm the bright and shining result of four years of their influence. I've been dominated by Uncle Maxwell, babied by Aunt Ellen, and alternately pitied, endured, or patronized by their friends; and a more useless or less ornamental piece of furniture it would be difficult to imagine."

In spite of himself, Barlow smiled.

"It isn't nearly so bad as that, sir. Really it isn't."

"Just the same, I'm bothered. The Angel expected

fine things of me, and I don't amount to a damn. She is the most generous and loyal soul in the world—she would not think of breaking a promise. But four years is a long time—*now* she may not want a husband with one hand; she may have met someone else. I couldn't endure the thought of her being ashamed of me. Not that she would show it—what she thought or felt, no one would ever guess—but I can't run the risk, Barlow; it means too much to me. Her happiness comes first, always."

"You are too sensitive, sir. Much too sensitive. You are a fine man. A hand is not so much; a leg would be a great deal worse, sir."

"Well, that's the story, Barlow. I've told you in the hope that you will understand the reasons for my irritation at times. You see, it hurts to have to have my shoes laced, and my belt fastened, and my necktie tied, like a child. I'd like to wait on myself. But, at that, I think you're right. I'm more sick in my heart than I am in my body."

Barlow's eyes filled as he answered.

"It's a pleasure to assist you, sir—you make my work very easy. I have appreciated being treated like a human being, sir. You know, there are people who treat their servants more like animals."

"You are a good man, Barlow, and you are not always going to be a servant. Don't forget that. But you'd better lead me to that bath. If I'm late, they'll say you forgot to bathe the child!"

Barlow busied himself about the room, while a great splashing went on in the tub. He was troubled. He saw, with an old man's keenness of vision, of what fine stuff Terence was made. The lessons he had learned among the sounds and silences of the forest had stayed with him, and they stood out among the shams and pretences of royalty like a mountain against a sunset sky. It was the missing hand that hurt him most—such supersensitiveness Barlow had never seen.

"If he were my own son," thought the old man, "I could not love him more. If I could only make him understand that it is far better to have a missing hand, than to be physically perfect on the outside and morally rotten on the inside, as is the case with many men of his age and acquaintance over here!"

That was quite true. Terence did know of their manner of living, and he did not approve of it. That was one reason that he had little to do with them. But it was also true that there were fine, clean men among them, and that Terence could have had a few real friends if he had so desired. That he did not was solely the fault of his sensitiveness over his deformity; his inability to join in their sports and games and his continual fear of their pity and sympathy.

Barlow was debating with himself: should he, or should he not, tell the boy what was on his mind? He finally decided that he would. He helped Terence to dress, and when they came again into the library, Barlow spoke.

"My boy, I'd like to give you the benefit of an old man's observation. All you think of is your hand. I've never had a child, but if I had a daughter I would rather see her married to a man like you than to a man with both hands who was diseased to the core morally, and I venture to say that would be the verdict of most men with daughters. Morals mean more than outward physical perfection. It is time for you to *forget* about your hand—the Angel was right, sir."

"You *are* a comfort, Barlow. I'll try." Terence touched Barlow's arm affectionately.

There was a tap at the door, but the two men did not hear it. It opened slowly, and Lady O'More looked in. There she saw master and servant, their arms affectionately across each other's shoulders, standing before the window, looking out across the country! Aunt Ellen was shocked.

"Oh, I beg your pardon! I—knocked—you must not have heard—I—do not wish to intrude."

The two men looked as guilty as a couple of little boys caught eating jam from the pantry shelf. But Terence smiled and motioned to Barlow to leave the room.

"Good-evening, Aunt Ellen." Terence walked over and gave her an indifferent peck on the forehead. "Don't look so horrified, Aunt Ellen. We're just two lonely men having a little chat. We've become quite good friends after four years. Really, there's no harm done at all."

"Good-evening, Terence, dear. I was quite surprised at seeing you so intimate with a servant. You know your uncle does not approve of it."

"Yes, I do know it—but strange as it may seem, that doesn't make a particle of difference to me. I am fond of Barlow, and he is fond of me, and that's that."

Aunt Ellen thought it best to change the subject.

"I've come to tell you about our guests for to-night," she hurried on, as if sensing the turbulence in the air. "They are old friends of ours, and they are bringing with them a young lady whose parents are dead, and who has no living relatives. She has been living with them for several months. She is a lovely girl. Her father was a boyhood chum of your uncle's. We want you to meet her—and—and like her. We are thinking of asking her to live with us—we think she will be a charming companion for you, dear. After dinner an orchestra from the city will be here, and some others are coming in for dancing."

"And what makes you think the young lady will like me?" Terence inquired. "I'm certainly not much to look at," and he glanced ruefully at the empty sleeve, tucked neatly in his coat pocket.

"*Terence*, you do distress me so! You are bitter tonight. You are a very charming gentleman—you have wealth, you know the best people, no one has better social standing——"

Had she tried deliberately, she could not have chosen phrases that would have irritated him more. He stopped her with an impatient gesture.

"Why shouldn't I be bitter? I'm only part of a man, and granting my brain is all right, I am not allowed the unprecedented privilege of using it. I am not permitted to do anything that keeps my brain active—and there are only a few sports in which a one-handed man can indulge to keep his body active. When I am only granted leave to be a model for expensive and exclusive tailors, how can I kid myself into believing I am a man?"

Aunt Ellen was startled. Terence's American frankness of expression often distressed her.

"And besides that, I don't care for the qualities of your so-called 'gentlemen'; they may be perfect examples of parlour etiquette, but their etiquette outside parlours is not so good. They don't amount to a damn—but then, neither do I!"

Aunt Ellen gasped. She had never seen her nephew quite so vehement before.

"Terence, dear, you must be hungry——"

"Yes, I'm hungry, but not for food."

Looking at him, Aunt Ellen saw that his eyes were not seeing her, or anything else in the room—they were seeing many miles into space—perhaps as far as across the ocean.

"And as for your young friend, ask her to live here by all means. No doubt she is lovely, but please don't expect me to entertain her. I am not interested——" Terence's voice trailed into silence.

Abruptly he rose. "Where is Uncle Maxwell?"

"In the garden, dear, but I think it best that you do not talk to him in your present mood!"

"Well, I don't agree with you! It may wake him up to find the mood I am in to-day is of the same piece as the one he is in all the time. No doubt he will stamp his foot, and grow purple in the face, but it's all a bluff. Anyway, I'm used to it. Funny why these explosive old men never realize that if they presented their arguments without assuming that they know everything in the world, and in a calm, sane manner, someone might pay a little attention to them sometime."

Aunt Ellen sighed. "Yes, dear. I've lived with your Uncle Maxwell forty years!"

"For which you deserve a lot of credit!"

CHAPTER IV

Wherein Terence Walks in the Moonlight and Writes a Letter

TERENCE went downstairs and strode out through the gardens, Rags at his heels. The awful gardens! They gave Terence the creeps each time he looked at them. Walks and flower beds were all laid out in geometrical designs, with faultless precision. The boxwood shrubs were trimmed by an imported and expensive gardener to represent various animals—it looked more like a zoo than a garden. Everything was artificial; nothing had the graceful beauty of things growing naturally. Even the flowers were not allowed to bloom as the Lord intended they should: all the buds were pinched off but one, so that there might be just one perfect blossom on a stem. They looked as stiff as a lot of sticks. Imperfect leaves were also removed, and the unfortunate little "runts" among the plants were ruthlessly pulled out and thrown away. There was not one friendly little weed or a stray "run-away" to mar the symmetry of the whole; the plants ran in rows as rigidly straight, or at just as acute angles, as the walks.

There were no birds living there, because the trees and hedges were trimmed so closely there were no secluded places for birds to hide their nests. To Terence, half the beauty of a garden was the voices of the birds singing and calling to each other; the babies chirping for food; and the few last sleepy twitters at sundown. He thought of the generous profusion of gay flower faces in the Bird Woman's garden, and sighed.

Exactly in the centre was a perfectly round pool, with a cement edge, and on the water floated two large white swans, as dignified and cold as their master and mistress. Terence held out his hand to one of the swans, but it rose out of the water until it seemed to be standing on its feet, flapped its wings aggressively, and struck at him viciously with its bill.

"Nice pet, you are! But then, maybe it's not your fault—maybe you've never been petted."

Terence and Rags walked around the pool and started down another path. Everywhere things had the same stilted, starched appearance. One would not believe it was within the realm of possibilities for trees, shrubs, and flowers to be actually growing and blooming outdoors, and still have all the silent, stiff perfection of artificial leaves and wax blossoms.

"Even the trees and shrubs have to grow as Uncle Maxwell says. They are not allowed to develop naturally; they get no more freedom than the members of this household. What a cheerless, spiritless place this is! If anyone around here discovered himself the victim of an honest emotion, he would die of fright!"

Unconsciously, Terence had thought out loud, so he was startled when he heard the curt tones of Uncle Maxwell's voice.

"Eh—er—what's that—what's that?"

"Good-evening, Uncle Maxwell. Pardon me. I sometimes get so lonely for someone to talk with around here that I talk to myself—or to Rags," and Terence sat down beside his uncle on one of the cold, straight benches with which the garden was decorated.

Uncle Maxwell glared, and Terence could not help wondering what pleasure the old man derived from keeping others unhappy. Surely he could not be ignorant of the fact that the entire household was discontented and afraid of him.

"Uncle Maxwell, I've decided that I can't stand this any longer. I thought the best thing to do was tell you so."

"Just what is 'this' that you seem unable to endure?"

"I've told you before—the idleness—nothing to do—having no incentive to live. Possibly you forget that I'm twenty-four now; I'm not a child any longer. You can't set me down, give me a toy to play with, and expect me to be good forever."

"What do you want, more money?"

"That's not it at all—I have more money than I need. But I *would* like some that I had earned by my own efforts, that was not passed out to me on a silver platter."

"Your friends do not earn their money."

"You mean *your* friends don't. That's their business, and has nothing to do with me."

"Wouldn't you be ashamed to have them know you were working, when they amuse themselves with sports?"

"If I could come home tired from a day's honest work, I would snap my fingers in their faces when they complained of being tired from the strenuous labour entailed by batting a tennis ball over a court, or chasing a poor, helpless little fox around until their dogs kill it. Must be an exhausting job for a he-man."

"Terence, how undignified you are at times."

"Yes, *at times*. I've discovered in the long run that the rewards of dignity are few and far between."

"It seems to me that you are a pretty lucky young man; I feel that I have done very well by you. You have everything done for your comfort, entertainment, and convenience. Most men in your shoes would consider themselves extremely fortunate," and Uncle Maxwell favoured Terence with a self-satisfied smile.

"I don't want 'everything done for my comfort, entertainment, and convenience.' The happiest years of my life were spent enduring quite a bit of discomfort and inconvenience; and my only entertainment was work. Do you think these men of whom you speak are content, or happy, with as useless and uneventful an existence as this?"

"They appear to be."

"You can't always judge by appearances; but if they are, they are pretty spineless individuals. We don't *live* at all—we just sort of slip over life on the surface. Don't you think it might be interesting to dig around a little, and see what one could find?"

"I can't see your viewpoint at all."

"I'm sorry, but I can't draw a diagram. It's simple enough. Uncle Maxwell, didn't it ever strike you that if a young man couldn't be interested in the right sort of thing, that he *might* become interested in—in the *wrong* sort of thing?"

"Such as——?"

"Well, to be frank, gambling, or drinking, or questionable women——"

"I must confess that it never '*struck*' me that any O'More would so far forget himself."

"Oh, bosh! You know better than that! Your friends' sons are of just as good blood as your son was, or as I am, but they 'forget' themselves deliberately and regularly."

"Are you meaning to say that you——?"

"I'm not meaning to say anything except that I am human, and full of energy and ambition. The logical person, at present, to direct my energies is you. If you fail to do it, they might direct themselves along the wrong road. It has been done. You ought to understand that—you were young once."

Uncle Maxwell reddened.

"We won't discuss me."

"No, I thought as much. Don't worry. I've no desire to pry into your past. I'm more concerned with my future than with your past. I didn't come out here to discuss morals. What I want to know is: are you, or are you not, going to allow me to live my own life in my own way? I don't ask your help—I only ask your permission."

"What do you want me to do?"

"Let me go into the city and go to work."

"At what?"

"I don't know. I'll hunt a job—any man can find a job if he wants it badly enough. I'm losing my pride and my self-respect, and I've got to get them back. I'm slowly dying of dry rot this way."

That far-away look came into Terence's eyes again.

"There is something I want to do—very badly—but I can't do it until I have made something of myself. I want to be able to stand on my own feet and accomplish some definite thing of which I can be proud. I can't do it if I remain here under existing conditions—a parasite."

"I cannot permit you to go to work; the men of our family have *never* worked."

"Then why not establish a precedent? I'm sure it would be appreciated by any real he-man. I know I don't fancy being either a lounge lizard or a tea hound, and there must be others who are deadly tired of spending their lives changing suits and telling beautiful lies to beautiful eyes."

"Lounge lizard?"

"In good old America we call idle men, with no ambition, who spend their time at cocktail parties and tea dances, making pretty speeches that they don't mean, lounge lizards. Fits them, don't you think? And it fits a large class over here, including you and many of your friends."

"Me?" sputtered Uncle Maxwell.

"Yes, you. What do you do with your time and your money that is any good to yourself, your family, or your country? If you had your mind on something in which you were really interested, you wouldn't have so much time and energy for ragging everybody. You just make people dislike you—it's too bad."

Terence could see that Uncle Maxwell was growing more furious and that he was about to blow up in one of his usual tantrums. But Terence had come into the garden for a purpose, and he did not intend to be sidetracked; the best thing to do was go ahead, and get it over with.

"Now *just* a minute, Uncle Maxwell. I'm the only person in this house who isn't afraid of you. I haven't talked to you very often because I don't *like* to quarrel, and I don't *like* to be rude or discourteous. I think you are the victim of circumstances, and I'm sorry for you; but I'm *not* afraid of you—get that straight. Your unlimited flow of hot air doesn't scare me a bit; neither does your stamping and swearing and banging doors—but you've got everybody else about this place buffaloed!"

"*You* sorry for *me?*"

"Of course I'm sorry for you. It must be pretty awful to have everyone afraid of you—even the animals."

"I was not aware that I was so obnoxious—your conversation is *very* enlightening."

"If you'd let it sink in, it might do you good. You're in a hole, but it's not so deep that you can't climb out of it if you want to, and I'd like to see you do it. You *could* be an extremely likable person, Uncle Maxwell."

"Thank you," with what was intended to be withering scorn.

"Don't mention it. However, I came out here to talk about me, not about *you*. I appreciate what you've done for me, and no doubt you thought you were right, but I am not contented or happy this way. I'd like your permission to get a job and go to work."

"The traditions of my family for generations cannot be set aside. As long as you remain under my roof you will obey me. I repeat, the gentlemen of my family have never worked."

Terence saw that it was useless to argue. Uncle Maxwell was working himself rapidly into a rage; his last appeal was futile. He rose.

"Very well, Uncle Maxwell, I'll never ask you again. But if anything happens you don't like, remember that you had your chance."

Just then dinner was announced, and they went into the drawing room where they found Aunt Ellen and her guests.

"Terence, my dear, I want you to know Lord and Lady Aridulane; they are old friends of ours."

They were a very attractive old couple, and they greeted Terence warmly. Terence hated guests, because he hated introductions. If he offered his left hand it was always confusing to guests, and it seemed a deliberate way of calling attention to his missing right hand. So he always stood at quite a distance, and bowed, when he would have preferred a friendly handshake, in the good old American way.

As Terence turned, he saw that the third guest was the young lady of the run-away. She was more tall and slender than he had imagined; her arms and shoulders were almost as white as the satin in which she was faultlessly gowned; her long dark hair lay in substantial-looking coils around her head; her lips were full and red; her limpid eyes met his quite frankly.

"And this, dear, is——"

"Oh, good-evening, Miss Strathern," Terence said formally.

"Good-evening, Lord O'More."

Aunt Ellen looked surprised.

"I was not aware that you and my nephew had met before."

"It was this afternoon—quite by accident. Black Prince decided to run away with me, and he made quite a success of it. Your nephew saved me a bad fall—he may even have saved my life. I am very grateful. I don't know just how to thank him," and Kathleen smiled into his eyes.

"He must have been wonderful," added Lady Aridulane. "Kathleen has talked of nothing else."

Kathleen and Terence were becoming very embarrassed.

"Why, Terence dear, why didn't you tell us about it?" asked Aunt Ellen.

"I only stopped her horse—there was nothing to tell." Terence answered shortly.

They strolled into the dining room, where Kathleen was seated beside him. She was much more effusive and friendly than she had been in the afternoon. Evidently someone had talked to her, or she had had a change of heart. The truth was that she had been thinking about Terence; there was something about the lad that made women think about him. Perhaps she was intrigued by his indifferent, cold manner, and wondered just what lay underneath it. Perhaps she had decided to find out. Kathleen leaned toward him.

"You know, really, you were marvellous this afternoon, Lord O'More. So calm, and so masterful. Black Prince knew instantly, when you grasped the reins, that he was beaten."

"It was nothing at all. I think you overestimate my ability. I have a well-trained horse, you see. I am quite happy that you have recovered from the shock of your unfortunate experience."

"Tell me, Lord O'More, why did you run away in such a hurry this afternoon?"

"What else was there for me to do? You did not introduce me to your friends, nor ask me to ride with you. Was it because I told you my name was *Terence* O'More?"

Kathleen felt the rebuke in his voice, and the bitterness. Yes, he would be difficult to manage, but it would be worth trying. What he said was true—she had been rude and impolite. She must apologize.

"I—I am sorry I was rude. I was a little shaky and unstrung by Black Prince's behaviour. When I locked for you, you were almost out of sight. Forgive me, please."

"That's quite all right."

But Terence knew it was not true. He and Barlow had walked their horses a long distance to give the panting Rags a chance to recover his breath. She could have ridden in his direction and caught up with him easily. Terence was unused to the polite social lies that women tell—the petty evasions and excuses that mean nothing and should be forgotten. So he took her statement seriously, instead of ignoring it and thinking no more of it.

"She's not on the square," he thought, "and if she is going to live with us, she will bear watching. Anyway, why is she so friendly now? She's had a quick change of heart since this afternoon." All of which was not quite fair to the young lady; but Terence's standards were his own.

Terence glanced around the table. The linen and lace, the silver and cut glass, the candles—the only natural thing on the table a bouquet of Aunt Ellen's favourite roses. Then he looked at the faces—all so proper, with so little animation. He thought of supper at the Duncans': the crackling wood fire; the red tablecloth; the little bunch of wild roses and elderberry blossoms in the earthen bowl; the sparkling eyes, rosy cheeks, and merry voices of the little Duncans; the kindly, booming voice of Duncan; and the ever-watchful eyes of Sarah, as she urged more steaming, savoury food upon her flock. Terence sighed. Aunt Ellen noted the sigh.

"You must be tired out from your experience this afternoon, Terence dear. It frightens me, when I think about it. You might have been injured."

"Well, an injury would not have hurt me any more than any other man—it's a chance we all have to take. I'm not a baby, you know."

Kathleen sensed his annoyance and the resentment in his tone. He seemed to be another of those petted, spoiled "gentlemen of leisure," but he was not enjoying it, and he was terribly conscious of his missing hand. He was certainly not handsome, but he was perfectly built—tall and muscular, without an ounce of superfluous flesh. His face was clean-cut and strong; no weak character looked out from those keen gray eyes. The carroty hair and freckles she did not admire so much, and his deformity was distasteful to her; but his money, his social position, his education, his friends—surely they would make up for a great deal. And she remembered his smile—only once had she seen a smile play over his face, but such a whimsical Irish smile it was! As if all the fairies in the mists of the moors were dancing through his eyes and tracing with their hands the little wrinkles about his eyes and mouth. She must make him smile again! But she was to discover that this was not an easy task. Kathleen looked at him again.

"You have a beautiful horse, Lord O'More."

"Yes, her name is Lady Bird. She is a great pet, and I'm very fond of her. I've spent months training her. She and Rags are my two best friends. Rags is not blessed with superior intelligence but he has two qualities I like—he's loyal, and he doesn't speak out of turn. Black Prince is a well set-up animal, too."

"Yes, but he behaves badly. I'm going to ride him

again to-morrow, and he's going to be taught that he cannot take the bit in his teeth and run any time he takes a notion."

Suddenly he laughed.

"What's the joke, Lord O'More?"

"I hope you will pardon me if I remind you that my name is *Terence* O'More."

"Do you object to 'Lord' O'More?"

"I do—strenuously."

"Then—Terence—my name is Kathleen, and I object to *Miss* strenuously."

"That's understood, then. It's just as well if you are coming to live with us. This household is over-run with formality now."

"Do you dislike formality?"

"Intensely."

Kathleen rather liked it, but she decided to agree with me.

"So do I—hate it."

"Good. I think we'll get along better after that."

But just then he saw her eyes on his right sleeve. He had learned to manage his food dexterously with his left hand, but he had never gotten over being sensitive and self-conscious about eating. Many times he refused to go to dinners with Uncle Maxwell and Aunt Ellen, and often when they had guests at home he refused to go down; he would ask Barlow to bring his dinner to his room, and he would feed Rags bits as he ate. All the bitterness rushed to the surface. How he hated their all too-apparent efforts to ignore his infirmity! How he hated their sympathetic glances and tactless comments! He wished he might have died when the falling tree crushed his chest; and then a half-smile twisted his lips as he thought of the Angel's admonition: "Freckles James Ross McLean, you just try dying, and you'll get a good slap!" How he longed to hear her eager voice; to see the sparkle in her unspoiled eyes; to run his fingers through her silken hair—hair shining like burnished copper in the sun! The Angel, who could look at him and talk to him for hours, and never even *see* his arm—the only person in the world who could make him forget it!

So ran his thoughts, and he was inattentive and unresponsive through the remainder of dinner. Kathleen made ineffectual attempts to interest him, but finding her efforts useless, she decided the next best thing to do was to be sweet to Lord and Lady O'More. Kathleen was quick enough to see that living in the O'More house was going to be an opportunity for her in more ways than one. She had not been so keen about it at first, but she had not known about the attractive nephew, who was just enough disinterested in her to make her extremely interested in him.

Dinner over, the others went into the music room, but Terence said, "Let's go outside for a little while, until the guests arrive. I hate having Aunt Ellen introduce me. She's sweet and lovely, and she means well, but she is so—so—*specific!* If we come in when they are all here, you can walk around with me quickly; I'll bow and it will be all over."

"But what will Lady O'More think, when she sees you are not in the receiving line?"

"She will just think I've wrecked another of her sacred ceremonial rites. She ought to be used to it by this time—it's a habit of mine. You don't know me—I'm really a very disagreeable fellow."

"I cannot possibly believe that: but I'll risk a walk in the moonlight."

Terence looked startled. He hadn't thought of that. He didn't want to walk with Kathleen in the moonlight. All he wanted was to escape the introductions—to slip in quietly after the music and dancing were started. And he had let himself in for a "walk in the moonlight" with, he must admit, a very beautiful girl with enigmatic eyes. Well, it was too late to get out of it now. He would go through with it, but he would think faster next time. He put Kathleen's cloak around her shoulders, and out they went.

Awful as the gardens were, the moonlight seemed to make them better, and the stars winking at the man in the moon added their friendly light. Kathleen put her arm through Terence's left and leaned against him as they walked. When he turned in her direction his nose just brushed the top of her head. What insidious perfume! He decided that he did not like it. There was a lovely sort of fresh fragrance about the Angel; but never perfume. He turned his head and smelled again. It didn't seem so strong this time; maybe it wasn't so bad as he had thought at first. Anyway, Kathleen was not the Angel's type.

They came to a bench.

"Let's sit down awhile—Terence."

"I'm afraid you'll catch cold."

"What a prosaic mind you have, to think of catching cold on such a glorious night as this."

Terence grinned in spite of himself, and Kathleen sat down. He sat down beside her. She sat closer—she almost snuggled.

"You are unhappy here, aren't you?"

"Perhaps not so unhappy as discontented."

"You should not be—you have everything here."

"I know it—that's what they all say. It might depend upon one's definition for 'everything,' however."

"I think you need someone to sympathize with you and to pet you. Lord O'More is too harsh—Lady O'More is too solicitous. Someone should strike a happy medium."

This time she *did* snuggle.

By George! the girl had sense! He hadn't thought of that before. It would be nice if someone understood. . . .

"I hadn't thought of that—perhaps you are right."

"Certainly, I am right. There are so many 'misunderstood' men in the world—and they are such helpless, pathetic creatures. I am sure I can understand you. I would love to have you confide in me, and I'll promise to sympathize and be a—a comfort to you."

Terence looked at her quickly.

"Are you serious, or just razzing me?"

"I'm serious. Why not? We will be in this house together, and we may as well console each other."

This was getting altogether too deep for Terence. She was *very* close to him now, and that perfume—he decided he liked the perfume; but he thought it was time to get out of the moonlight. He stood up suddenly.

"I think it's time to go in now."

Kathleen went—reluctantly. There was nothing else for her to do.

When they entered the music room they did not see Lady O'More, so they went about speaking to those they knew. Terence loved music and he loved to dance. As he put the maimed arm around Kathleen's waist, he felt her wince slightly. It was the last straw. He dropped his arms, turned on his heel, and dashed out of the room, leaving her standing there staring after him.

Terence ran upstairs, three steps at a time, and slammed the door of the library behind him. He sat down at his desk, drew out his stationery, picked up a pen, and then paused—staring at the two feathers—thinking. Yes, he was right. He had kept the Angel waiting four years. And it wasn't fair to keep her waiting any longer. Even if he broke away from the O'Mores, as he firmly intended to do, no telling how long it would take him to find a suitable position, or work that he could do. He had tried job-hunting once before, and he knew what it meant. He would have to go through all the old bitterness again. Big business men would either frankly say, "Sorry, but we can't use a man with one hand," or they would squirm and choke and stutter some such palpable excuse as "You're not strong enough," or "too young," or "too" something else. It seemed to Terence that he could not face it again, but he knew it had to be done. If he ever did make a success of anything, he would go to her, and if she had married someone else—well, it would serve him right; he would jolly well deserve it for making such a mess of his life.

Of course, dear old McLean would give him a job in a minute, but he was too proud to go back and ask for it. They had sent him away expecting great things of him—he could not go back with nothing.

There was one thing he must do—he must be square with the Angel. He must tell her the truth, and set her free. But he must be diplomatic about it. If he let her know how he loved her, her generosity and loyalty would make her cling to him. He must make it easy for her by making her think he did not care; it would hurt her for a time, but she would get over it. He would rather die than marry her, and then see the look in her eyes he had seen in the eyes of other girls. He dipped his pen in the ink and wrote:

DEAREST ANGEL:

There is no use mincing words, Angel—I am a failure. I am doing nothing, and am fitted to do nothing. I seem to be stifled by conventions, by the unyielding, inherited laws of aristocracy, and by Uncle Maxwell's relentless, domineering personality.

You would not know me now. I'm no fit companion for anyone. I've grown cynical, sarcastic, and ill-tempered. One thing remains clear before me: I know that I cannot risk hurting your pride, or being a burden to you. Anyway, why should a young and beautiful girl want a cripple for a husband? It is best for you to forget me. I cannot allow your loyalty and generosity to overshadow your better judgment, and mine.

I hope you do not think I am ungrateful or unappreciative; I'm not. I am trusting you to understand, as always.

My love and affectionate regards to all my dear friends in the Limberlost, of whom you are the shining light.

FRECKLES.

Then he sealed and stamped it, and lest he grow cowardly and change his mind, he gave it to Barlow with instructions to send it out on the morning post. Then he came back to his desk and sat staring at the two feathers for a long time. Again, he wondered . . .

CHAPTER V

Wherein the Angel Encourages a Romance

"WELL, how are all the patients this morning?" called the Angel gaily. She had come for a morning call on the Bird Woman, and not finding her in the house, she had gone around through the garden to the back yard, where she found the Bird Woman standing in front of several improvised bird cages, mostly boxes lying on their sides, with sand on the bottom, and wire across the front: a sort of hospital ward for birds.

The Bird Woman was the friend of all the wounded or crippled birds in the country. Boys of the neighbourhood brought them to her. Although we seldom stop to think about sick or hurt birds, perhaps because we see so few of them, the fact remains that baby birds get into trouble just as human babies do—and grown birds make mistakes and have accidents, even as human grown-ups. So the Bird Woman kept the cages in readiness, and it was seldom that one or more of them was not occupied. A few of the patients died, to be sure, for bird surgery is a delicate task requiring skill and practice, but many of the little fellows grew strong and fat, and were set free to go about their business.

The Bird Woman turned to look as she heard the Angel's call. The Angel was a sight for tired eyes any time. This morning it seemed to the Bird Woman she looked particularly delectable—the crisp, bright curls were in a halo around her face; her round blue eyes sparkled with the vigour of an enormous vitality; her cheeks glowed with the natural rose of perfect health; and when she smiled, full red lips parted to disclose even white teeth, and a tiny dimple appeared in one cheek. She was as fresh and clear as the morning itself in her blue and white print frock as she waved a large hat of the sunshade variety at the Bird Woman. There was nothing blasé or nonchalant about the Angel: she was too frankly interested in life, and was not ashamed to show her emotions; she could frown, or brush away a tear, or laugh with equal honesty and spontaneity.

"Hello, Pretty Thing! Come and see the latest addition to my Bird Orphanage."

On a branch in one of the boxes sat seven baby screech owls, blinking their shining round eyes in ridiculous solemnity.

"Oh, I've never seen anything so cunning! But how do you feed them? I thought owls couldn't see in daylight."

"They can't, but they can smell—just watch me."

The Bird Woman picked up a bit of beefsteak with a pair of small tweezers and held it in front of one little fellow's nose. He snapped at it savagely.

"You see what he would do to my fingers if I didn't use the tweezers, don't you?"

"I should say I do—the little cannibals! But do let me help feed them," the Angel coaxed.

"Sorry, but I've only one pair of tweezers."

"I'll soon fix that," and the Angel reached over and picked a hairpin from the dark coils on the Bird Woman's head. "You see, you don't know *all* the tricks."

The Bird Woman smiled.

"Hairpins have such a lot of uses," went on the Angel, as she speared a piece of meat and watched the littlest one of all make a savage dive for it. "I often think I should let my hair grow, just so that I would always have a supply of them on hand in case of emergency."

The Bird Woman looked at the Angel's bright hair blown in ringlets around her face.

"I think it's very lovely as it is, dear."

"Oh, all right, but Dad likes it long."

"You have plenty of time to let it grow longer."

"Thanks. I'll tell Dad you said that—I notice he thinks whatever you say is about right."

The Angel's quick eyes caught the blush that crept over the Bird Woman's face as she quickly changed the subject.

"Now, let's see what can be done for the next one."

The little fellow in the next box looked very unhappy. He was a baby blackbird who had blistered his mouth and throat on a poison berry.

"O-oh—isn't that awful? The poor wee thing! My friend Kay uses an expression that would describe him to a T."

"What is it?"

"Well, Kay would say he was 'in the middle of a bad fix.'"

Both laughed. The Bird Woman lifted him gently and pried his beak open with her finger nail. Then she took a needle and punctured three blisters. After that she washed his mouth carefully with a small piece of cotton saturated in boric acid solution.

"Now for your breakfast, you silly little bird; and next time don't select sumac berries for your supper—

they are a pretty colour, but no good for babies to eat," and once more she pried his beak open and with an eye dropper put drops of warm milk far back in his throat. He swallowed them eagerly, and when he had all he wanted, she put some vaseline in the sore mouth and set him back on his perch. There were salves which might have healed it more quickly, such as zinc oxide, but one has to be very careful with birds; anything strong kills them at once.

"I never heard of giving birds milk," said the Angel.

"I never did either. It's an invention of my own. In desperation, in cases like this, when they couldn't swallow food, I tried milk, and they not only took it but seemed to like it."

"Will he live?"

"I think so, but he has had rather a bad time and I will have to repeat this performance three or four days longer. Next I'll give him boiled potato, mashed with the yolk of a hard-boiled egg and moistened with saliva."

"Where did you learn that?"

"It's what I give my female canaries to feed their babies. They get fat on it and it makes their feathers sleek. I have eight tiny ones now, too cute for words. I feed them sometimes with a toothpick. I moisten all food for baby birds with saliva."

"How awful!"

"There's nothing awful about it—it's warm and it helps the food to digest. It is what digests your own food. Many mother birds regurgitate food to feed their babies. Food moistened with saliva is the nearest substitute."

"How do you make the baby canaries open their mouths?"

"Easiest thing in the world. Just tap a little on the edge of the nest; they think it's their mother alighting on the nest, and up come the heads with the mouths wide open."

They went on to the next cage.

"Now this is my most interesting case; it's a mother bat with her two babies. Bats seem to be half animal and half bird. The mothers carry their young in pouches, like kangaroos. The babies nurse, and they are as greedy as baby pigs. The youngsters haven't much consideration for their mothers, either; they crawl all over her and cling fast to her back with sharp little claws."

"What's the matter with her?"

"I don't know. Some boys got her out of a tree. She is hurt in some way and can't fly She has a vicious temper. Just watch this."

The Bird Woman took an orange-wood stick and gently poked the bat's mouth. She snapped at it and sunk her sharp little teeth in it. Then the Bird Woman took her eye dropper and let drops of milk run down the stick into the bat's mouth, and she swallowed them.

The Angel laughed. "No one would have thought of that but you."

"Well, she wouldn't eat herself, and I had to figure out a way to feed her so that she couldn't bite me—they make a nasty bite, like a mouse—and she was nursing her babies, so I thought she needed milk. I couldn't feed her with an eye dropper. First time she snapped at it she'd break it and, like as not, cut her mouth. So if I let her bite the stick, that keeps her mouth open; I let the milk run in and she *has* to swallow it, and if she feels disposed to bite, she can help herself to the stick."

"Well, commend me to you for bat psychology!"

"Goodness knows, I couldn't be sure of the proper diet for bat mothers with nursing children, but they will eat beefsteak—it's the nearest substitute for worms," and the Bird Woman proceeded to give Mrs. Bat her allowance of meat in the same manner as she fed the owls.

"That's all for a couple of hours. I have to gorge them. There is nothing like the capacity of a baby bird, and it wouldn't do for mother to run short of milk."

Arm in arm they walked toward the gate.

"What a delight your garden is!" and the Angel stopped to look. The flowers, like Topsy, "just grew." Winding, narrow paths of sand ran through it as carelessly as streamers of ribbon carried by a truant summer breeze. The fence on one side was completely hidden by hollyhocks and morning glories of all colours; and in charming disarray there grew cosmos, phlox, poppies, daisies, marigolds, zinnias, four o'clocks, asters, sweet-Williams—all the old-fashioned flowers that delighted the hearts of our grandmothers. It had been allowed to seed itself, so that when one plant died, there was always another to take its place.

"It's lovely," said the Angel softly. "It looks like a garden God might have made."

"Well, He did—mostly. I don't like to interfere with Nature. Whenever I do, I find I make a mess of things."

They walked on to the gate.

"What are you doing this afternoon?" queried the Angel.

"I am going to the Limberlost to take pictures of some orchids. There is a large patch of them near Freckles' room—want to come along?"

"Love to. I'll go have lunch with Dad, and then I'll be back."

"Never mind coming back. I'll meet you at the bank at two o'clock," promised the Bird Woman as she went into the house.

It was just a little country town nestled beside the old Wabash River, and the Angel walked the three blocks to the bank, of which her father was president and cashier. As she opened the door she did not see him, but she noticed Fred Mason, the assistant cashier and bookkeeper, in earnest conversation with Bill Dillon and Tom Ryder, two of the village "bad eggs." Immediately the Angel was suspicious. Her ears were trained by the Bird Woman so that she heard things more readily than most people. She had helped in the bank often enough that she knew all the customers and their financial ratings, and she could post the books, make up the exchanges, count the cash, use the adding machine, or wait on customers just as well as Fred. Now she pretended to catch her dress in the door, and fussed with it as she listened.

Distinctly she heard Bill say: "We need more cash, and we've got to have it."

And Tom: "We asked the old man for a loan and he said No."

Then Bill again: "You better come through, or it will be just too bad for you."

And Fred: "All right—*all right!* Now shut up and beat it. I'll see you later."

"Hello, Fred," said the Angel, nodding to Bill and Tom as they passed her. "What's all the heavy argument about?"

"Well, none of my 'heavy arguments' are about business, so don't worry."

But the Angel looked troubled as she walked on

through to her father's private office. She found him sitting at his desk with his head in his hands.

"Hello, Dad—what's up? Last oil well come in a dry hole, or something?"

The Angel's dad rose and kissed her. He was a man nearing fifty, of slightly over average height, with a narrow, aristocratic nose and a high forehead. He wore a moustache, brown like his thinning hair, which covered up the friendly curve of his mouth. His eyes, a clear, candid blue, always met another's squarely. At once he inspired confidence and respect.

"Not a thing wrong—go to lunch with me?"

"That's what I came for, Dad."

He put on his hat and they went out together. The Angel was bareheaded, as usual. Her dad said she only bought hats so that she could take them off.

They went into the village restaurant and sat down at a secluded table. The Angel studied her dad as he ordered lunch. The hair above his ears was showing considerable gray, and his forehead had a few new wrinkles—but that was to be expected at his age. What worried the Angel was the look in his eyes. Usually a brilliant blue, to-day they were a sort of dull gray with no lights in them at all.

"Come, Dad, out with it! Something's wrong. You can't fool me."

"Well, to tell the truth, it's you!"

The Angel looked surprised. "Me? I thought I was a model chee-ild. I say my prayers at night, and brush my teeth in the morning—what more do you want?"

But her dad was not in a "kidding" mood.

"Really, I'm serious. When you were little I managed you all right. When you were away at college I was beastly lonely, but my one consoling thought was that you were being properly educated and trained." He broke a roll, buttered a small piece, and munched it thoughtfully.

"And now that I'm home again, why am I so much worse to take care of than I was before I left? I can weep on your shoulder just the same, or dash in and interrupt you when you're busy, or ask for money at the wrong time!"

"Because you are older, my dear. You are no longer a child; you are a young lady. Your problems are not the same; there's quite a difference."

The waitress served their meal, and when she had gone he continued: "I don't know about your clothes, or about the parties you should give or attend. Girls your age, it seems to me, need a woman."

"Oh, so you want to marry the Bird Woman, and are using me for an alibi!"

They both laughed.

"You are very sagacious, my dear. I'll admit I've been lonely these past eighteen years since your mother died. You were only two, you know, when she left us."

The Angel sobered instantly. "Forgive me, Dad. How selfish I've been! Of course you have been terribly lonesome. Why didn't you do it long ago? I've loved the Bird Woman ever since I can remember her. You go right ahead and do it. It's perfectly all right with me."

"Well, it's great that you approve. I didn't want to hurt you." He lighted a cigar and looked at the Angel quizzically.

"Now that that's settled, I overheard part of a conversation between Fred and Bill Dillon and Tom

Ryder as I came in. Seemed to be about money. Did either of them ask you for a loan?"

"Yes, and I refused. I have reason to believe they are bootlegging, and neither of them has anything but a bad reputation."

"I'm sure they asked Fred for money."

"Fred cannot make a loan without my O. K., but I'll speak to him about it. You're a great girl—always on the job, aren't you?"

"I've got to keep busy at something—I'll be running this bank yet!"

They looked at each other in amusement.

"What is the last news from Freckles?"

"I had a letter this week, but there was no news in it. I think those people have had an awful effect on him. There is no sparkle or vigour in his letters; they are just *blah*—he writes like an old woman!"

"Is he doing anything yet?"

"Gracious, no! His uncle thinks work is a disgrace. I think I'll have to write him to come back here, so we can pep him up!" The Angel laughed ruefully.

"You're right. A man never gets in a rut and loses his perspective so quickly as when he has nothing to do. I had to take a six months' vacation once, and the cure was worse than the disease."

"I'm sure of it, but I don't feel that it's up to me to make suggestions yet. He has just finished his education, and it will take a little time for him to find something suitable. If Ireland is anything like this country, he will find that jobs don't fall off trees and land in your lap these days. A man who wants a job has to *hunt* it."

"You're right. What are you doing this afternoon?"

Seeing the Angel looked worried, he thought it wise to change the subject.

"I'm going to the Limberlost with the Bird Woman. Want me to plead your case?"

"Oh, a few well-chosen words delivered in your usual diplomatic manner wouldn't do a bit of harm. If she can resist you, she can do more than I ever could."

As they came out of the café, they saw the Bird Woman seated in her car waiting for them in front of the bank. She would not have a chauffeur; she said he would scare the birds, and she could not be bothered. So the faithful little horse and buggy in which she used to jog around over the country had been replaced by a shining roadster.

The Angel waved, and her dad lifted his hat as they walked over to the car, the rumble seat of which was filled with boxes and shovels and photographic paraphernalia.

"Again the Limberlost surrenders to the invasion of modern modes and methods."

"Well, it ought to be accustomed to it by this time. I've been invading it regularly for five years now, and its attractions are still numerous and varied," said the Bird Woman as she opened the car door for the Angel, who climbed into her seat and blew a kiss to her dad.

"Good-bye! Good luck, and take good care of my child," he called after them.

"Your orders shall be obeyed," answered the Bird Woman as she stepped on the gas.

"Does your dad ever think about anyone but you?" she asked the Angel.

"Oh, yes, indeed! And the other subject for his thoughts isn't more than a million miles away, either."

"Just what is the meaning of that cryptic remark?"

"Well, he thinks about *you* a lot."

"How do you know?"

"Maybe he thinks out loud!" The Angel laughed, as the Bird Woman blushed. "I don't want to butt in on your party, but that house is pretty lonesome for the two of us. I like you and you like me—at least, I think you do. But, of course, the essential thing is whether or not you and Dad love each other."

"I don't know because I've never allowed myself to think of him in that way. But I believe it would be very easy to love him. I've known him for twenty years, and he is the finest man I know."

The Angel nodded. "Yes, they don't make them any better than dear old Dad. And he needs a vacation—he hasn't had one since I can remember. A wedding trip would be just the thing!"

"Don't make plans too soon. The gentleman in question hasn't spoken yet, you know."

"Well, his tongue was in good working order this noon, and with a little well-disguised encouragement, he should arrive at the well-known climax not later than this evening."

"What did he say this noon?"

"That would be telling—I couldn't double-cross Dad, you know."

"Of course you couldn't, and I didn't mean to be inquisitive. I was just—just curious."

"I don't blame you a bit," and the Angel gave the Bird Woman's arm an affectionate squeeze.

"I suppose I'm a fairly self-sufficient individual. I have my photography, my nature study, my writing, my flowers, my reading, and a house to keep me busy. But

I do get terribly lonely at times—one misses human companionship."

"I don't believe people were meant to live alone—least of all anyone with the human feeling and generous impulses you have."

"Don't flatter me, dear."

"I'm not. I mean every word of it. I think you and Dad are meant for each other. That's my story, and I'm going to stick to it!"

CHAPTER VI

Wherein the Bird Woman Takes the Angel to the Limberlost

AS THEY approached the Swamp, the Bird Woman drove slowly. Nothing escaped her eye or ears, trained as they were by her years of outdoor work to catch all the sights and sounds of Nature. She watched for rare flowers, moth or butterfly cocoons, bird nests, odd varieties of shrubs or ferns. She stopped to examine anything that looked unusual. They turned off the highway into the narrow road that led into the Swamp; it was not used much, and grass and flowers grew between the wheel tracks.

The Angel drew a deep breath of the fresh, woodsy air. "Oh!" she said. "It's great to be alive on a day like this!"

"Indeed it is! Especially if you are lucky enough to be where you can get into the country, away from the smoke and noise and grime of a city. Cities drive me crazy!"

"I like cities for a few weeks at a time. I like to shop and go to theatres and concerts, and get a taste of cabarets and all that, but I'm always glad to get back."

"Me, too—just look at that," and the Bird Woman pointed to the road ahead of them.

On either side ran wide ditches, partly filled with

water, and just inside the ditches ran ancient rail fences, moss- and lichen-covered, a haven for birds, snakes, rabbits, squirrels, butterflies, and all wild things.

"When they take down these fences I'll be ruined," she continued. "Half the bird nests I've photogaphed were in the corners of them; rabbits and quail nest on the ground under the tall grass; vines and wild roses make beautiful backgrounds, as well as furnishing grand hiding places for the nests of smaller birds; butterflies and bees hover over the flowers. You know, my dear, there is nothing so soothing as the droning hum of bees; I can't see why people are so afraid of them."

"Perhaps because they sting."

"They don't sting if they are let alone. You know what happens if you interfere with other people's business—well, a bee can't make a sarcastic remark, so he stings."

The Angel laughed. "Yes, it's quick and effective, all right."

"*And* just what a lot of people deserve. A bee is dependent for his life, and for his work, on the pollen he gathers from flowers with which he makes honey. He doesn't bother anyone; and he doesn't hurt the flowers. He's industrious and a willing worker. I think anyone who interferes with a bee deserves all he gets. But I believe I was talking about rail fences. Look at this one—you've never seen a more picturesque sight than that."

The Angel glanced in the direction the Bird Woman indicated. The old tumbledown fence *was* a picture. The pink of wild roses mingled with the creamy white of alder bushes; a variety of ferns and feathery grasses grew among the variously coloured wild flowers. In the water of the ditch was reflected the blue of the wild iris, the pink of the mallows, joe-pye weed and ironwort, and the yellow of the goldenrod. Back in the swamp the bird calls were incessant, and a mass of red bud and dogwood in full bloom mingled with the pussy willows to make a charming background for it all.

"These straight wire fences are terrible; the light shining on them scares the birds and hurts your eyes; they get so hot from the sun the vines cannot cling to them, and they burn the birds' feet. There is no place to hide nests, so they drive the little wild things back to the woods. I suppose they do make room for a few more furrows to plant in a wheat field, or for a few more rows of corn. One great trouble with our country is that we have to commercialize everything. We're in such a mad rush to earn money, no one thinks about the beauty of a rail fence if its destruction means a few more bushels of corn."

The Bird Woman suddenly realized that she was philosophizing to herself. The Angel's eyes had grown dreamy; she was not hearing a word.

"The old Swamp was never lovelier than it is this year. I wish Freckles could see it now. There is talk of draining it, and then it will be ruined. There were some agricultural experts in town last week, and they reported that if this soil were drained, it would be ideal for onions and celery. Can you imagine the old Swamp covered with fields of celery and onions?"

"Makes me sick to think about it. And that's not the worst—Dad says a Chicago oil company wants to drill oil wells all over it. The smell of oil and onions ought to be great!"

"Well, let's not think about it until we have to. Anyway, Mr. McLean still holds his lease on it, and he refuses to give permission for the oil wells. He is very sentimental about the Swamp."

"He's a darling, the finest man I know next to Dad. He is hoping Freckles will come back, and he wants the Swamp here to greet him, I guess. I love the Swamp, too, but I'm afraid His Lordship, Terence Maxwell O'More, will have lost his taste for rattlesnakes and vultures and outlaws by the time he comes back—if he ever does."

"Do you know when he is coming?"

"I do not. His letters are peculiar; they don't sound like him. His people are not like us; they may have changed him. After all, he has their blood in his veins. You know, he was a poor boy. Wealth and all that goes with it may not have been good for him. Here he had to work for everything he had, so he knew how to appreciate it. Now he has a fat allowance from his uncle every month, aside from half of his grandfather's estate which was given to him when he was twenty-one. There are servants in the house, grooms and gardeners; Freckles has his own personal valet. It's a very different life from ours."

The Bird Woman stopped the car in the shade of an aged sycamore tree and faced the Angel.

"Now see here, my dear, don't be bitter. If I know Freckles, and I believe I do, I know he is not the kind to change fundamentally. He might lose his perspective for a time, but that isn't serious—we all do that—it won't last. Underneath he is the same. I'm sure of it. I've worked in the fields and woods for many years, and they get a hold on you that never is broken. Men come back to the earth for solace for their soiled and ruffled souls and for rest from the tumult of the whirlpool of life, just as a little child runs to its mother and cries out its troubles on her shoulder. Aside from that, Freckles has *you*, and you can hold any man you choose—he would go through hell on earth, and still come back to you."

"Well, perhaps you are right. I'm not very old, but I've seen a few strange things happen—there's no accounting for human nature sometimes. I write to Freckles just as I always have, but I've no desire to keep him if he doesn't want to be kept."

"That's the natural pride of youth. Wonderful youth! There is nothing like its high confidence, its independence, its ambition, and its pride."

"Yes, I suppose I have pride—most folks have. But I buried my pride once to save Freckles, when he was homeless, nameless, sick in body and sick in soul. Now he has not only a name but a title; he has a huge estate for a home; he has wealth, health, social position, and aristocratic friends. That's about all the background anyone needs, and I don't feel free to make advances. All he lacks is a hand, and that is nothing compared to the handicaps of some of the boys I know."

"Yes, dear, that's all true, but it is usually the woman's task to pull these men out of holes that they dig for themselves, either intentionally or otherwise. Have you forgotten how sensitive he was? He may need to be saved from himself."

"I've forgotten nothing. But if that young gentleman needs saving again, the job is likely to fall on his own shoulders, or those of some other girl!"

"Do you think there is another girl?"

"How do I know? *Something* is radically wrong with his letters. Just to show you what I mean, I'll read you a choice morsel from his last letter." The Angel extracted a folded letter from her pocket, and read:

"DEAREST ANGEL:——

"Now you must admit that's not what you might call *ardent* after four years, is it? All the boys write to me like that, only they say Dot or Dorothy. No one else calls me Angel but you and Dad."

The Bird Woman repressed a smile as the Angel read on:

"It's evening, and I'm sitting in front of my fire with Rags asleep beside me. According to the rules and regulations for the day, which are prescribed by Uncle Maxwell's standards, I should be thoroughly exhausted. Just listen to the strenuous routine: I woke up at seven-thirty and had breakfast in bed. I'm not supposed to wake up until eight-thirty—it isn't done—but I insist upon being contrary and coming to life an hour earlier than the rules allow. Then I was bathed and shaved and dressed in a black velvet dressing gown, which I was permitted to wear until I had read the papers. Then I was dressed again and took a short walk. Then I was dressed again and had lunch. Then I was dressed again and took a ride. Then I was dressed again and had tea. Then I was dressed again and had dinner. And here I am, about to be dressed again for the night—oh, yes, I'm not even allowed to dress for bed by myself. Barlow gets all the exercise, but Uncle Maxwell considers that a day's work. Exciting day for a six-footer, wasn't it? I can hear the Boss laughing now—thinking of the day's work I used to do.

"That's a great spirit, isn't it? Makes one feel so cheerful and hopeful."

"That *does* sound a bit down at the mouth, but I wouldn't let it worry me. It's just a momentary mood, and probably had passed by morning."

"Perhaps—but his letters the past six months have had the same strain running through them. I'm getting fed up on them. I don't know what he has on his mind, but I wish he would say it straight out. I'm no good at groping in the dark."

The Bird Woman was troubled. She saw that the Angel was unconvinced. That may or may not be a fault of youth. Is it better for them to profit by the experience of their elders, or is it better for them to learn life's lessons for themselves? The Bird Woman did not believe in mixing too much in the Angel's affairs; but she did like to smooth over the rough spots when she could. The Angel slipped an arm around the Bird Woman.

"Oh, I'm so sorry! I didn't mean to bother you with my troubles, but you're such a peach and I've no one to talk to but Dad, and while Dad is great, he doesn't understand girls' problems as well as a woman. You've made a marvellous success of your life all by yourself: your books and pictures have entertained thousands. Everyone loves you!"

The Bird Woman smiled.

"Let's not talk about me; let's talk about you. I hope you won't mind if I ask a question."

"Not at all."

"What about Dick Summerfield?"

The Angel looked squarely into her eyes.

"He is the best friend I have, and I like him best of any of the boys."

"I see—handsome, isn't he?"

"Yes—*very*. One of those perfect brunette men that you are sure to read a description of in almost any novel you pick up."

"Go out with him much?"

"Why—yes—I suppose I do. Every place I go, I go with Dick. No one else asks me. You see, there are just a small crowd of us, and we're usually paired off the same way. If I didn't go with Dick, I'd stay at home, and that would be pretty lonesome business."

"Yes, it would. You couldn't be expected to stay at home; soon you wouldn't have any friends at all. I was thinking about Dick."

"Dick is all right. Dad says he is a fine fellow, and that he is to be trusted anywhere."

"No doubt he is, but that's not what I mean. I know what you think about Dick. Now the question is: what does Dick think about you?"

"I don't know—I've never thought about it."

"Well, I'll bet he has thought about it—plenty."

"What do you mean?"

"I don't want to flatter you, my dear, but you are a very attractive girl in many ways. What does Dick know about Freckles?"

"Nothing. I don't speak of him to anyone. I can't say anything—what would I say? Things are so indefinite, they would only laugh at my credulity. You see, the crowd in town knew very little of Freckles. You know that I saw him mostly in the Swamp, when I was with you. It was there we first learned to love each other. What happy kids we were! When he recovered from his injury, he left immediately, and I went away to school. Things changed here. The discovery of oil brought many new people, and many of the old friends had moved away. When I came back, I met almost an entire new crowd of young folks, and they know nothing about Freckles. Can you imagine the reaction the simple love story of Freckles and me would have on them? I can hear Lolly now: 'The country maiden awaits her titled lover from a foreign land', etc., etc., etc. I *can't* tell them

—I'd be the target for their wisecracks from now on. I couldn't stand it. You see, they don't know Freckles. I wonder sometimes if I know him myself."

The Angel turned away and bit her lip, trying to hold back the tears. The Bird Woman patted the Angel's shoulder.

"Let's forget it and go to work—there's nothing like a good round of real work to soothe one's ruffled feelings. We've got to keep smiling—the same old sun will still be shining in the morning."

They loaded themselves with the camera, cases of plate holders, tripod, and extra lenses, the usual paraphernalia the Bird Woman carried, and followed the little path to Freckles' room.

Freckles' room remained much the same as he had left it, but the natural growth in four years' time made it look a little different. The same moss- and lichen-covered logs were there for seats; the specimen case was in the same old spot; the carpet of moss had flourished and the flowers and grasses were growing in profusion. The vines had made a network entirely over the top, so that it looked like a real room—with shrubs and trees for walls.

The orchids were growing in huge clumps just at the edge of Freckles' room, and they were covered with a profusion of delicate white and lavender blossoms, the shape of Dutch wooden shoes, hence their name—Lady Slippers. One wondered how anything so fragile and dainty could come from the black muck and slime of the Swamp. As the Bird Woman stepped on the moss around them it was like stepping on a huge sponge filled with water; her feet sank a couple of inches, and the water oozed up around them.

The Bird Woman focussed her camera and took her pictures, with one eye on the Angel. She was catching tiny turtles from a murky pool. She looked such a child as she stood there. She had stripped her feet and rolled up her sleeves, and had waded out in the water almost to her knees. Truly she was the Swamp Angel—simple, beautiful, and as unafraid of life as she was of the Swamp. It was a shame for her to be unhappy, but life cannot always be a beautiful dream for any of us.

The Angel came over and stood watching the Bird Woman, her hands full of the squirming, pawing turtles, her arms dripping muddy water, and her feet and legs black from the mire.

"You're a fine sight! What are you going to do with those?"

"They are for my goldfish bowls, and if I have any left over, I'll put them in the old tub out by the well. I always have a supply of turtles. They don't grow very fast in captivity, and when they get too big to be cute I bring them out here and put them back in the pool. Then they can get acquainted with their families again."

The Bird Woman smiled and the Angel's eyes sparkled as she went on.

"It's lots of fun to watch them snap at flies—one of my daily occupations is to kill flies for them, and once I got a long fish worm and gave one end to one turtle, and the other end to another turtle."

"*Angel!* How awful! I'm surprised at you. What did they do?"

"They swallowed and swallowed until they came together, and then started pawing. It was a tough worm, and I was afraid they would scratch each other's eyes out before it broke, so I cut it in two."

"That was a fine performance—I hope you don't repeat it often."

"Never again. But you needn't be so shocked. I've often seen you string poor suffering worms on fish hooks, and that isn't exactly pleasant."

"You win."

The Angel took a key from her sweater pocket and opened a rough wooden case that was nailed to a huge tree in one corner of the room. Some of Freckles' things were still in it. She took out a can, put the turtles in it, and set it on a log. Then she took a towel and set about drying her feet and dressing them. As the Bird Woman began packing up her things, the Angel asked:

"Do you ever see Mr. McLean?"

"Oh, yes. He calls occasionally with your dad."

"Does he ever mention Freckles?"

"He used to talk of him all the time, but recently not a word."

"I feel very sorry for him. You see, Freckles was all in the world he had to love. You see how perfectly this room is kept? Well, McLean hires Duncan to do it; and he still rides out here on Nelly and spends hours fussing around, arranging the shrubs and vines—there isn't a weed in sight. And he's fighting the oil men and the county officials who want the Swamp drained. He says he won't have the Swamp ruined. Life doesn't hold so much for him just now, and it's too bad. He is such a splendid fellow. He had such great plans for Freckles, and now that he is gone, McLean seems lost. I think he is very unhappy."

"He is. It wouldn't be so bad if he thought the boy was happy, but I suppose the letters he writes to McLean have the same under-current as those he writes to you. No doubt McLean is troubled, and is trying to find out what is wrong and why."

"Well, I wish him luck, and I hope wnen ne finds out he will tell me. Do you see that trail over there?" The Angel indicated a little path leading directly through the heart of the Swamp. The Bird Woman nodded.

"That's a short cut to Duncan's house. He and McLean blazed it themselves, and it was no easy task. They had to drain two pools, and pile in logs and stumps in lots of places."

"What did they do it for?"

"It's much shorter than the trail around the Swamp. Duncan can come through this way in half the time. It's just another of McLean's Scotch precautions. I guess he thought if Duncan had to come the long way around he wouldn't come so often. Duncan loved Freckles, but he is not nearly so sentimental about him as McLean. It's a good trail now, though—I travel it myself."

The Bird Woman looked amazed.

"What do you mean, 'you travel it yourself'?"

"Just what I say. I call on Sarah Duncan regularly. I take all my half-worn clothes to her Mary. She is in school in town now, and she is thrilled to death over my light-coloured things. Sarah only buys dark things because they are more practical. I come this way because it's so much shorter than the pike."

"And for no other reason?" inquired the Bird Woman sweetly. "Are you sure McLean is the only sentimental one?"

The Angel blushed, but she was honest.

"Yes, I come here, too—sometimes when things get too much for me. I bring his letters here and read them, and try to make them fit into the old Freckles I knew; but letters don't change with environment—as—as people seem to. I look off into the old Swamp and dream about what I'd like his letters to say, but when I look at them again, the same old words are there in cold black and white, indifferent, sarcastic, and bitter. So it isn't a very successful plan. I can't understand him—I just *can't*."

"I know it's difficult, dear, but you must be brave. I still have a feeling that he has not changed, that way down deep he is the same, and that he will come out of it in time, and be his own old self again. But I don't like your coming here alone. It's dangerous. You know this old Swamp is just as thick as it ever was."

"I never thought about it."

"No, you wouldn't."

"But sometimes I bring my revolver just to do a little target practice. I'm quite proud of myself because I can still hit the bottom of a Campbell soup can at forty paces—right in the middle, too!"

The Bird Woman had to smile. That was the Angel—tears one minute and smiles the next.

"All the same, Angel, I wish you'd promise to take your revolver with you whenever you come here. I'd feel safer about you."

"All right. Henceforth the trusty gat accompanies its dangerous owner!"

By this time the Angel had emptied the can of turtles in her lap, and they were crawling all over her.

"Good. Now put down the darling pets and hand that short-handled shovel to me, will you?"

"What are you going to do?"

"Dig up a clump of these orchids—I've a moist spot all ready for them at home, where they can have their toes in the water."

"I wouldn't bother to do that now—you might not be living in your house very long, and there is a grand place for them in the low spot below our orchard. I have a wild garden started there, and we can finish it together."

The Bird Woman laughed.

"Your poor dad! What chances has he with two women conspiring against him!"

"Well, he seems to like it. At least, I don't notice him struggling desperately to free himself from our clutches."

"What a darling you are! Let's go."

"All right. Dad said he wouldn't be home to dinner. Wonder where he can be going?" teased the Angel.

"Won't you come along, dear?"

"Couldn't think of interrupting the proceedings. Besides, I have a heavy date myself; Dick and the gang are coming to dinner, and we'll be all set to razz Dad when he comes home to-night. You'd better come over with him; he may need your moral support!"

CHAPTER VII

Wherein the Man of Affairs and the Bird Woman Are Married

WHEN Mr. Kingsley came in, just at the conclusion of his daughter's dinner party, and announced that he was going to be married, there was immediate excitement. The Angel's friends were all likable youngsters, most of them a little older than she. There was Lolly the wisecracking one, with Adele, the quietest girl of them all, who smiled at his jokes and adored him silently. There was Lolly's sister, Kay, comely and comical, with Al, who was as tall and slim as Kay was short and fat. There was big Bill, the captain of the football team, with tiny Kitty, the daughter of the Methodist preacher. (She often pretended to be shocked, but she really was not.) There was pretty red-haired Joan, with Jewish Sam Goldberg. There was blue-eyed Irish Molly, born in the *city* of Limerick, if you please, with Leo Latti, dark-skinned Italian. And there was Dick—ever shadowing the Angel. All sensed his adoration for her, but she was either oblivious of it, or chose to ignore it.

Mr. Kingsley was the sort of man whom all young people adore. They knew him to be a firm yet kind father, considerate, understanding, and invariably just. They had a way of slipping into the bank and asking his advice, and they never were disappointed or disconcerted. Youth feels a vast importance which it likes respected; it does not like its opinions undervalued nor its problems underestimated. This Mr. Kingsley understood. It is a rare gift in a man and one youth never fails to recognize and appreciate. When any of "the boys" came into the bank, Mr. Kingsley always had time to see them; he treated their problems with the same interest and consideration as those of his elderly and wealthy customers. The young folks were never made to feel that either they or their affairs were trivial or insignificant. So when he came into their party with a sudden and brief announcement, "Hello, young folks! I've good news—I'm going to be married!" there was pandemonium, and he was nearly mobbed as they closed in around him with their greetings and congratulations.

"The Bird Woman!" was the cry in one breath.

"How did you guess it? You youngsters work too fast for me—can't keep any secrets at all these days!"

"How could we help it? We're not blind!"

"When is the grand and glorious occasion? I want to be Master of Ceremonies." This from Lolly, the irrepressible one.

"All I can say is, they have my sympathy if *you* have anything to do with it."

"Well, you haven't much time to prepare the fireworks. We are having the ceremony in three days."

"Soon as that, Dad?" queried the Angel.

"Didn't think I could work so fast, did you, dear?" That was funny, too, but he didn't know that he had done just *what* the Angel and the Bird Woman wanted him to do, and just *when* they had decided he would. He went on:

"Once he gets started, your old dad isn't so slow. But is that too soon to suit you?"

"No, indeed. I was only surprised for the moment. There is no reason in the world why you should wait." She turned to her guests. "A wedding in three days means a lot of work——"

"Oh, no," Mr. Kingsley interrupted. "We thought we would just go quietly to Reverend Cain's——"

"Well, *I* think you will do no such thing! That's ridiculous, and I won't stand for it at all. We will have the wedding right here." The Angel could be very decisive at times.

"Now that that's settled, what's the next topic for discussion?"

"Lolly, *will* you be quiet?"

"Have it your own way, youngsters. I'm sure the bride won't object. But please don't fuss; we want it very quiet."

"Oh, I'll see that it's quiet—*and how*—I'm always quiet!" Lolly again.

"Well, I choose to give away the bride," Dick announced.

"Don't be so choosy—you might find yourself singin' in the rain."

"You'd give her away all right! You'd probably trip her and let her fall downstairs."

"You're always the cheerful prognosticator!"

And so the congratulations, suggestions, and nonsense continued, until Mr. Kingsley escaped to his den for a quiet hour with his paper and pipe.

Then the Angel spoke: "Now it's time to forget the kidding and settle down to the business in hand. So gather round me, children, and let's plan something really spiffy for the Bird Woman and Dad. Three days is not much time."

"With such fast workers as my present henchmen," said Lolly, rising and gesturing elaborately, "we can accomplish hitherto unheard-of feats by way of decoration, entertainment, and nourishment. The way I can count calories since my sister Kay is reducing is most amazing. I can suggest non-fattening foods by the score. For instance, we could serve frozen fruit salad (dressing made with lemon juice), gluten-bread sandwiches, and black coffee, with saccharine, or——"

"Oh, *do* be serious!"

"Never more serious in my life. There are among us a few of the female persuasion who cannot afford to gain avoirdupois. We have 'gag' men, 'yes' men, 'know' men——"

"Well, you belong to the 'gag' class!"

"*Per*-haps. But gags inspired by me don't end as disastrously or violently as *some* gags I could mention."

The Angel stood up and rapped for order.

"Lolly, sit down. I've an idea. The Bird Woman likes things to be 'different.' Something original *always* makes a hit with her. Now I suggest a wild wedding."

"Then why sit me in the corner? That was my idea *exactly*. *Wild*. But not altogether unrestrained; boisterous, but not turbulent; stormy, but with mild breezes ——"

"Lolly, *do* be quiet, and let me finish what I started. I meant wild *decorations*. The Bird Woman loves the outdoors and all wild things. Wild flowers are dainty and delicate, and there are loads of them right now. If you'll all help, we can transform this house into a fairyland of wild flowers. What do you say?"

"To fairyland we go
With a song of joy, heigho——"

Lolly rose and did a spring dance.

"Bill," said the Angel, "will you kindly get your best football tackle hold on Lolly, and *keep* him in his chair for a few minutes?"

"You and who else? You may temporarily incapacitate my limbs, fair lady, but you can't my organ of speech. Now why confine the decorations to flowers? Why not a few snakes and lizards crawling among the flowers? And what could be sweeter than a few tree toads clinging to the bride's bosom? They could crawl around and amuse themselves during the ceremony!"

Dick fired a book at Lolly.

They went on making plans until well past midnight.

"Now it's time for you all to go home so we can get a good sleep. There's strenuous labour ahead of us. All of you who can get away meet me here at nine in the morning, and don't wear your Sunday-go-to-meeting frocks or French heels, either. Hiking boots and breeches are best to invade the Swamp; if you haven't those, skirts and sweaters and flat-heeled shoes. Now, skip—all of you!"

But Dick was not so easily disposed of; he lingered after the others had gone.

"What do you really think of them getting married, dear?"

"I really think it's splendid. The Bird Woman and I are great pals. Dad and I both are often lonely, and she is, too. I think it's an ideal arrangement."

"I just wanted to be sure it was all right with you; I couldn't bear to see you unhappy."

"You're a dear, Dick, always looking out for me. It's a nice feeling."

"Don't know of anything I'd rather do, dear. I——"

"Now you run along, too," the Angel interrupted. "See you in the morning," and the Angel fairly pushed him out the door.

So it happened that the usually well-ordered Kingsley household was in a turmoil. The Angel requested the Bird Woman not to come at all, saying they wanted to do everything. Dick borrowed a truck, and all the volunteers brought their cars.

It was quite a procession that left the Angel's house the next morning. First came the truck with a wheelbarrow on it, buckets to carry water, lunch boxes, and a varied assortment of spades and shovels. Then came the Ford with the Angel's gardener and the Bird Woman's gardener, who was loaned to them for the occasion. The Angel and several others were sitting on the back of the truck with their legs dangling, laughing and singing, a noisy crowd. After the Ford came a couple of cars for the young people to ride in coming back when the truck would be loaded.

The noise attracted a lot of attention, and the neighbours ran out to look. But the whole town knew and loved the Angel; whatever she did was all right. As they passed the Kings', Cora paused in her daily task of hanging a washing on the line and lifted little Cliff, with the crooked knee, so that he could see better.

"Oh," he lisped, "ith pretty Mith Dottie, ithn't it? The alwayth givth me pennith. I bet the'd give me thome now, if the thaw me."

"Yes, I 'spect she would, Cliffie," and Cora took the last clothes pin out of her mouth and deftly fastened the corner of Mrs. Black's best linen tablecloth to the swaying line.

In the Thompsons' back yard, Jake King, Cora's father-in-law, was digging a cistern for "soft" water, so that the two Thompson flappers wouldn't get their skin rough using borax to "break" the water. As usual, the rim of the hole was lined with children, and old Jake, who loved them all, told them stories as he tossed great shovels full of dirt over his head. It never mattered whether old Jake was digging a cistern or a grave—the edge of the hole was lined with children, just the same. Jake's unshaved face, with the bleary eyes, and tobacco juice dripping from the corners of his mouth, peered out of the hole, and he smiled as the children called and the Angel waved her hand.

"Miss Dottie's the finest girl in this town," he said. "She's the only one of her crowd that speaks to me. Don't never git too stuck up to speak to folks you know, children," and Jake went on with his digging and his story.

And so it was all through the poor section of town. Everyone smiled at the Angel, and she waved back. Even when they came to the unpainted shacks where the shutters always were kept closed, it was the same. But they could not see the dead eyes of the white-lipped women light up with wistful smiles of real affection as they peered through cracks in the shutters and saw the Angel, perhaps thinking of a tiny grave somewhere, wherein frustrated hopes and cherished ambitions were buried with a little body. For they had no way of knowing that on the last day of every month Minnie, one of these bits of human wreckage, slipped unobtrusively up the alley, through the garage, and tapped at the Angel's back door; nor that the Angel was always there to greet her with all of that month's magazines, a few books, and candy or nuts or fruit—there was always a treat of some sort; nor that the Angel always went with Minnie into the garden and cut for her an armload of flowers, so that when Minnie went home she carried a touch of colour and a breath of perfume into its dreary dinginess.

"You sure know your 'four hundred,' Dot. Why don't you introduce us?"

"Principally because I've never been introduced myself. It really isn't necessary; I know them just as you know them; only difference is, I speak and you don't. It doesn't hurt me a bit, and it pleases them—and besides that, you never know when you're going to need a friend."

"Speech! Speech!"

"Well, whenever you ask me a question, you're likely to get an answer."

As they went on, the Angel suddenly laughed.

"If I asked you why you laughed, would I get an answer?"

"Yea, verily, that you would. I was just thinking of a momentous occasion—I was ten years old, and I'd saved all my money for a bicycle. One day when I had learned to ride it fairly well, I started out this way, and I realized to my horror that I kept going faster and faster, and I couldn't stop and the road was too narrow to turn around! Just as I was trying to decide what to do, I saw Ned Sims driving his team toward me, hitched to an enormous load of hay. The road was sloping on each side and it was the law that loaded wagons had the right of way; so I knew he wouldn't turn out an inch for me. There was only one thing to do—I aimed that bicycle at the softest looking fence corner I could see, and shut my eyes——"

"What happened?"

"Well, my aim was fairly good. When the bicycle hit the ditch, I landed in an ignominious heap in the fence corner. I picked myself up, rescued the bike, and discovered I couldn't mount or get started back. So I ran down the road shrieking frantically at Ned. When he finally heard me, he stopped his team and started me back down the road ahead of him—so he 'could keep an eye on me.'"

"You always find a gallant knight to come to the rescue, don't you, fair maiden?"

"Well, when you keep friends with them, you can ask favours of them. Ned's help saved me a long, hot walk back to town."

"So endeth the first lesson."

"Yes—it was a good lesson, too. I didn't venture so far away from home again until I knew my stuff."

Work at the Swamp was fast and furious. They filled the smallest boxes and pots with yellow, white, and blue violets, planting all sorts of small, dainty ferns among them. If the soil seemed dry, they poured water on it, so that the dirt would not fall from the roots when they were lifted. If the dirt did fall away, the roots were quickly dipped in water and rolled in dry dirt to shut out the air. Thus they moved blooming plants galore—anything they saw that attracted them—so that before they knew it the most delicate flowers of the Limberlost were blossoming their prettiest in the Angel's music room. She chose that room for the ceremony because it was done in shades of green and gold, which would make the most suitable background for the colour scheme.

With hatchets they loosened fungous growths from old stumps; they gathered mosses and lichens and banked the mantels and other available spots so that they seemed to be sections cut from the old Swamp. There were bluebells, marsh buttercups, lady slippers of various colours, and pitcher plants. In the bay window they arranged a pool with all sorts of water hyacinths and other delicate plants that required their toes in water. The Angel added her collection of fancy goggle-eyed, fan-tailed Japanese goldfish and a few frogs and turtles from the pools in the Swamp.

At the last minute they brought in branches of dogwood with its snowy blossoms, and red bud with its tiny rose-coloured bells; and instead of smilax they used fronds of wild cucumber, covered with lacy, cream-white flowers, and the larger leaved "rattle-box" vine. At the same time they added quantities of cut flowers. Wild flowers wither very quickly after they are gathered, but if properly cared for they last a long time. They should be cut just as you would cut flowers from your garden, and should be immediately plunged into buckets or cans of water provided for that purpose. If kept in the shade, and set outside at night, most varieties will last as long as garden flowers. Fern fronds of the large varieties will do the same; but you are only sure of maidenhair fern when it is planted in pots—this may be done very successfully. The corners of the room they banked with larger ferns, and the swamp mallows, which grow on tall stocks and have rose-coloured flowers not unlike our tame hollyhocks.

The Angel made the bride's bouquet, and never did a bride have a lovelier one. It was large, to be carried, and made with a background of ferns and baby's breath, then yellow lady slipper orchids and yellow and white violets, all freshly gathered from the Swamp; the whole tied with huge loops of yellow and green tulle from which hung streamers knotted with tufts of fragrant creamy wild honeysuckle.

The Bird Woman was lovely in soft folds of pale yellow satin, with her heavy coils of dark hair dressed in its usual simple and becoming manner. The bridegroom was handsome in his brusque mannish way, and the two made an ideal pair. They were delighted with the Angel's idea, and the young people were pleased as possible over the praises they heard on all sides for their work and skill.

Mr. and Mrs. Kingsley thought at first they would slip away and not tell anyone the time of their departure; but Mr. Kingsley finally decided that it would be mean to deprive the kids of their fun, after all the work they had done; so they very accommodatingly allowed the gang to escort them to the train, and to shower them with rice and confetti until the train carried them away.

Dick, who had worked at the Angel's elbow for the entire time, was radiant. He had been escorting the Angel to various functions for several months, but never had she seemed so beautiful as now, and never so kind and so friendly; she seemed bubbling over with exuberance and affection, and she was so grateful for his help and devoted attention.

"Oh, Dick, you *are* a dear! I never could have done it if it hadn't been for you; and the gang are all bricks, too!" the Angel said as she sank into a divan after coming from the train. "I'm so happy, and I know Dad and my new mother are going to be happy, too. And I'm so thrilled at the thought of having a mother! I was only two, you know, when mine left us. She will be a comfort to Dad, after having had me on his hands for so long: I must have been a terrible trial at times."

"I can't possibly imagine you being a 'trial' to anyone. I think you are just perfect. Maybe—someday ——"

But the Angel changed the subject. She didn't want Dick to be serious yet.

"Now, Dick, if you will help me one more day the worst will be over. I don't want these lovely things to die, and they will if they are not outdoors soon. I've got Brenner spading the low place behind the orchard, and while he's a good gardener, he doesn't know beans about wild flowers. So to-morrow let's put them all out where they'll be happy again. It will be a good start on the wild-flower garden Mother and I are going to have out there."

"I'm sure that will be great: you think of everything, don't you? You're even kind to the wild flowers. Are you always so kind—to—to people?"

"I try to be; I never hurt anyone intentionally. But then, that comes easy, because everyone is always so lovely to me. 'Love begets love,' you know."

"Well, that's a great piece of news——"

But again the Angel interrupted.

"You run along now, Dick. I want a good rest before to-morrow. Plan to stay to lunch, you know."

"Yes, dear."

Being in the Swamp the past few days had set the Angel thinking of Freckles. She had avoided going near his "room" so that no explanations to her crowd, or to Dick, would be necessary. She set about opening all the windows, so that the plants and flowers would be refreshed by the dewy dampness of the night air. Then, tired as she was, she wrote to Freckles before she went to bed.

CHAPTER VIII

Wherein a Fire Rages and Suspicions Are Aroused

DURING the weeks her father and mother were gone on their honeymoon, the Angel was in a queer mood. Part of it was due to lonesomeness; part of it was due to Dick—he was becoming more and more of a problem; and part of it was due to what the Angel graphically described as a "hunch." She was restless and uneasy; constantly moving about aimlessly.

"I feel as if something were going to happen," she explained to Dick. "I've never felt like this before. At school they called me the 'three C's'—calm, cool, and collected—because no matter what happened, I always kept my head level; but I'm certainly not that now. I've got a prize case of fidgets. As soon as I start one thing, I want to do something else; it's really an awful feeling."

"Oh, I'm sure it's nothing to worry about, dear. I think you've worked pretty strenuously over the wedding, and there's bound to be a reaction. You're just nervous and exhausted."

"Well, I hope you're right."

"Are you afraid in the house at night? One of the girls would be glad to stay with you."

"No, indeed. I've never known what fear was, and I'm sure I'm amply protected. Old Toni sleeps with one of his longest, sharpest knives beside his bed; Marie's room is not far from mine, and she is a faithful servant if there ever was one. Besides, I have a revolver of my own, you know."

"That's fine. Now let's go to lunch, and we'll take a ride afterward. It will do you good."

As they passed the bank, the Angel looked in; one could see the entire front room through the window. Mr. Kingsley had designed the building, and he was very proud of his window. It was wide at the bottom and ran to a peak at the top, like a huge inverted heart. There was a wide sill across the bottom. When his farmer friends grew an especially fine specimen of fruit or vegetable, they brought it in "for Miss Dottie," but before "Miss Dottie" got it, it lay in state for a day or two in the window, with a card saying who grew it and where, its weight or length or other distinguishing feature set forth in careful lettering. So sometimes the bank window looked like an exhibit at the county fair; but it pleased the farmers, and gave them an incentive to try for finer fruit and vegetables. And when the Angel turned the battery of her clear-eyed, dimpled smile on them and said, "Now, Mr. Shoemaker, that was the loveliest, rosy-cheeked peach I've ever seen. And the *flavour*—it was delicious!" Mr. Shoemaker went home and told his wife what a fine girl the banker's daughter was, and how next year he was going to "raise the finest peaches in the country; there's a new fertilizer out," etc., etc.

Now, as the Angel looked over the display in the window she saw the two state bank examiners. They rode on a little way in silence. And then the Angel said:

"Dick, those two men in the bank are Mr. Snyder and Mr. Logan, from Indianapolis—bank examiners.

I'm sure they aren't due yet. Dad spoke of it before he left; told me he would be back before they came."

"Well, they may have changed their schedule, or something."

"Yes, maybe. But I don't just like the looks of it. They always notify Dad a few days before they come, and they are due every six months. It's only three months since they were here last. Dick, would you mind driving back past the bank? I'd like to talk to them, and anyway, Fred will want to help them and I'd better wait on the customers."

"Anything you say. Here we go, right about face!" and Dick swung his car around. In a few minutes they were at the bank. "You've gotten me curious now. I'll sit here and wait. You can come out and tell me what it's all about after you talk to them."

"Thanks, Dick."

The Angel spoke to the men in her usual radiant manner. It was easy to see that Mr. Logan, the younger of the two, thought she was about perfection, for he was especially friendly.

"I'm surprised to see you here. You aren't due for some time. Why the hurry?"

"Oh, we've been vacationing at one of the northern lakes, and we thought we'd stop on our way home. Where is your father?"

"Dad is away on his honeymoon. Couldn't think of disturbing him. I've a brand-new mother and I'm tickled pink . . ." so the Angel ran on about the Bird Woman, the wedding, and so on.

"I think I'll dismiss my Sir Galahad, who awaits without, and wait on customers; then you can have Fred to help you."

"No, indeed. Don't think of it. We've just gotten in from a long ride on the train, and we are not going to work until morning. So you run right along and enjoy yourself."

Mr. Snyder, who had said little, strolled over.

"By the way, *where* did you say your father was?"

"I didn't say—I just said he was romping around on a wedding trip. He hasn't had a vacation in years."

"I see—when will he be back?"

"I don't know. Well, I'll run along now, and come back in the morning. Good-bye," and the Angel was gone.

"Well, anything in particular?" asked Dick.

"I don't know. I noticed they asked twice where Dad was, and when he'd be home, but I guess that's only natural."

"You decided not to stay?"

"Yes. They said they were not going into the books until morning, so we can have our lunch and ride, as we had planned."

But as soon as she was gone, Mr. Logan and Mr. Snyder literally buried themselves in the books. At four o'clock they went out and left Fred to lock up.

"Logan, what do you think?"

"Darned if I know!"

"No—all you know is that you're *sunk* every time you see that girl. Now, come out of it. This is *business*, not a kindergarten."

"You don't *know* anything yourself yet. Don't be so damned suspicious. You know the old man is honest as the day is long—and the girl, too."

"I don't *know* anything. I think they are, but that doesn't *prove* anything. You're young. I've been in this game a long time. and I've seen some queer things happen; always where they were least expected. Fred was nervous as an old woman this afternoon. You know, I've been suspicious ever since we were here before, and now that we have made a special trip, we have to make a thorough investigation. That's why we're here."

"Let's forget it. No use arguing now. We'll get to the bottom of it to-morrow and then we'll know where we stand. But I warn you now, you old steam shovel, that I'll fight for the girl and I'll not believe anything wrong of her until it's jammed down my throat. And if you think Fred is 'so nervous,' why don't you have him watched to-night? Wouldn't do for the old, experienced brains of the outfit to slip up on anything."

"Don't get so fresh. It's serious business. You can't do anything until you're *sure*."

"O. K. Let's eat."

It was early in the evening when Dick and Dot, sitting on the veranda, saw dark clouds of smoke, cut by the red and gold of flames, leaping toward the sky.

"Looks like the whole town's on fire. Let's go."

"Just a second."

The Angel ran into the house. "Marie, you and Toni turn on every light in the house, and *stay here*. Thieves sometimes set fires so that they can rob houses while their owners are watching the fire. Mr. Dick and I are going. I can't tell just when we'll be back."

They rushed to Dick's car.

"I'm so worried, Dick. You know Dad owns two or three other store buildings down town, aside from the one the hotel and bank are in. It looks like a bad night for dear old Dad."

It was. As they turned the corner and came out on the main street, the fire was raging furiously. The bank building was in the middle of the block and was the only structure all of brick and concrete. The fire had started midway between the building and the east end of the block, which ended in the railroad station and the tracks. The hotel was in the bank building.

They took in the situation at a glance.

"I think the wide space at the tracks will stop it on the east, but we'll have to stop it at the hotel. If the wind changes it's going to be pretty tough. Once it gets into the bank building, we'll be almost helpless. The other stores are frame, and there's only a narrow alley between them and the houses on the south."

The Angel saw Dick was right.

"The whole south end of the town, as well as the store buildings on the west of the bank, will be in danger unless it can be stopped at the bank, and our house is less than three blocks away. We must work, Dick, and use our heads."

Men and women were running aimlessly about, while the small streams from the chemical engines made feeble headway against the flames.

"Dick, you talk to the men in front, and have them concentrate on the bank building. It's our one chance. You know the east wall is solid, not even one window. Explain to them how it is."

A crowd had gathered around Dot and Dick, for they knew Mr. Kingsley was away. Dot looked around her. She saw Lolly and several others of her crowd; the whole town seemed to be there, from the "best citizens" to the bums and loafers.

"It's going to be a fight, boys, and we all love a fight!

First, I want all the buckets and tubs from all the stores in town. Dick will take charge in front. I want about fifty men to go to the well at the back; we'll need fifteen or twenty men on the roof, and more to form a bucket brigade to pass water up the fire escape. All of you get buckets and meet me at the back. Lolly, you and some others come with me. Hurry!"

The Angel worked like a human dynamo. She went first to the hotel clerk.

"I want the master key to the rooms." The clerk handed it over. "Lolly, take this key, open every room, and yank the blankets off the beds. Take some to the back window and throw them down. Open the trap doors to the roof and put up the ladders that you will find beside them. Carry the remainder of the blankets to the roof, and I'll get water to the men up there as fast as I can. Ted, come with me."

For once, Lolly forgot his nonsense and worked. The Angel and Ted went to the linen closet and got all the blankets from there. When they reached the kitchen, she grabbed a knife.

"Now, boys, each of you take a blanket," and she began slashing holes for eyes and nose. "It's going to be hot up there; put on gloves and keep yourselves as well covered as you can. Send somebody to the ten-cent store for their stock of cotton gloves."

Men came running with the things she had ordered, and she set men to pumping into tubs, other men to dipping up buckets full of water, and in a short time there was a steady procession of men passing buckets to those on the roof. It was heart-breaking work. Men came down from the roof with burned clothes and blistered hands and faces.

"All right, boys, second relay for the roof, up you go!" and the Angel kept things moving—men to man the pump; fresh men to replace those passing buckets of water. Once she went to the roof herself, and came back with grim face.

"The boys up there need something to beat the flames. Sparks are falling on the roof and must be put out. Someone find Joe Stern and tell him I want all the empty grain sacks from his grain elevator. Wet sacks will be good for that; and, Lolly, you run to the hardware store and get all their mops—wet mops will help. And keep hustling the water to the roof. The east wall is getting very hot."

It was not long before the men on the roof were supplied with grain sacks and mops. The Angel set the cook to making coffee and sandwiches in the hotel kitchen, and though he was terrified, he did as he was told. The owner of the bakery was sent for all the doughnuts and other food that could be eaten easily.

Serious as it was, funny things happened, too. Once, as the Angel came from the kitchen, she saw that a falling ember had set fire to the back steps. All the buckets were in use.

"Jesse," she called to the second cook, "open the lid to the reservoir back of the stove, take your soup ladle and pour some water here on the steps where they are burning. Hurry!"

A few mintues later she looked again, and there was Jesse with a huge crock of milk from the refrigerator.

"Why on earth are you pouring *milk* on the steps, Jesse?"

"Well, Miss Dottie, because it's cold; the water in the reservoir is boiling hot!"

The heat grew more intense. Sparks began to ignite rubbish back of the building, and even the board walk broke into flames a few times. Three doctors were dressing burns, and one came to say that they were out of bandages and oil.

"Lolly," directed the Angel, "go break into my Dad's drug store and get all the bandages you can find, and anything else that's good for cuts and burns."

In a few minutes Lolly was back.

"Sorry, Dot, the store is flat!"

The Angel drew her sleeve across her purple, perspiring face. "Poor Dad! Every building he had is gone but this one!" She dashed upstairs and came down with an armload of sheets and began tearing them in strips for the doctors. She noticed Mr. Snyder at her elbow. He was just as tired and dirty as the others.

"Where's Mr. Logan?" she asked.

"He and Fred are out in front with Dick."

"How's the wind?"

"Almost gone—I believe we have a good chance. The wall is mighty hot, but it hasn't cracked or broken. If it holds an hour more, we are safe. And you are some general. By George! you're marvellous!"

"I hope nobody is seriously hurt——" and the Angel toppled over in Mr. Snyder's arms.

When Dot awoke, she was in her own bed. The events of the night before began to flash through her mind. She called Marie.

"Marie, quick, did the bank burn?"

"No, miss."

"How did I get home?"

"Mr. Dick and another gentleman brought you home

and carried you upstairs. Then I put you to bed and the doctor came. He said you were not hurt; only tired. He said you must rest, and to be sure you would, he gave you a hypodermic in your arm. He said you were wonderful——"

The door bell rang.

"See who that is, Marie. If they want me, bring them up."

Presently Marie came back with Mr. Logan.

"How is our charming heroine this morning?"

"Right as rain. All I need is a life-sized breakfast. Marie, tell Toni I'm starved and bring up the result. What time is it?"

"Eight-thirty. You must think this is an early call, but—but—Fred hasn't appeared, and we—we—can't get in the bank. We don't know where he lives."

"Well, I do. Maybe he was hurt last night, or overslept. Would you hand me my purse? Thanks. Here is the key so you can get in the bank, but the books are in the vault and the time lock is set for nine o'clock. I know the combination for the vault and the safe both. I'll eat a bite, look up Fred, and be at the bank at nine."

"That's quite a large order, so I'll run along and let you dress. See you later."

Mr. Snyder was waiting at the bank door. He had been watching men trying to clean up the débris; men hunting something to save out of the wreckage of their stores; and other tight-lipped men who had lost all they had, wandering around aimlessly. It was a pathetic sight and it did not add to Mr. Snyder's already aggravated state of mind.

"How's the girl?" he asked Mr. Logan.

"Fine. Says she's going to eat, look up Fred, and come right down."

"Well, I'd just as soon take a crack at those books before she gets here. Get a key?"

"Sure, that's what I went after," and Logan grinned. "But you can't get the books now; they're in the vault, and the time lock is set for nine o'clock. Miss Kingsley said she'd be here then; she knows the combination to everything around the place."

Snyder went in first.

"Who the h—— said the books were in the vault? Here they are—right here on the desk."

"Miss Kingsley said they were kept in the vault."

"Well, this business looks queer to me. First the old man is gone; then a lot of the entries look fishy; then there's a fire and the books are left out of the vault; and then the bookkeeper doesn't show up."

"Do you mean to say you think the fire was set, and that the books were left out on purpose? You *would* think of something like that!"

"Now look here, Logan, strange as it may seem, I've done a lot of things this morning besides smoke a cigar and read a paper. I *know* the fire was set, and a lot of others know it, too. We found tin tomato cans stuffed with coal-oil-soaked rags under some of the buildings on the *west* side of the bank. For some reason they weren't lighted. So you can be damned sure this bank was intended to burn. Also, I'm informed, it's very well insured."

"That's another dirty crack. If Fred wanted the books to disappear, he could have taken them away yesterday. And old man Kingsley has better things to occupy his time than a low-down trick like having his bank burned so he can collect insurance. You have a filthy mind, sometimes."

"Yes? But if the building burned just accidentally it would be easier to say he forgot to put the books in the vault, wouldn't it?"

"Sh-sh! Here comes Miss Kingsley! Let's get busy."

When Dot came in, the first thing she saw was the books. She seemed relieved.

"Good-morning, Mr. Snyder. Fred's here, then?"

"No, he isn't."

"But the—the books?"

"Found them just where we left them. They never were put in the vault at all. But what made you ask if Fred was here?"

"I thought he must have opened the vault, when I saw the books."

"Well, he hasn't been here. Did you look for him?"

The Angel's heart sank, but she looked the men straight in the eyes.

"I went to Fred's boarding house. He is not there, and he has not been there all night. His grip and his clothes are gone. I can't understand it."

"Hear anything from your father?"

"No."

The Angel opened the vault, and the safe: the cash was all there. She arranged things for the day's business. Men began coming into the bank, all full of talk about the fire. They praised her and said how proud her father would be, and so on, indefinitely. Insurance men came in, and from them she learned that undoubtedly the fire had been set. In the afternoon several customers became insistent as to where Fred was and when her father would be home. Women came in and repeated all the gossip they had heard. The hotel clerk had spread the report that the bank examiners were not due for three more months. People began to get uneasy; there were mutterings and whisperings. Dot was frantic, but she kept calm outwardly and had a friendly word for everyone.

About three o'clock Dick came in. Mr. Logan and Mr. Snyder, deep in the books, had said little.

"It's three o'clock now. I'll close the doors. Are you gentlemen ready to quit for the day?"

"Almost."

"All right. I'm going out for a few minutes, and then I'll be back to close the safe and vault. Dick, will you run me over to Mr. McLean's hotel?"

It was only when Dot spoke his name that she realized that all during the hours of the fire, and all during the day, she had not seen McLean. Suddenly, the Angel felt weak, and an icy hand seemed clutching at her throat. She knew McLean was gone.

When Dot and Dick went out, Mr. Snyder looked up from his ledger.

"Well, are you convinced now that some of these entries are false as hell?"

"Yes, I am."

"So am I. I think it's time we quit playing and got an officer. Somebody is guilty around here. At least the girl ought to be watched."

"It won't do any good to stir things up to-night. Let the poor kid get some rest; she's about all in."

"Well, it looks bad for somebody—Fred, or the old man, or her."

"Say, calamity, you say what you please about the

others, but you'll *stop* making insinuations against the girl right now."

"Well, why doesn't she tell where her old man is then; or when he's coming home; or send for him? Why all the secrecy? It's the queerest mess I've ever seen."

"She probably has her reasons—but here she comes. Let's let her lock up and beat it."

The Angel was right. McLean was gone and he had left no address. There seemed to be a feeling of hostility in the air. Dorothy, accustomed all her life to kindness, love, and laughter was bewildered.

Dick stayed with her until she finished at the bank, and then took her home.

"Oh, Dick," and she put her arms around his neck and leaned her head against his shoulder, "I couldn't stand it if you didn't stick by me. I feel so alone!"

Dick dropped his head on hers.

"Listen, honey girl, tell me one thing. Don't you really know when your dad is coming home, or where he is; or won't you tell?"

"Why do you ask that?"

"Oh, I don't know." But when Dorothy looked up at him, he wouldn't look in her face.

"Dick Summerfield, look me in the eye! What's on your mind?"

"Nothing much, but people talk such a lot. I wonder why the bank examiners didn't finish their work in a few hours, as they usually do, and leave?"

"Dick—why, *Dick*—you don't mean—is there anything wrong with the books?"

"I'm afraid there is. I don't like the attitude of those

two examiners, coming ahead of time, staying so long, and Fred not showing up to-day."

"I'm beginning to see. There's something crooked—and—and—why, Dick, does anyone *dare* to think it's my dad?"

"The people in this town are pretty thoroughly incensed over the fire, and their losses in that. They're excited and nervous. They're just in the mood to believe anything. Your dad's absence won't add to their peace of mind when they hear this report to-morrow. If you know where he is, or when he is coming, I think you ought to tell them. It would help to calm them."

"You mean there may be trouble?"

"I don't know, but it's as well to be prepared."

"Oh, Dick, I'm *so* worried!"

"Well, you lie down awhile and get some rest and a hot bath to relax you. I'll come back about seven and take you out for dinner. I'll try to think out what is best."

Dot started to lie down, but her mind was too active. She thought she'd try the bath first, but before she got started, she had another idea. Duncan might know where Mr. McLean was. He was Dad's best friend, and if Dad *was* in trouble he would want McLean. So she would go to the Duncans'; if she took the short cut through Freckles' room, she would be back before Dick came. At the door she paused, went back to her dressing table, and picked her revolver out of its hiding place. At the foot of the stairs she met Marie.

"I'm going to Duncan's on an errand, Marie. I'll be back by seven."

"Yes, Miss Dorothy. You will need a coat, won't

you? It's cool these evenings. I'll run up and get one for you."

"Never mind, I'm in a hurry."

She picked up a coat of her dad's that was hanging in the hall, and slipped the revolver in the pocket as she left.

CHAPTER IX

Wherein His Lordship Dives, and Kathleen Rushes to Rescue Him

FOR the next few days after Terence wrote his ultimatum to the Angel, he was in a frenzied state of nerves. One minute he regretted sending it, and the next minute he was glad he had had the courage to do it. He was not sure of himself. No sooner did he make up his mind than he changed it again. He was completely disgusted with himself. All this did not improve his disposition; he was inexcusably irritable and irritating. Barlow saw it all. He was a perfect mirror for Terence's moods anyway. When Terence was happy and in good spirits, Barlow beamed and went whole-heartedly about his duties; when Terence was morose and cross, the faithful old soul was down in the dumps, too.

Barlow was watching Terence now as he laid down one magazine and picked up another; patted Rags; chose a book and read a few words and threw that down; went over to the window and stood looking out. Barlow hovered in the background, so he would be there if he was wanted. He was sure something was on his master's mind, but he was afraid to ask questions. He had to content himself with the hope that if he stayed around the boy would tell him. Finally Terence spoke.

"Barlow, I'm nothing but a vacillating old woman; I'm disgusted with myself!"

"What is wrong, sir?"

"There goes that 'sir' again! Thought I told you to cut that out. I can't make up my mind and stick to it, that's all. Can you feature a *man* changing his mind with the wind?"

"What about, my boy?"

"That's better; much better. About—a—a letter—to the Angel."

Terence explained what he had done and what he had said.

"One minute I think I'm right, and the next I think I'm wrong. What do you think?"

"Pardon me for saying so, but I think you were wrong."

"Why?"

"You know what you think and feel, but you don't know what the young lady thinks or feels. You assumed too much. I'm afraid she will be hurt."

Terence groaned.

"Well, it's done. I guess I'll have to stick to it."

"You do not have to stick to something you think is wrong."

"Well, I'm not convinced yet that it's wrong. My head feels as if there was a whirlpool inside it. I think I'll go for a ride; maybe that will clear the cobwebs out of my brain. And when I come back I'm going in to the city and stay there until I find work."

"Leave here?"

"Yes, at least temporarily. If Uncle Maxwell sees I mean business, he may change his mind and welcome the prodigal. *Yes*, he would! I can see him now!" Terence smiled sarcastically.

"Your leaving will be a shock to them."

"Uncle Maxwell needs a shock. I'll explain to Aunt Ellen. I think she will understand."

"And Miss Kathleen?"

Barlow had been doubtful about her at first, but now he was sure the boy did not like her. He had watched her pretty carefully, and he had seen her studied efforts to meet Terence wherever and whenever she could. And he also saw that she only annoyed Terence. He needed youthful companionship, and a wholesome friendship with her would have done the boy good. But Barlow knew that she wanted more than that; she wanted a husband, not a friend. She was distinctly not the type to be Terence's wife. So Barlow was immensely relieved when the boy replied:

"If she doesn't miss me any more than I'll miss her, both of us will be happy. But I'm determined to go to work. That's the only point on which my mind is clear. Now for that ride."

"Do I go with you?"

"No. I want you to stay here and pack our bags. I'm taking you with me to the city, if you'll go."

"I am happy to go with you; I'd be heart-broken left behind."

"That's settled. Now, if you'll help me into my riding togs, I'm off. And keep Rags here with you; I'm going to ride long and hard."

"Yes, sir."

He did ride long and hard, and after two hours he came in, dusty and hot. He saw little flecks of foam dotting Lady Bird's sleek coat as he fed her the daily ration of sugar. As he was hurrying up the path to the house, he saw Kathleen coming toward him. He had managed to avoid a talk with her since the night he had rudely left her standing alone on the dance floor.

"Confound that girl! I would manage to bump into her just at the wrong time. Just my rotten luck. Now I'll have to apologize to her for being so rude the other night!"

"Hello, Terence."

"Hello, Kathleen."

Not much enthusiasm there.

"Been for a ride?"

She *would* make an obvious remark like that. Terence's irritation grew.

"Yes, how did you guess it? I escaped my bodyguard for once. I took a ride alone. Nothing happened. I am returned alive. Isn't it amazing?"

"Come and sit beside me and tell me why you are so cynical: one is almost afraid to speak to you."

Terence sat down.

"I owe you an apology for my abrupt departure the other evening. I'm sorry."

"You did leave in rather a hurry. Was anything wrong?"

"Yes. *Plenty*."

"Anything I did?"

"Probably nothing you could help."

"Please tell me."

"I'd much rather not."

"But *please*, you're not fair."

"Very well, then. If you must have it, here goes: It was only that I saw the look in your eyes and felt you wince when I put my right arm around your waist. It's the thing that always happens to me, and seeing *you* do it, when you have come to stay here—well, it was too much—and I chucked it."

Kathleen coloured. She must wiggle out of that hole at all costs.

"Oh, Terence, did I? *How awful!* I was utterly unconscious of it. Your right arm does not bother me at all. Some day maybe I'll *prove* it to you. *Do please* forgive me if I really did such a careless, heartless thing."

She sounded sincere, and, anyway, a gentleman must accept a lady's apology.

"You're forgiven—let's forget it."

Kathleen moved closer and ran her hand through his ruffled hair.

"How silky your hair is!"

"Yes, it's about as silky as the stubble in a wheatfield."

"What is 'stubble in a wheatfield'?"

"Well, assuming that you know what wheat is—am I right?"

"Yes."

"Stubble is the stiff stocks that are left after the wheat is cut; and as for colour, it looks like a fine, large Indiana pumpkin after a frost. Lovely, isn't it?"

"Terence," reprovingly, "why can't you be serious?"

"I am serious. That's what is the matter with me."

"This is your country, and we are your people, but you do not seem a bit like us."

"That's because I had twenty years' American training. It was darn good training, too. Only trouble is, I haven't stuck to it tight enough."

Freckles could not help laughing at Kathleen's expression.

"*I* think this is a lovely place; you have everything here."

"That's exactly the point. I don't want everything. I want to work for something I haven't got."

"I cannot understand that at all."

"No, I don't suppose you can."

"Terence, I would like to be better friends with you. I would like——"

"If you'll excuse me," Terence interrupted, "I'd like to remove a few layers of dust. Come, Rags," and Terence rose and walked into the house, Rags galloping behind him.

Kathleen walked to the farthest end of the garden and stood peering through the hedge. She was thinking of Terence: how pessimistic he was, and how unapproachable. Surely there was some way to pierce that outer mask of cold indifference. He seemed unhappy; why did he keep so aloof? Surely he would like friends. It must be someone in America; she had seen letters from there addressed in a feminine hand.

She heard Rags barking, and looked more closely through the hedge. Terence in a bathing suit! His bathrobe billowed behind him, and Rags was snapping at a bath towel which swung from his hand. The other sleeve was fluttering aimlessly in the breeze. Kathleen shuddered. The missing hand was terribly distasteful to her, but she was intrigued by the thought of his country house, his wealth and social position. And there was something else; she couldn't define it exactly, but there was *something* that made him an extremely attractive young man. Even she could see that Terence was far different from the other young men she knew. He did not care to indulge in their dissipations, so he let them alone. He was indifferent and sarcastic, but his manners were perfect. His voice had a soft, penetrating quality that somehow reminded one of low lullabies sung at dusk; and on the rare occasions when he did smile—well, his chief charm was his smile, and it was irresistible. He smiled all over his face; little wrinkles came at the corners of his mouth, and his eyes became alive and warm.

At first Kathleen had decided that she would like Terence for a husband because of his wealth, standing, and so on; but she was beginning really to like him. And the more she tried to be nice to him, the more aloof he was. This was her chance. She would follow him, and, no matter how she really felt about his arm, she must prove to him that the sight of it was not offensive to her. She hurried into the house to put on her suit.

Terence loved to swim, but he would not wear a swimming suit in public. He had taught himself to swim in the river that ran beside the Limberlost. His arm seemed no handicap at all. He had a powerful leg stroke that carried him through the water at a great speed, and his left arm served to guide him. He simply held it rigidly in whatever direction he wished to go, began a rapid scissors kick, and away he went. He loved the water, and he had missed his swims when he came to Ireland. But, exploring the country around the estate, he had found a secluded spot at the foot of the cliff just back of Uncle Maxwell's house. A narrow, winding path led down to it, and there Terence and Rags went alone for their swim. The clear, cold water refreshed and invigorated him as nothing else did.

Kathleen was rushing out of the house when she met Aunt Ellen coming from the garden with a basket of roses. It was the one duty Aunt Ellen insisted upon performing herself; the only one that took her into the air and sunshine. Despite Uncle Maxwell's opposition, she *would* cut and arrange her roses herself.

"Why, Kathleen, where are you going to swim?"

"I don't know, Aunt Ellen. I was standing in the garden when I saw Terence come out of the house in his bathing suit. I watched him out of sight over the cliff. He must have a place to swim that none of us know about."

Aunt Ellen could not help noticing how lovely Kathleen looked in her scarlet suit. A satin scarf, striped in brilliant colours, was bound around her head and tied in a saucy bow below one ear. Over her suit she wore a knee-length cape of red and black, colours very becoming to her dark hair and white skin.

"Does he know you are coming?"

"No; but he thinks his right arm is abhorrent to me, someway I've got to prove to him that it is not. It occurred to me when I saw him going for a swim, that would be my chance. If I swim with him and don't notice it, perhaps he will be convinced that it really makes no difference to me. I've tried so hard to be nice to him, and he is *so* indifferent."

"And that hurts your vanity? You think he wants you to follow him?"

"Sometimes men don't know what they want. Anyway, I'm going to follow him—I think it's worth trying."

As she watched Kathleen dash through the garden and out the gate, Aunt Ellen looked dubious. She sighed. The two of them were becoming something of a problem; her thoughts were disturbed as she arranged her roses. She had thought Kathleen would be company for Terence. In fact, she and Uncle Maxwell really hoped that the two would fall in love. Kathleen was not wealthy, but she was from an excellent family and money need not be a consideration. Terence had sufficient for both. Aunt Ellen had mildly hinted something of their idea to Kathleen and she seemed agreeable. But Aunt Ellen could see that Kathleen was overdoing it. She fairly haunted the boy; Terence was annoyed. *No* girl got very far with Terence; he was the difficult one; he seemed utterly indifferent to girls.

"Poor boy," mused Aunt Ellen, "so lonely, so proud, and so sensitive; wanting friendship, yet seeming afraid of it. Love would mean so much to him—a home, children. I wonder if it's that girl in America. She was beautiful; her father seemed a gentleman. They said he was quite wealthy, too."

Terence's bitter words the evening of their last talk ran through her mind. She did not know what he had said to Maxwell. He had said nothing about their conversation in the garden. It was not his custom to discuss anything with her, particularly concerning Terence, for the last times they had argued about the boy, she had upheld him, and this Uncle Maxwell did not like. He thought that because she was his wife, she should agree with everything he said: if she had conflicting opinions of her own, let her keep them to herself.

As she thought it all over, she decided she should speak to Maxwell. It would do no harm to remind him that Terence had O'More blood in his veins; if he was driven too far, he might do something rash. Yes, she must speak to Maxwell, but how she dreaded it! He would probably storm, with plenty of thunder and lightning, and ultimately she would accomplish nothing. But she was fond of the boy. Her eyes filled as she thought of her own boy.

She selected a small vase and arranged several perfect buds in it—she would use them for an excuse. She carried them to her husband's study, and listened. She did not hear voices; he must be alone. She knocked timidly on the door.

Meantime, Kathleen followed Terence. The path down the cliff was steep and difficult; little stones rolled under her feet, and she stumbled and slipped on smooth rocks. It was her first experience with a precipitous path, and she did not like it. Once she glanced down and became very dizzy; desperately she grasped a scrubby bush to keep from falling. She was terrified by the distance to the water. Her loose straw sandals kept slipping off, and her feet were scratched and bruised. Whatever she was, she was not a coward, and she had no thought of turning back.

Suddenly, rounding an abrupt turn in the path, she looked down and saw him. He had climbed some high rocks and was poised to dive, Rags barking and splashing below him. Absorbed in talking to Rags, Terence did not see her. What a splendid specimen of manhood he was: tall and muscular, straight as an Indian. He lifted his arms above his head. A second he stood thus; abruptly he dived. His lean body cut the water in a perfect "jack-knife," leaving scarcely a ripple. Kathleen stood fascinated—watching. Suddenly she realized that he had not come up! She screamed frantically: "Find him, Rags! You *must* find him!" Then she raced, stumbling and slipping, down the path.

Lord O'More was reading when he heard the knock

on his study door. It did not sound like his secretary's knock, so instead of calling out as he usually did, he laid down his book and opened the door himself. He was much surprised when he saw his wife standing there; it was not often that she invaded his own particular retreat.

"Oh, come in, my dear."

Lady O'More entered rather hesitatingly, and as she crossed to his desk and set the roses on it she looked closely at her husband, as if trying to determine just what mood he was in to-day. Not having seen him since lunch, she could not be sure. He seemed coldly polite and formal, about as usual. There was no warmth or affection in Uncle Maxwell's "my dear": it was merely what he considered proper form.

"I've brought some roses for you, Maxwell."

Aunt Ellen stood nervously fingering the buds.

"Is that the only object of this unexpected visit?"

"No, not the only one, Maxwell. I want to talk to you about Terence."

"Sit down, my dear."

Aunt Ellen sat down uncomfortably on the edge of a chair and fingered the lace at the throat of her gown. She felt a bit frightened, but she was determined to go through with it. She knew it was silly, but she could not help it. She was accustomed to his tantrums, and she always thought she was prepared for them—but, some way, when they came she never was prepared, and each succeeding one terrified and hurt her as much as the last.

"Maxwell," she began, "what did Terence say to you the other evening?"

"What other evening?"

She was perfectly sure he knew what evening she meant, but she would give him the benefit of the doubt.

"The evening Lord and Lady Aridulane were here to dinner. He told me he wanted to talk to you, and asked me where you were."

"Then perhaps he told you what he wanted to say."

"No, he did not. If I already knew, Maxwell, I should not have taken the trouble to come and inquire."

"Quite so—quite so. Well, the young man had the effrontery to come and ask me again to allow him to go into the city and 'get a job'—using the same elegant phraseology in which he customarily expresses himself."

Aunt Ellen ignored his inflection.

"What did you say?"

"What do you suppose I said? I said it was impossible, of course."

"But *is* it impossible? It need not be manual labour. The boy has ambition, it would be a pity to break his spirit. Besides, he is lonely here; to be out with other men would take his mind off himself; it would broaden him."

"He does not need 'broadening.' There is no reason why he should not be content with what the other men of our family have had."

"Our ideas are the result of tradition and heredity for generations past. The youth of to-day seem to progress; at least, they *want* to progress, but we of the old school make it very difficult for them. *I* can see why a young man wants to make a place for himself in the world."

"You always could see a lot of things no one else

could. Terence, with one hand gone, has a perfectly legitimate excuse for not working."

"That is precisely the reason he should be doing something; he thinks about that missing hand all the time. Work would take his mind off himself, and that is exactly what he needs. Remember, Maxwell, your own father drove his son from home by his unbearable domination: if I were you, I would not drive Terence too far."

"His twenty years in America," said Lord O'More, neatly avoiding her issue, "have put those plebeian ideas into his head. Young people in America are terribly rude and undisciplined."

"*I* thought young Americans delightful. Their parents seemed sort of depending on them, instead of having to protect and shelter them every minute. One young lady I distinctly remember was anything but 'rude and undisciplined.' On the contrary, she was polite, respectful, and altogether enchanting—aside from being extremely beautiful."

Aunt Ellen looked at her husband, but he had missed her point entirely, and she could see that he was fast reaching the stage where he stamped and blustered. Well, evidently she had not done the slightest good, but she had said what she thought, and that helped some. However, a tiny fear persisted—Terence *was* different—she hoped he would not do anything rash.

"Very well, Maxwell, you have had your own way always but that does not prove that you have been right always. I am going now, so you need not explode at me."

Maxwell spluttered and gasped; his wife had never spoken to him quite like that before. He looked at her and saw that she was eyeing him calmly and coldly, although within she was seething. She was going slowly and deliberately toward the door when Katheen's voice rang through the house in one long, terrible scream. Then a thud—and silence.

CHAPTER X

Wherein Science, without Love, Strives to Mend a Broken Head

NEITHER Lord nor Lady O'More were demonstrative people. What emotions they had were perfectly controlled; that is, all but Lord O'More's temper. If any other poor, defenceless little emotion tried to show itself, it had a terrible struggle; and it struggled in vain. It was immediately smothered; it never saw the light of day.

So Kathleen's ear-splitting scream was something of a shock. They proceeded to the door with such speed as their dignity allowed.

"That's Kathleen's voice," said Aunt Ellen.

"Well, why the deuce does she scream like that?"

"Probably for the same reason most women scream, *not* just for amusement. I think we should investigate."

Uncle Maxwell opened the door.

Barlow was coming downstairs two steps at a time, knowing that he was making an undue lot of noise, and not caring if he was. Kathleen was lying on the floor in a dead faint, a little pool of water slowly accumulating around her from her wet bathing suit. Her cap was gone and her hair fell in long, wet tags around her shoulders and across her face. Her arms and legs were scratched and bleeding. Aunt Ellen could not resist saying to her husband:

"No doubt you recall having heard Terence tell how one young American lady managed everything in a crisis when he was injured. Here is a fine sample of our discipline and training. Something terrible has happened, and Kathleen faints—that's a great help!"

Lord O'More glared at her, but she ignored him and said: "Anna, bring a blanket to cover your mistress, and some water."

Barlow was frantic. He felt certain something had happened to Terence and that they would have to revive Kathleen before they could find out what it was. The two must have gone swimming together, although Terence had said nothing about Kathleen's accompanying him. Barlow was none too gentle in his efforts to arouse Kathleen. He darted into the dining room, grasped the large silver pitcher of ice water which always stood there, and poured it on Kathleen's face. She opened her eyes and gasped:

"Quickly—down the path over the cliff to Terence. He is unconscious—will have to be carried——" and she fainted again.

Barlow waited for no more. He snatched a rug from the floor, called the butler to come with him, and they ran past the stables, where the two grooms joined them. As fast as possible they made their way down the steep, rocky path. When they rounded the curve, they could see Terence lying on his back, his head in a little pool of blood and poor, frenzied Rags on guard.

"She should have left him on his stomach, so the water could run out of his lungs," muttered Barlow, pathetic in his anxiety. He felt the boy's pulse and listened to his heart—it was beating steadily. Life-saving methods brought no results; there seemed to be no water in his lungs. Barlow examined a long gash across the boy's head, which was bleeding freely.

"It must be his head that is causing the trouble. We must get him to the house at once and stop the bleeding. Careful, boys. He's just like my own son——"

Gently they laid him on the rug and the others watched silently as Barlow ran to the water, moistened his handkerchief, and placed it over the boy's forehead and eyes. He could not stand the sight of those awful, wide-open eyes staring into space, and seeing nothing. They grasped the corners of the rug and began the tedious climb up the hill. It was a task for the four of them, as there was no place to put him down while they shifted positions or rested. Rags followed dejectedly.

In the house, Lord O'More and Anna had carried Kathleen to her room and put her to bed. She had come out of the second faint, and was strugglng to get up and dress.

"Have you any idea what is wrong?" Lord O'More asked his wife.

"Yes. Kathleen saw Terence going down over the cliff in his bathing suit. He and Rags were evidently going for a swim by themselves. vou know Terence will not swim in public——"

"Well—well—leave out the details—then what?"

"Kathleen put on her suit and followed. She thought it a good opportunity to show him that the sight of his arm would not offend people——"

"Fool! Idiot! Imbecile! Worst thing she could have done!"

"No doubt you are correct, as usual; but if she had not gone, Terence might be dead now—maybe he is—you can see she has had a dreadful shock."

"Well, what then?"

"I don't know. The last I saw was Kathleen running toward the cliff. That was just a little while before I went to your study."

Lord O'More walked across the room to where Kathleen was fighting with Anna.

"Lie still, young woman, and tell us what has happened." The flat, unemotional voice cut through the room like a whiplash. It quieted Kathleen immediately.

"I ran down the cliff a little more than halfway, to a place where the path curves around a huge rock. There I saw Terence ready to dive—he must have been twenty feet from the water. I was fascinated by his body as it flashed through the air and cut the water without a splash—I waited for him to come up—but he didn't. I screamed, but of course no one heard me. I scarcely remember any more—I stumbled and fell trying to run down the path, and I called frantically to Rags to find him. When I got there, Rags was circling the exact spot where he went down. The water was clear and I could see him. When I got hold of him Rags fastened his teeth in one shoulder strap and helped me, or I am not sure I could have made it; he is a wonderful dog. I dragged Terence up on the shore, but I had no idea what to do for a drowning man. His head is badly cut where he hit a rock when he dived, and I had nothing to use for a bandage. He is unconscious. But where is he? Have they gone after him? Tell them to hurry!"

Kathleen fainted again.

Uncle Maxwell began pacing the floor ineffectually and Aunt Ellen left Anna to care for Kathleen. Suddenly Kathleen and her needs became vastly unimportant as compared to Terence. Aunt Ellen telephoned for doctors and nurses. Then she hurried into the boy's room. There she turned back the bedding and busied herself laying out extra blankets, strips of cloth for bandages, and whatever else she could find that might be needed in an emergency.

Barlow and the grooms, almost thoroughly exhausted, were just able to carry their still unconscious burden upstairs and lay it on the bed. Uncle Maxwell ordered Rags to be taken from the room, but he howled so horribly that Aunt Ellen, remembering what Kathleen had said about him, told Barlow to let him in again. With a dog's intuition, Rags knew something had happened to his beloved master, and he intended to stay until things were right again. He stretched himself at the foot of the bed and refused to leave.

Aunt Ellen completely forgot her formality when she looked at the white face of the boy, streaked with blood, and drawn as if he were in terrible pain. She became strangely efficient and rose to the occasion magnificently. She and Barlow put Terence to bed, and it was Aunt Ellen who bathed his face, washed the clotted blood from his hair, and made him as comfortable as she could.

The doctors came and then the nurses; but Aunt Ellen and Barlow left the bedside only when it was necessary, and Rags' appealing eyes followed them constantly. The surgeon made his report shortly. Terence had a four-inch crack in his skull, caused by striking a rock when he dived. Aside from that, there was no other injury. It required several stitches to close the gash in his head, and when that was done there was nothing to do but wait. There was quiet confusion; an accompaniment of strange, subdued voices; soft footfalls; shaded lights; and then silence and inaction —waiting—waiting. Thirty hours—just waiting; for he lay unconscious almost two days. He had no fever and his pulse held steadily. There was nothing to do but hope that consciousness would return, and with it sanity.

Kathleen, weak and shaken, crept to the door, her frightened face with the huge dark eyes looking ghost-like in the dim light of the room. When they told her there was no change, she crept away silently again, only to return later to hear the same report.

The monotony of it was nerve-racking—the awful helpless feeling. If there were only something to do! Uncle Maxwell alternately cursed the doctors and paced the garden. He would stride up the stairs, take one look at the still, white face, and disappear again. Beneath his formal and dignified exterior he was slowly realizing that his nephew was a splendid chap, and that he was really very fond of him and proud of his ambition and independent spirit! When the boy got well, he would let him go his own way. By Jove! he would! The youngster had courage and spunk—no doubt about it. Uncle Maxwell had plenty of time for reflection—and then an icy finger would clutch his heart. What if the boy just—just slept away?

It was a long vigil they kept at the boy's bedside, for none of them tried to sleep. At last they were rewarded for their faithfulness. Toward the close of the second day, Terence opened his eyes and looked about him. But they were lustreless, half-conscious eyes, and he did not recognize any of them.

He was desperately ill. For a second time devoted friends battled for his life, and for a second time they battled alone: they got no help from the boy. Mostly he was in terrible agony, and it required two or three to hold him on the bed, save when he was under the influence of opiates. After a few days he had lucid intervals, during which he was acquiescent, but indifferent. He refused food, and languidly allowed them to dress his wound and make him as comfortable as they could. But when they asked him if he wanted anything, the answer was inevitably a short No. The pain in his head was intense. When he was delirious he fought them, and when conscious he lay quietly enduring it, his fingers twisting in Rags' shaggy hair.

All through the nights he tossed, while his semiconscious mind roamed the trails of his loved Swamp. He was tortured constantly by snatches of bird songs, the snapping of hickory bark on camp fires, the friendly rattle of dishes in cook tents, the rustle of wings, the stealthy step of wild things, and the whispering of soft winds through the trees. Again he walked the paths; he could feel the fresh breezes on his face and through his hair; he stopped beside the pool at noontime and ate his lunch to the accompaniment of a wild orchestra, the music of the great outdoors. And at dusk he followed the trail home!—home to Sarah Duncan's warm smile; home to the delighted shrieks of Sarah's children; home to a friendly fire and steaming food; home to the all-encompassing love of a genuine welcome. And through it all the Angel ran before him, always just out of reach—beckoning—beckoning. Constantly he ran after her, but he never quite caught her. No matter where he wandered through conscious dreams or delirious visions, it was always the merry eyes of the Angel that haunted him.

The kindly doctors were puzzled. Slowly their patient gained, but he had no interest in life, and they had to force him to take nourishment—he had no appetite for any sort of food. Aunt Ellen and Kathleen spent hours trying to think of tempting dishes, but it was no use. Uncle Maxwell, in his usual volcanic manner, tried to reason with Terence, and made him so much worse that the doctor ordered His Lordship out of the room. That did not set so well, but he had to go.

"It's a most peculiar case," said the elder doctor, "most peculiar. It is very unusual for one so young to be so indifferent. He doesn't seem to care whether he he lives or dies—makes our work extremely difficult—*extremely*."

It was against the doctor's orders for Terence to have any mail, but one day the Angel's letter came. Barlow knew the doctor's orders; but he also knew the Angel's writing! He put the letter in his pocket and said nothing about it. Then he waited his chance. It came sooner than he expected. The doctor saw that Barlow worried Terence less than any of the others, so he asked that his patient be left alone with Barlow while the nurse went to meals or for walks. That afternoon, when the others were all out, Barlow took Terence's hand.

"How do you feel, my boy?"

"Oh—all right, I guess. I don't see why they won't let me die; I've tried it twice now."

"It's because we all love you. We see that you are too fine to die. See this?"

Barlow held up the Angel's letter. For the first time in many weeks Terence looked interested.

"Shall I read it to you, laddie?"

"Oh, yes—quickly—no—slowly. I want it to last a long time. It's from our Angel, Rags, old boy."

Rags leaped to the bedside at the sound of his name and stood licking Terence's hand. The boy's face relaxed and he was perfectly quiet as he listened to the familiar phrases of the Angel.

"Dearest Limberlost Guard:

"I'm so tired to-night, Freckles, dear, but I've such grand news. I couldn't go to bed without telling you. I have a mother at last! Isn't it wonderful? Dad and the Bird Woman were married to-day: she is a perfect treasure. I've always loved her, and I know all of us are going to be 'happy forever after.' I wanted her to be married among the flowers of her loved Swamp, so the gang all helped, and there wasn't a tame thing in the house—not even me.

"It *is* a joy to have someone to call 'Mother'; and you should see Dad. A human being more pleased with himself you've never seen. He's just touching the high spots!

"They have gone on a short trip to the northern lakes. I'll miss them, but I'll help in the bank, and play some tennis, and get their rooms all ready for them; so I'll be busy. Then I'm having all the ground in that low spot below the orchard spaded, so that Mother can have a marvellous wild flower garden there. She wouldn't be happy without one, you know. Dick is coming to help me to-morrow, and we are going to plant all the flowers we dug to decorate the house for the wedding."

Barlow paused and looked at Terence. A little frown had appeared between his eyes.

"Who—who is Dick?"

"I don't know, Barlow. She has never mentioned him before. But, of course, all the boys must be crazy about her—they wouldn't be human if they weren't. But go on with the letter."

"Speaking of the orchard reminds me: I found that the robin family in the maidenblush apple tree have hatched their second brood of babies. Fat, bunchy Mrs. Robin was busy plucking the casings off the babies' pin-feathers—they were looking quite dressed up. As I passed she chirped to me, 'How is Freckles?' I told her all the big things you were going to do hadn't materialized yet, but that I was sure they would soon. They will, won't they?

"Your room in the Limberlost is lovelier than ever. McLean makes the lumbermen stay away from it, and allows no one in the Swamp but Mother and me. Your big black vultures still hang high in the sky; sometimes they fly low and drop a feather to me for good luck. I have one stuck in the side of my field hat; it perches there rather defiantly.

"I'm hoping for a letter with great news soon.

"As always, my best love to you,

SWAMP ANGEL—but I don't look a speck like an Angel this summer—I've been out a lot, and I'm all 'browned up.'"

Kathleen, who was almost constantly in the room, came in just as Barlow was finishing, and she discerned the effect of the letter. So he *was* in love with the American girl, and it was her letter that had soothed and quieted him, when all she could do had failed. That was a disturbing thought. Well, *she* would watch the mail after this, and see that any future letters from America were kept away from him. She tried to take possession of Terence, and she hovered over him constantly. Barlow disliked her more and more; he could see that his master was more at ease when she was out of the room.

"Barlow, why did you read Mr. Terence that letter? You know that he is not to be bothered with mail."

Kathleen was provoked; Barlow knew what she said was true, but he had thought the letter would do Terence good, and it had.

"He asked me if there was any mail from America,

miss, and when I told him there was, he asked me to read it to him.—And may the Lord forgive me for that lie!" he added under his breath.

"Well, see that it doesn't happen again. We want the doctor's orders obeyed implicitly."

"Yes, miss," but he put the precious letter in his pocket. The poor sick boy would be wanting him to read it again, and what he wanted he should have if it was within Barlow's power to give it to him.

Kathleen seated herself on a low stool beside the bed and took Terence's hand in hers. She tried to push Rags out of her way, but Rags refused to be pushed. Terence slowly drew his hand away from her, and began pulling at Rags' ears.

"You *are* better to-day, aren't you, dear?" Kathleen leaned over and stroked his cheek; his head was a mass of bandages. But he was impatient under her touch, and turned his head without answering.

Aunt Ellen came in, looking wan and pale.

"If we could only *do* something—this waiting is becoming unendurable."

At the sound of her voice, Terence's eyes opened and he attempted a smile. He seemed to sense the fact that at heart she was on his side. He felt a large sympathy for her: living with Uncle Maxwell could not be easy. He held out his hand to Aunt Ellen, and although she saw that he had been stroking the dog, she took it without a murmur. Terence noticed, but he was not inclined to comment on it.

"Sorry I'm being such a nuisance," he whispered. "Take a nap—you look tired."

He would talk only at rare intervals. Mostly he lay with his eyes closed, and it was difficult to tell whether he was sleeping or merely pretending because he wanted to be let alone. But his pulse was steady, and he had no fever.

That evening he asked Barlow to read the Angel's letter again, and when it was finished, he whispered:

"Barlow, would you bring those two feathers of mine in here and set them where I can see them?"

Watching them, and caressing Rags, he fell asleep.

CHAPTER XI

Wherein the Angel Goes to the Swamp, and Discovers a Plot

HAVING made her decision, the Angel hurried out to the garage. She smiled as she looked at her little car, her "baby Fiat" as she called it, a birthday present from her father. Dear old Dad! What a shock he would get when he came home and found almost half the business block of the town burned; three of his own buildings gone, and not a scrap saved from any of them. She knew he had always carried insurance. Of course, that would help. But most of the storekeepers had no insurance. The rate was almost prohibitive on small frame structures with inadequate fire protection; so the fire had meant a total loss to several men with families to support. Her dad still had his farm and oil wells: she was sure he could loan them money from the bank to make a new start. The bank . . . she wished she knew just how much foundation there was for Dick's uneasiness; and how much of it was imagination. Well, if they did not tell her pretty soon she would ask them. She had nothing to conceal, and she was not afraid of anything they had to say. She would fight for her dad through anything. But let them say what they had on their minds. None of them could get anywhere working in the dark.

She stepped into her car; it was so small, just pint

size, her dad said, large enough for her and, maybe, one other. Old Brenner took great pride in keeping it polished. No speck of dust or finger marks ever marred the shining paint, and the nickel trimmings shone like mirrors. No other car got any attention at all until the Angel's was spotless. It was painted the same fresh shade of green as the pussy willows that grew along the banks of the river in spring. Really, when she drove to the Swamp and stopped it near Freckles' room among the flowers and underbrush, it looked as if it had grown there and was just a part of the picture.

As she scudded along the south road, she noticed the sun was setting and the fireflies were beginning to wink over the clover fields. The perfumed air seemed to blow away the cobwebs in the Angel's head, and as she breathed more deeply, she seemed to see things more clearly. She must not get nervous; she must keep her head on her shoulders and be calm and cool. Surely not much could be wrong. Still it was inexcusable for Fred to go away, without any explanation, when her father was gone and while the examiners were there. She did not like it.

She turned off the main road and took the narrow road to Freckles' room. She knew she should not go through the Swamp after dark, but she loved the little trail at twilight—its charm was irresistible—and she had never been afraid. She stopped the Fiat at the end of the road and went directly to Freckles' room; the night calls of the whippoorwills and the pleasant chirps of the katydids and didn'ts all reminded her of Freckles. Dear old Freckles! If he were only here to help her now, what a comfort he would be! She wondered where he could be, and if he had ever found a place as lovely and as quietly satisfying as the old Swamp. She could have stayed there for hours, but it was getting dark. She roused herself and took the path toward the Duncans'. It was so lovely she could not hurry. It made her forget. Soon she saw lights from the cabin windows. Thank goodness, they were home!

"Hello, Sarah Duncan," she gasped, almost smothered in Mrs. Duncan's huge embrace. "It's good to see you."

"It's grand to see you, too. The old Swamp doesn't see its Guardian Angel much these days."

"Hello, Mary! Hello, young Sarah! How they grow, and sweet as peaches, too!" The Angel kissed each of them. "Where is Tad?"

"Tad's gone to town with his father. But what brings my girl out here alone at this time of the eveing? It's almost dark. I'll bet you came through the Swamp, too."

The Angel laughed.

"You guessed right, Sarah. I did—and it was delightful. You say Duncan is not here?"

"He went to town on some errands; he will be back any minute. Did you want to see him?"

"I only wanted to ask if he knows where Mr. McLean is."

"Yes, he does, for he told me. Mr. McLean went to Grand Rapids on some business about his furniture factory there."

"Do you know when he is coming back?"

"Yes. This evening. He said he would be out here to-morrow to see about some new work for the good husband."

"Well, that's a relief," and the Angel sighed largely.

"I suppose he will be in at eight-thirty: we can meet the train."

"Anything wrong, Angel, dearie?"

The Angel did not want to worry Mrs. Duncan, so she only said: "You know Dad is gone and I am taking his place in the bank. I just wanted to ask Mr. McLean's advice about something."

"I don't want to hurry you, Angel, but I think you'd better be getting back. I knew you had come by the path when I didn't hear your car."

"I left the little buzz wagon at the edge of the Swamp. I'll go now, so you won't worry."

Sarah Duncan strolled with her to the end of the clearing. It was dark now and a million stars were twinkling above them.

"Oh, look, Sarah—a new moon! It's good luck. Let's make a wish."

"Let's wish our boy would come home, Angel. He was just like one of my own. I'm that homesick to see him, sometimes I think I can't stand it."

"So am I, Sarah, but I don't dare admit it even to myself. Four years is a long time. Maybe—maybe he—isn't coming back!"

Sarah's quick eyes flashed.

"Angel! What an awful thing to say! Of course he's coming back!"

"He is very slow about it, seems to me. He never mentions it in his letters."

"Then they have done something to him. Never was a finer laddie than Freckles. If they have spoiled him with their riches and fine feathers, or perhaps made him feel ashamed of his arm—well, may all the curses of the ages fall on their heads!"

"Why, *Sarah*——!"

"I mean every word of it: nothing could be too great punishment for spoiling that lad."

The Angel drew Sarah's head down and whispered in her ear. "Deep down in my heart I think so, too."

Sarah patted the Angel's shoulder and smoothed her bright hair.

"I wish Mr. McLean had never let him go. He was our boy, and we should have kept him with us."

"It's done now, Sarah, and we have to make the best of it. I'm not sure that it isn't a good thing for him. We all understood him, and loved him, and petted him. Maybe *we* spoiled him. Seeing the world and making new friends will either make him appreciate us more, or less. Now it's up to him to take us or leave us. We are still here, but, Sarah, we don't want him back unless he wants us."

"I'll never believe he doesn't want us."

"I wish I had your loyalty and unbounded faith. There are times when I need them. But I must run along now. Marie will worry."

The Angel did not mention the fact that Dick would be waiting, too, and that he would be worried if she were late. Something seemed to tell her this was not the time; Sarah would not approve. She kissed Sarah affectionately and started back along the narrow trail.

At seven-thirty Dick rang the Kingsley door bell. Marie answered it.

"Miss Dorothy is not back yet, Mr. Summerfield."

"Back yet? She promised me she would take a nap. Did she go out?"

"Yes, sir."

"Do you know where she went?"

"She went to the Duncans' on an errand. She said she would be back at seven."

"Did she go alone?"

"Yes, sir."

Dick looked at his watch.

"It's seven-forty now—it's not like the Angel to be late. Do you remember at what time she left?"

"Not exactly, sir, but it must have been between five and five-thirty."

"She has had plenty of time to get back. I don't like her being out there after dark alone. I think I'll drive toward the swamp. If I don't meet her on the way, I'll leave my car out there and drive back with her."

"Yes, sir. I wish you would. I feel extra responsible when Mr. and Mrs. Kingsley are away."

As Dick drove, he wondered which road she had taken. He knew there were two ways to go, one through the Swamp, and one around it; but he decided that, as it was evening, she would not go through the Swamp. So he kept to the road and followed the pike around the Swamp. Being a man, and not knowing of Freckles, or of his room, or of how the Angel loved to go there, he *would* get it wrong.

The Angel, walking along the path unconcernedly, was amazed to see a light in Freckles' room. Almost unconsciously, her hand closed over her revolver. Advancing cautiously, she heard men's voices. It never occurred to the Angel that there might be danger, or that she could turn and run back to the Duncans and safety. She went straight ahead, and when she was sufficiently close to see and hear, she stopped.

Tom Ryder, Bill Dillon, and Fred!

They were seated on logs around a flickering lantern. She could see that Fred was pale and that he looked nervous and worried.

"Better not talk so loud, Tom."

"That's all right—I come here often on my way to the still with the gang. Never saw anybody around here after dark. The Bird Woman an' the old man's daughter often poke around here in the daytime, but they don't come near our business, so we don't interfere with them."

"Now look here, Tom," said Fred, "I'm in a hell of a hole, and it's up to you and Bill to help me out. The bank examiners are here, and they will find I'm short, if they haven't already discovered it. I want to beat it, and make it look like the old man did it, and I haven't any dough. Now it's up to you to help a pal out."

"That's swell reasonin', but we ain't got it."

"Why not? Where is it? You guys got most of what I took."

"I told you we bought a new still, an' that was straight goods. We won't have any cash till we deliver the next batch of hootch."

"That will be too late to do me any good."

"That's your tough luck. I'm sorry, but we ain't got what we ain't got."

"I don't believe you."

"That's just too bad, too. What are ya thinkin' of doin' about it? Goin' to start a little private *in*vestigation, or something?"

"Don't get smart. How'd you like a poke in the jaw?"

"Landed by you, *and* who else? I'll say what I please, and you'll like it."

"There's no use of us quarrelling."

"Not when there's two of us, an' one of you."

"I'll have to rob the bank. I've got the keys, and I know the combinations. About two o'clock I'll sneak in the back door and grab off some jack. At three o'clock I'll hop the fast freight at the water tank. Then it's a new start for me. I'm sick of this crooked business."

"Oh, don't get so darned virtuous all of a sudden! You make me sick! You're nervous as an old woman now. Got any smellin' salts, Bill?"

"Shut up!—You'd be nervous, too, if you were in my shoes."

"There's game crooks, an' there's yellow ones, just like in everything else. Now you're in it, stick it out *white*, not yellow."

"Well, let's have a smoke—there's no hurry," and Fred passed his cigarettes.

Tom and Bill exchanged quick glances.

"We'll go to the still and work till you come."

But they did not add what was running through both their minds: that when Fred boarded that freight, he would be unconscious and *without* the money.

The Angel stood as if petrified, but her brain was working like lightning. The moon was gone, and it was quite dark. Quickly she debated the possibilities. Her one thought was that she must get to town in time to stop that robbery. After her father had trusted Fred for years, he would rob the bank and make it look as if her father did it. How awful! She felt like shooting him then and there, but she was sensible enough to see that that would be wrong: she could not prove her story, and they were three to her one, and undoubtedly armed. It would be much better to catch him in the act, and not try to fight them. It would not help to go back to Duncan's; Duncan was gone with the flivver; horses would be too slow. She must get to her car at once. If she got away in it, no one could catch her; and she could depend on the engine to purr immediately she put her foot on the starter. She thanked heaven that in her hurry she had put on her dad's dark coat, rather than run upstairs for one of her own. As she put her hand in the pocket, she felt something and pulled it out. More luck! It was one of her dad's caps. She put it on quickly and stuffed her hair underneath it—driving rapidly she did not want hair blowing in her eyes.

She dreaded to step off the path, fearing a twig would snap under her feet, or that she would make some slight sound which would reveal her presence. But she had to take that chance. She had learned from the Bird Woman how to walk through the woods noiselessly, and now her training was valuable She reached her car without accidents, climbed in, and laid her revolver on the seat beside her. But she forgot that they probably had a "look-out"; and they had. As she leaned over to release her brake, she felt a blow on the head, and then—nothing. A dark figure walked nonchalantly back to Freckles' room.

"Well, some guy's went to sleep suddenly out here," he announced.

"What's that, Bud?"

"I was settin' in your car, Fred, when I seen some bozo sneak through the weeds and get in a car. I jes' crept up behind him, and knocked him cuckoo. What do you want done with the remains?"

"Holy jumpin' Jupiter! Ain't dead, is he?"

"Nah—jes' temporairily incapaci*tated*, as 'twere——"

"Let's take a squint at him—and don't be funny."

Fred, following closely behind Bud, saw a figure slumped over the wheel. He grabbed a shoulder, and yanked the limp form. As the head fell back, the cap dropped off, and over Fred's hand and arm there spread a shower of clinging, glittering hair!

"God! Dorothy Kingsley!"

Tom and Bill came up as Fred was withdrawing his hand, staring as if entranced by the crisp yellow curls that seemed to wind themselves around his fingers.

"Hell's bells and buckets of blood!"

"Pictures-*que* swearin', I calls it—where'd you learn that? From some of your highbrow friends in the bank?"

"Shut your trap! Now we *are* in a mess. What will we do now?"

"I suggest a conference, gentlemen——"

"Well, you'll suggest one thing too many pretty soon."

"No telling how long she was back there, or how much she heard."

"We can't do her no harm, that's a cinch—her old man would raise heaven and earth——"

"Not to mention hell——"

"Shut up! I didn't know you were a comedian. Anyone would think this was a vaudeville stunt."

"Well, I'll bet you wish it was, brother," and Bud lighted his pipe.

"Let's tie her hands and carry her back to the still—'tain't far. I'll get to town, do that bank job right away and get back. You boys push her car back in the bushes out of sight. And put on your masks. When I get back, we'll let her go."

"I'm not so hot for takin' her to the still; s'pose she

comes to an' sees where she is—then it's all up with us."

"Blindfold her, then, so she can't tell where she is."

"Fair enough."

So Fred and Bud started to town. Tom and Bill bound the Angel and blindfolded her.

"We better gag her, too, Tom. Wimmin always yell their damn fool heads off!"

"All right, but let's wait till she starts comin' out of it—I don't want to stop her breathin'."

"Suits me."

They carried her as gently as possible back to the still, laid her on a pile of empty sacks, and sat down to wait.

When Dick arrived at the Duncans', the Angel's car was nowhere in sight and he had not passed her on the road. He began to feel very uneasy as he knocked. Sarah Duncan heard his car, and she knew it was not Duncan. She was at the door by the time she heard his knock, and when she opened it she was surprised to see a very handsome young gentleman standing there, hat in his hand, and smiling winningly.

"Are you Mrs. Duncan?"

"I am."

"I am Dick Summerfield, Mrs. Duncan. I am a friend of Miss Kingsley's."

Sarah appraised him quickly as she asked him to come in, but she did not offer her hand.

"No, thank you, I won't come in. I'm in a—a hurry. I just want to know if Miss Kingsley's been here this afternoon, Mrs. Duncan."

"Yes, but she has gone."

"I wonder if you could tell me at what time she left?"

"Not exactly, young man. I wonder if you could tell me why you are asking so many questions?"

"Pardon my curiosity, Mrs. Duncan. You see, I am a little worried. I called at her house to take her to dinner at seven-thirty. The maid said she had left to come out here about five o'clock. I left there at seven-forty and she was not back yet, and I have not passed her on the way."

Sarah Duncan looked thoughtful. She glanced at the clock. It was a quarter-past eight.

"Miss Kingsley came to the Swamp by the other road, and walked here on the little path from F— from the place she left her car." It was on the tip of her tongue to say "Freckles' room," but she did not know whether or not Dick knew about Freckles, and she was not taking any chances.

"I think I'll follow the path, Mrs. Duncan. I'm nervous about her."

"Have you ever been in the Swamp?"

"Not very far—just on the edges to dig flowers with Miss Kingsley."

"Then I'd better go along with you; just a minute until I light a lantern, it's pretty dark. I know the way Miss Kingsley always goes, and just where she leaves her car."

"That will be fine, Mrs. Duncan."

Dick was doing his utmost to make friends, but he was not getting the slightest encouragement from Sarah. Grimly loyal to Freckles, she did not propose to be too friendly with any other handsome gentlemen friends of the Angel's. Grudgingly she had to admit to herself that she did not blame him for being crazy about the Angel. What sane man wouldn't be? And then, in all fairness to the Angel, she also had to admit to herself that this Dick was very attractive—good-looking, polite, and courteous; and Freckles *had* stayed away four years. Men were such idiots! Why didn't he come home? Even if he did deserve it, it hurt. It was a rather sulky Sarah that marched down the path ahead of Dick. But she forgot to be provoked with the Angel when they reached Freckles' room and found no sign of her or her car.

"Well, I guess she has gone—I'm sorry to have troubled you, Mrs. Duncan."

But Sarah Duncan was not so sure. Many peculiar things had happened in the old Swamp during the ten years she had lived on its borders. As they came through Freckles' room again, she held the lantern low and looked around.

"Isn't this an entrancing spot, Mrs. Duncan? It looks like a natural room—isn't it strange?"

Sarah Duncan did not answer. She had no information to offer, and besides she was busily examining the floor and the contents of the room, momentarily growing more worried. Finally she spoke.

"Young man, there are fresh footprints in this moss—made by men's shoes—and here is a cigarette butt—and here is a lantern, still warm from being lighted. Looks to me like you better cut out for town, and be *sure* Miss Kingsley has gotten home safely."

Dick "cut out."

CHAPTER XII

Wherein the Bank Is Robbed and the Angel Leads the Man-Hunt

BY THIS time Dick was thoroughly frightened. He had heard several very unsavoury tales about the Swamp and criminals of various sorts who had used it for a rendezvous at one time or another. Many thoughts flashed through his head as he dashed back over the path to the Duncans', jumped in his car, and started to town at top speed. He had known for a long time that he loved Dorothy; but now that something might have happened to her, it seemed to him that he could not endure it. About halfway to town he passed Duncan going home, but he did not stop. It seemed to him that he would never reach the Kingsley house, but he finally did. Again Marie answered the bell.

"Has Miss Kingsley come back?"

"No, Mr. Summerfield. Wasn't she at the Duncans'?"

"She had been, but she had gone."

"Oh, Mr. Dick! Excuse me, but has anything happened? I'm *so* frightened!" and Marie burst into tears. Before Dick could reply, they heard a car stop at the gate.

"Thank goodness, that's Mr. McLean's car! He must have come in on the eight-thirty train."

"Oh, Mr. McLean, I'm so glad to see you!"

"As soon as I got off the train I saw the remains of the fire. I hurried right here to see the girl. She must be worried about her father's losses."

"Yes, sir, she is. And she is worried about other things, too."

Briefly, Dick explained to McLean what had happened during the past few days: Dorothy's predicament at the bank; Fred's disappearance; and his own present anxiety.

"Shall we get the sheriff and organize a posse, Mr. McLean?"

"No. I don't think it wise to further incense the people: they are sufficiently aroused over the fire and current rumours. The chances are that if the Angel has been kidnapped, she has been hidden in the Swamp."

"But her car was gone."

"It may have been driven away, but it probably was pushed back into the Swamp. It's small and light, you know. No one knows the old Swamp as Duncan and I know it. If she is in there, we can find her."

"Very well, Mr. McLean, whatever you say. Marie, you had better stay at home, and don't mention a word of this to anyone."

"Yes, sir."

"Come, Dick, there's no time to lose. We will both go straight to Duncan's in your car—by the main road. I want Duncan with us."

On the way McLean was thoughtful.

"Dick, of late there has been bootleg whisky among the oil men and the teamsters; rotten stuff, too, dangerous to drink. I've had a couple of men sick from it. I've reason to believe there is a still around here, and if there is, what more likely place than the Swamp? I've meant to investigate myself, but just haven't gotten around to it."

"But what has that to do with Dorothy?"

"You may not know it, but she is accustomed to going there frequently. She may have come across that still, and if one of the gang saw her, they may have kidnapped her, either to keep her from talking until they can move it, or to hold her for ransom."

"Do you think she would wander into the Swamp at night?"

"I'm sure I don't know. I know she *shouldn't* wander in it at all—but she does. All her life she has done exactly as she pleased, and no matter where she went, or what she did, everyone has respected her. She is just the kind who never pleases to do anything wrong, so she always gets away with it."

"She was simply wonderful at the fire. Nobody else would ever have thought of the things she did. Wet blankets, gloves, bandages, doctors, buckets, tubs, ladders, hot coffee, food. Such courage! Her cheery words kept the men going when they were ready to drop."

"Yes, my boy, and those same men won't make it particularly healthy for anyone who interferes with her. Don't forget that."

"She is responsible for stopping the fire at the bank building, and if she hadn't no one knows *where* it might have stopped."

"I've known her since she was a tiny thing, and she's always been like that. She sees instantly what to do in a crisis, and by some miraculous method all her own, she has everyone following her."

"Mr. McLean, what do you think about the situation at the bank?"

"I don't know much about it. I was just coming to find out how much the child knew. When I got off the train, I heard ugly rumours."

"What did you hear?"

"A lot of things, more or less of a jumble: that the funds are short; that Fred has skipped off while Kingsley is gone to make it look as if he were guilty; that Fred set the fire to burn up the books; that Dorothy refuses to tell where her father is, or when he will be home, and so thinks he is guilty and is trying to shield him; that thieves set the fire, thinking they would rob the bank during the excitement. You could pay your money and take your choice out of the edifying collection of stories I heard!"

"Well, one thing out of the lot is true. Dorothy won't tell where her father is, or when he will be here, and she is sure to know. I tried to coax her to tell me, but she won't. Do *you* know?"

"I am not talking until I see her. She must have reasons. Anyway, he will see the news about the fire in the papers, and he will start for home as soon as he reads it, that's sure."

"Well, it's a big relief to me that you are here."

"You know, Dick, last week when I went to Grand Rapids, I went on the midnight train. I was restless and couldn't sleep. I was worried about F—about a friend of mine. I was looking out the window, and just after we stopped at the water tank I remember seeing lights flickering through the darkness. I wondered at the time what it could be. That might be the place. Anyway, we'll go there first."

Mrs. Duncan evidently had been listening for a car; she opened the door and ran out just as Dick stopped.

"Oh, Mr. McLean! Our lassie *is* in the Swamp! Here is her revolver, and she had it with her when she was here—I saw it in her pocket," and she held out the Angel's revolver.

"Tell us, Sarah, quickly, all you know. Duncan, get your revolvers and ammunition."

"After the young gentleman left I was too worried to sew or read. I went back to Freckles' room. I hunted and hunted, and finally I found her little green car pushed way back under the bushes. The door was open. On the seat was her revolver, and on the ground just beside the car was this cap." Sarah extended the cap, held gingerly between two fingers, as if she were afraid it might bite her.

"That's Kingsley's cap!" cried McLean. "I was with him when he bought it."

Duncan handed each man a revolver.

"Must have been the providence of the Lord, Mr. McLean. It was only last week I cleaned and reloaded them."

"Good! Let's go. Dick, you follow us, and keep your eyes and ears open. Have you a flashlight in your car?"

"Yes."

"Better get it and meet us at the back of the house."

After he had gone, McLean said to Duncan: "Did you hear anything in town?"

"Hear anything? The whole town's buzzing like a swarm of angry bees. Is any of it true?"

"I'm afraid part of it is, but let's not discuss it before the boy—he's coming. He knows enough now."

McLean took the light.

"Now follow me quickly and quietly. I'll only flash the light when it's necessary."

Grimly they set out. The old Swamp seemed calm and serene; the owls and the whippoorwills were having their usual evening vocal contest, and there was an occasional dismal wail from a dove. The katydids, crickets, and frogs were beginning their nightly concerts, but there were no unusual sights or sounds. The men were running now, and Duncan was breathing heavily. Presently they came to a clearing.

"This is the railroad track, Dick, just up there is the water tank. A few more minutes will tell whether my hunch was right."

By the time Tom and Bill got the Angel to the still, they had decided it was a bad job.

"This isn't so hot, Tom. Here we are left with the innocent victim, who happens to be the daughter of the richest guy in town. We ain't got anything against the girl."

"No, we ain't; an' you can be darn sure it won't be long before someone is hunting her. We better put her down and beat it."

"I hate to let that son-of-a-gun Fred get away with the bank roll."

"He'll hop the train at the tank. We can find him around there later on an' take it away from him."

"We better hop the train, too; it ain't gonna be any too healthy for us around here. Say, ain't it about time for this dame to come to?"

"Yes, an' I ain't achin' for her to lamp us, either."

"We got masks on, an' she's blindfolded."

"Yes, but she's smart as they make 'em—an' she's seen us before, an' heard our voices; blinds slip sometimes, too!"

"Shall we gag her now? If she hears us, she'll scream like hell."

"No, I don't think she will. She'd know no one would hear her, an' I don't believe she's the screamin' kind."

"Anyhow, let's beat it an' let her scream if she wants to—I hope she does get help. I don't want to see her lie here an' starve."

"Don't worry, she'll get help all right. She ain't gonna be gone long before the whole town's lookin' for her. She knows everybody in the town, an' speaks to all of 'em. Let's ramble."

"O. K."

They started for the tank, but just as they reached the edge of the clearing, they saw the figures of three men approaching. They drew back in the bushes and waited until they had passed.

"You know those birds, don't you?"

"Sure."

"Well, the dame'll have help now. They'll take her back to town: that makes things pretty safe for us to-night."

"*Yes*, it does! Safe till the whole town comes back lookin' for the thief, after the bank's robbed. We're about as safe here as we'd be in a lion's cage. I tell you, I think we better get out while the gettin's good."

"You give me a pain in the neck! Let's hide near the tank an' get that jack off Fred."

"I think I'll make tracks now."

"How'll you get away? You ain't got a car."

"Maybe I'll hop the train farther on. I dunno, but I got a hunch to beat it now."

"Not this baby! I'm stickin' around till I get a slice of that dough."

"We could take the girl's car and make a getaway in that."

"Don't be an ass! I bet that's the only foreign car in this state; everybody on the road would see it and remember it. You sure are blessed with dumb ideas!"

"All right, I'll stick. I can take a chance if you can."

McLean, striding ahead, saw the light first.

"Here we are, boys, draw your guns—but look for the Angel before you shoot, and be quiet."

The Angel sat up just as they came into sight.

"Dot, are you hurt?" It was Dick's voice.

"Only my feelings. You are just in time, I hope. They thought I was unconscious, but I wasn't—only for a minute. I figured the best way was to fool them and listen to what they had to say. Untie me—I'm no Houdini—and take this dirty rag off my eyes."

"Who was it?"

"Bill Dillon, Tom Ryder, and Fred—and another one I didn't see, the one that struck me on the head. But don't ask me questions! We've got to hustle. Fred's going to rob the bank. We've got to get there in time to stop him."

As they hurried back to Duncan's, the Angel told all she had heard.

"Dirty skunks!"

"How do you happen to have your dad's coat and cap?"

"I started in a rush and thought I might need a coat. I didn't want to go upstairs after mine, so I just snatched one of Dad's from the hall. I didn't know I had the cap until I put my hand in the pocket. Guess it was a good thing I put it on and twisted my hair under it. It probably saved me a worse crack than I got," and the Angel rubbed a welt that was slowly rising on the back of her head.

She rode back to town with Dick, McLean and Duncan following in the flivver.

"Oh, Dick! Such a hectic time!" The Angel cuddled against Dick and put her head on his shoulder.

"Head ache, dear?"

"A little. But don't mind me. My! but it was good to see McLean, wasn't it?"

"Sure was! And he says your father will be certain to read about the fire in the newspapers and take the first train home."

"Yes, he will; and what a homecoming! Three buildings in ashes, books short, bookkeeper skipped. Do hurry, dear, before the bank is robbed; that would be just too much!"

"I'll take you home first and you get to bed. McLean and I will attend to the remainder of the night's work."

"Thanks, but I couldn't think of going home, except long enough to tell Marie not to worry, and to get the bank keys."

As usual, the Angel had her way. When they reached the house, Marie handed her a letter.

"Toni went to the post office, Miss Dorothy. This came on the evening train."

The Angel glanced at it. It was from Freckles. She stuck it in her pocket.

When they turned the corner to Main Street, they saw a large crowd of people gathered before the bank and heard ugly voices.

"Stop the car quickly, Dick! We'll slip up the alley and in the back door. We'd never get through that mob to the front door. Are we too late?"

Fred had been too quick for them. The back door was open, the vault was open, and so was the safe. The money was gone.

The village marshal was trying to hold the crowd back from the front door, and McLean and Duncan took places beside him. The mutterings grew louder and more threatening. McLean finally opened the door and tried to talk to them; but they were too excited to listen to reason. They were mostly day labourers with families, who worked hard and economized rigidly for what they had, and believing their savings were gone made maniacs of them. The marshal called to several men, trying to press them into service, but he might just as well have called to an empty street; no one even took the trouble to answer him or look in his direction.

The Angel took a hurried look through the safe. Several thousand dollars in bills were gone. They had not taken the silver.

Someone in the crowd threw a brick. It struck the large plate-glass window a terrific smash fairly in the centre. There was a crash, and the shattered glass flew in all directions. One flying piece of glass just grazed the Angel's cheek and a thin line of blood dropped, unheeded, down the front of her white blouse. McLean's face tightened, and he began fingering his revolver.

"You mustn't shoot, McLean, they are not armed. It would just be cold-blooded murder!"

"Well, they've got to be stopped someway. The idiots will destroy the building."

"Wait—let me try!"

The Angel climbed on a chair and faced the crowd It was a weird sight: the angry, threatening mob collected in the village street, excited faces gleaming from among the lights and shadows of the flickering street lamps, and facing them, the Angel, her face framed by the jagged points of the broken glass window; her hair falling like a shower of spun gold around her head and shoulders; face pale, one cheek split by the thin line of drying blood; eyes sparkling with excitement. She was inwardly seething with worry and anger, but she faced their rage calmly and unafraid. Quickly she appraised the crowd. She knew most of them by name, and all of them by sight. A few of them were drunk, but even a drunken man can be useful if he is started in the right direction.

The shouts subsided a bit as she appeared, and when they saw she wanted to speak to them, there was absolute quiet. The Angel smiled.

"Boys, you're great, but I'm surprised at you; you're wasting your energy. It won't do you any good, or get the money back, to tear down this building, or go to jail for hitting someone with a brick, or refusing to obey orders when our marshal asks for help. We've a large night ahead of us, and we need help."

There were shouts of assent.

Deliberately the Angel picked the three roughest, toughest of the lot.

"Jerry, you and Joe and Mooney go over there to the marshal and help guard that door."

The three looked at each other sheepishly, but the important thing was that they went.

"Now, boys," and she smiled again, "we can't waste time here. We've got to catch the thief. I've just been struck on the head and bound——"

Quickly the Angel pulled back her hair and let them see the bruise on her head; she threw off her coat and extended two white, round arms with ugly red welts around the wrists to prove her words. There was an angry murmur of "Lynch him!" and "Hang him!" as the crowd pressed closer.

"God, she's magnificent! That was a stroke of genius. Any man in the crowd would do murder for her now." McLean was right.

"You all know my father is an honest man. You all know where he is and why. We've got to protect him, as well as all of you. The thief is Fred, and he is hopping the fast freight at the water tank in the Swamp. But first Tom Ryder and Bill Dillon are planning to rob him. Our chance is to get to the Swamp and catch them before the train comes. Is the telegraph operator in the crowd, gentlemen?"

There was a gasp at the "gentlemen," and the telegraph operator took off his hat as he stepped forward.

"You wire the train to look out for the thieves and wire descriptions. Wire Decatur to have officers board the train there, and a few of you men get on when it stops here. And remember, all three of them have guns."

"Is Mr. Pierce in the crowd?"

"Yes, Miss Dottie."

"You get all the revolvers and shotguns in your store, load them, and give them to the men who can shoot. All of you who have guns at home get them."

The Angel paused. She had shouted until she was hoarse.

"McLean and Duncan and Dick Summerfield know just where to go. They can lead three squads into the Swamp from three different directions. Now, let's get all the cars in town and head for the Limberlost. Dick and I will go first. And when we get near the Swamp, be quiet."

A half hour later a motley procession started toward the Swamp, led by McLean, Dick and the Angel, and Duncan; old and young, rich and poor, some in cars, some on horseback, and some walking, armed with everything from a gun to a fence picket, but all intent on one thing. The laundry wagon, the bakery wagon, every delivery wagon in town was loaded with grim-faced men. The Angel had swung them into line. There would be no futile destroying of property now; they would fight for their money and for the honour of their friend and their friend's daughter—"God bless her! the prettiest and the smartest girl in the whole gol-darned country!"

CHAPTER XIII

Wherein Sarah Duncan Falls Asleep, and the Angel Captures the Thief

MURRAY," said McLean to the marshal as they drove rapidly toward the Swamp, "I'll take a squad in from this end. Dick can lead the way from Duncan's house, as he's just been over that ground, and let Duncan take his men in from the end of the South Road. He is the only man who can come through the Swamp from that direction. That plan sound all right to you?"

"Yes, sir—but you must make the young lady stay with Mrs. Duncan."

"Certainly; that is, I'll do my best."

As they came to the crossroads, Mr. McLean halted them.

"Now, boys, I'm taking about a third of you with me. We'll take the west fork of the road and go into the Swamp from this end."

As he spoke the men began to climb down from the cars and trucks.

"I have no particular instructions. We are here to *get three men.* But remember to shoot low and accurately, if you shoot—the Swamp is going to have a lot of men wandering through it, and stray bullets would be very dangerous. Now, come along, men. The remainder of you are in charge of Duncan and the marshal."

When the remainder of the procession arrived at Duncan's, the marshal divided the men.

"I'll take half of you, and Dick can show us the way from here. Duncan will take the other half to the south end. Remember Mr. McLean's instructions to shoot low—we don't want any accidents."

Duncan and Dick were busy trying to persuade the Angel to stay with Sarah Duncan. She had listened quietly to McLean's instructions, but when they asked her to stay with Sarah, she protested.

"Please don't argue, dear, we're in a hurry. Promise me you'll stay here."

"But I don't want to miss the fun. Please take me along!"

She looked pleadingly at Dick. He had never refused her anything. He had always been happy to do just as she said. But this time he could not. He knew there was likely to be serious trouble.

"Dot, darling, *do* be reasonable. Promise me, quickly! Murray is waiting for me," and as he saw the Angel was still hesitating, Dick added, "If you don't promise, I'll stay here with you."

That would never do. The Angel knew he was needed to guide Murray's squad.

"All right; anything to please you."

Impulsively, Dick gave her a quick kiss.

"That's a dear! Take good care of her, Mrs. Duncan."

"I will. Good luck and be careful."

They waved to the men as they went into the house.

"All the kiddies in bed, Sarah?"

"All sound asleep long ago."

The Angel walked over to the table and picked up her revolver.

"Where did you get this?"

"Lying on the seat of your car."

"By the way, where is my car?"

"I suppose it's still pushed back in the bushes. It is well hidden. I hunted a long time before I found it."

"Were you looking for it?"

"I wasn't looking for anything in particular: I was uneasy after the young gentleman left, so I just went back to see what I could find. After hunting about I found your car, and a man's cap on the ground beside it."

"Yes, that is Dad's cap: it was in his coat pocket. It came in very conveniently, too."

"By the way, Angel, dearie, who is this Mr. Summerfield?"

"Just a friend of mine."

"Just a friend?"

"Yes, Sarah, just a friend."

"He is handsome and has nice ways."

'Yes, I think Dick is a peach."

"I saw him kiss you out there."

The Angel reddened.

'He shouldn't have done that. If you were looking you saw that I didn't kiss back. Anyway, kisses these days don't mean as much as they used to."

"Maybe not—to some folks. But I remember once Freckles asked me if kisses washed off. I never did know why he asked me that."

Again the Angel blushed.

"What did you tell him, Sarah?"

"I told him kisses from those we love *never* wash off, that they struck deep into our hearts and stayed there. Isn't that true, Angel, dearie?"

"Yes, Sarah, it's true."

Sarah started to make another remark, but swallowed it. She could see that the Angel was excited: she was pacing up and down the room, still with her father's coat on.

"What happened to your face, dearie?"

"I'd forgotten all about it," and the Angel told Sarah the details about the bank being robbed, the angry mob, and the brick thrown through the window. As she talked she walked over to the mirror.

"Would you bring me a basin of warm water and a cloth, please, Sarah? I'd like to see just how deep this is."

They washed away the dried blood and found only an ugly scratch, but it ran from her eye to her chin.

"Lucky for me that it's no deeper. I might have had a scar like one of Germany's prize duellists. Sarah, where did you say my car was?"

"Pushed back in the bushes at the east side of Freckles' room."

"Well, after the men get a good start, let's go and get it. I don't like to have it out all night in the dew—and we might need it."

"I promised Duncan we would stay here. There's likely to be trouble in the Swamp."

"Oh, yes?"

The Angel took off her coat, sat down, and picked up a magazine. Mrs. Duncan did likewise. The Angel, watching out of the corner of her eye, saw Sarah Duncan nodding. It was long past her regular bedtime.

"That's great," thought the Angel. "Sarah will be fast asleep soon."

"Sarah, did I ever tell you about Dad's wedding;

all the wild flowers we gathered, and about the dresses, and supper, and everything?"

"No, dearie, you never did."

"Well, this is a good time."

The Angel began in a low, crooning voice. She told Sarah all the details of the decorations; how they had worked; and how her crowd had all helped. Before she was half finished, Sarah was fast asleep.

The Angel walked quietly over to the table, put on her coat, picked up her revolver, and put it in her pocket. She felt Freckles' letter. She had forgotten it. She sat down again and read it. What an awful letter! How dare he write to her like that? She walked over to the window and looked out, her eyes searching the sky as if seeking courage and advice from the few stars and scattered clouds, the whispering breezes and flutter of wings. She glanced again at the letter, "Failure—conventions—domineering personality—ill-tempered—crippled—cannot risk hurting your pride or being a burden—forget me."

"What an emotionless, passionless existence!" she muttered. "Ceremony, formality, dignity—all the things we taught him were trivial and inconsequential. What a change for him! How he has suffered! What agony and chaos of mind have driven him to write like this!"

How little we know what we do when we write letters. Perhaps our own mood changes before they are received. We cannot tell how the person to whom we write is feeling, or under what circumstances our letters are read. If Freckles had known where and when the Angel would read his letter, he never would have written it. But he had not known.

It was almost the last straw, after all she had been through. She brushed her hand across her forehead; this was no time for sentimentalizing. There was much to be done before the night was over. She glanced at Sarah Duncan; there would be no interference from her; she was safe in dreamland.

The Angel picked up her father's cap and for the second time that evening she pulled it well over her head and tucked her curls under it. Then she went to the door stealthily, stepped out into the darkness, and quietly closed it behind her.

Tom Ryder and Bill Dillon kept well in the background while they watched McLean, Duncan, Dick, and the Angel go back to the Duncan cabin. Then they waited until they saw Dick and the Angel start out in Dick's car, McLean and Duncan following in Duncan's Ford.

"Well, that clears the Swamp of them babies. Now we'll go back an' make ourselves comfortable in that room for a spell. We got lots of time."

As they seated themselves on the mossy logs, Bill remarked: "Too bad we ain't got some Morris chairs an' upholstered settees out here—might as well have all the comforts of home."

"I wish I *was* home. I ain't all-fired sure we're so bloomin' safe out here as you are. You don't know how much the girl heard. Maybe they'll go to town and get a posse and come back here."

"Our job'll be done before they can do that. Fred's been gone more'n two hours now. He ought to be back here any minute."

"What about Bud?"

"I dunno, an' don't care. The two of us is good as them two. You got a gat, ain't you?"

"Yes."

"Well, so've I. Yes, an' it's got a silencer on it, too."

"So's mine."

"An' you can shoot, can't you?"

"Yes. An' so can Fred an' Bud; an' they've got silencers, too."

"Good! That makes it even all round. Now, look here, sappo, bootleggin' ain't no Sunday-school picnic, an' you ought to know it. You wasn't born yesterday. Now stay in, or get out, but quit your infernal bellyachin'. I'm tired hearin' it. Now let's mosey toward the tank."

They had gone only a short distance when they heard a car stop.

"That's them now. Come on, let's get it over."

Bill's hand closed on Tom's shoulder.

"You ain't got the sense of a louse! Don't be in such a damned hurry. It's too open there. Wait till they get back in the Swamp. Anyway, I want to hear what they say. We want to be sure they got the stuff before we rush 'em."

They went back to the side of Freckles' room, keeping well hidden in the shadows. Fred was turning the car around and heading it out toward the road.

"Good thing we came back; looks like they're plannin' to beat it in the car. They think we're at the still, twiddlin' our thumbs and waitin' for 'em. I bet it's never entered their thick heads that we're layin' for them to get that dough—the darn fools!" and Bill laughed.

"I'm glad you think it's funny."

"So am I. No use cryin'. I can remember a school

teacher I had once when I was a kid tellin' us to always keep a 'sense of humour.' She explained what it meant. Said no matter what 'career' we chose as our life work, a sense of humour would always help us. She was a sour-lookin' egg herself, but I've never forgot what she said. The ol' dame was right."

"I don't suppose she was referrin' to thieves."

"No, I don't suppose she was—that's the joke. You must be English."

Fred took a satchel from the back of the car and started toward the room, followed by Bud.

"Yes, sir, goin' to divide the jack an' then beat it. We'll get 'em while they're dividin' it. They'll be stoopin' over. I'll cover 'em an' make 'em throw away their guns, an' we'll tie 'em an' get out."

But while Bill was talking, Bud took out his revolver and gave Fred a quick blow behind his ear. Fred crumpled in a heap. Bud picked up the satchel and started back to the car.

"Pretty work, sonny," said Bill. "Too bad you can't get away with it. Drop that satchel an' put 'em up!"

But Bud was not so easily frightened. He turned quickly and fired several shots in the direction of the voice. It was too much for Tom. He turned and ran. Bill stood his ground and fired back. One of his bullets went through Bud's leg and he dropped. Instantly Bill was on him. He took Bud's revolver and gave him a rap on the head before Bud had time to see who it was. Then he took a quick look at Fred—he was still unconscious. So he took Fred's gun from his pocket, and leaving the two of them lying there, Bill picked up the satchel. He was wondering whether to escape in Fred's car or through the Swamp, but that question was answered for him. He heard the car start and knew that Tom had taken it. He turned and started back through the Swamp. When he came to a pool, he threw the two stolen revolvers into it.

Fred was not badly hurt, and he soon regained consciousness. He sat up, rubbed his head in a dazed fashion, and tried to figure out what had happened. The satchel was gone; his revolver was gone; his car was gone. He took a few steps and stumbled over Bud's limp body. He knelt and examined Bud; he was breathing. His gun was gone, too.

"I'm in a h— of a swell fix," he muttered. "Guess I'll look around for the grip." Just then he heard cars coming, and voices. "That's the gang coming to hunt for me!" Quickly he grabbed Bud and carried him into the high swamp grass. Then he lay down on his stomach and waited. He could not hear what McLean said to the men, but he watched them well into the Swamp before he moved.

Bill was not very familiar with the Swamp. All he knew was the way to the still and the direction to the railroad tracks. He had not gone far before he heard twigs cracking and dried leaves rustling beneath stealthy footsteps. So they were here already! Quick work! He did not have any idea which direction was safe, and it was very dark. But he was near a large tree. He shoved the satchel into a hollow log, closed the hole with a chunk of decayed wood, climbed the tree, and flattened himself along the largest limb.

The posse was not much scattered, and it was not very large. He could not tell who any of them were as they were keeping quiet and he heard no voices. He lay there for quite a time after they were out of hearing, trying to decide what to do. He did not want to risk being seen by Fred or Bud. They could think what they pleased, but they did not *know* that he had taken the satchel. He was worried about Bud, not knowing just how badly he was hurt.

When the Angel left the Duncan cabin she had no definite plan in her mind. She was nervous and restless; she could not sit there any longer. Instinctively her feet carried her to the path leading to Freckles' room. She could not hear anything; the men were being very quiet. She thought she would get her car and drive it back to Duncan's. It would give her something to do.

As she approached Freckles' room she saw a light flashing on and off. A signal, she thought. She went closer. In the centre of the room a man lay stretched, evidently unconscious. One trouser leg was rolled up and Fred, in his shirt sleeves, was bending over him, trying to stop the bleeding from a wound between his knee and ankle. The door of Freckles' case was hanging by one hinge, and Fred was using bandages taken from it. He had lighted a lantern and was using his flashlight on the other side.

The Angel took in the situation at a glance. One man unconscious; one on his knees. She had the advantage—this time she would not try to go for help. She kept well out of sight. She would try it, anyway.

"Put up your hands, Fred."

Fred put them up.

"Now take your *left* hand and throw away your gun."

"I haven't got a gun."

"That's a good story—a criminal in a Swamp without a gun! Well, *I have one,* and I know how to use it. Now, do as I say, and no monkey business!"

"I tell you, I haven't got a gun. Somebody knocked me out and took mine. You can see Bud—his is gone, too."

The Angel looked at Fred's pants pockets. All of them were flat.

"Where's your coat?"

"Over there on that log."

The Angel examined it—no gun there.

"Now, you back over there by that case, and *keep your hands up.*"

She had forgotten to be cautious. She stepped over to Bud, rolled him over with her foot, and with her foot kicked all his pockets. No gun.

"I can scarcely believe it, Fred, but I guess you told the truth."

"Oh, Miss Dorothy! I didn't mean to steal—I got in a bad crowd—I didn't mean to do any harm. Honest, I didn't!"

"Oh, no! You just meant to rob the bank and get out, so it would look as if my father did it. Now you keep quiet, before I forget that I'm a lady. And just remember that I can shoot—I'll give you a sample. See the knothole in that door beside you? Keep your eye on it."

There was no silencer on the Angel's revolver, and the shot set the echoes ringing through the Swamp. She hoped some of the gang would hear it and come to investigate. The bullet went through the hole fairly.

"Now, where is the money?"

"I don't know. I suppose the same guy's got it who shot Bud and took our guns."

"Who shot Bud? *You?*"

"*No—no*—I think Bud hit me and took the satchel, and someone got him afterward."

"Well, who do you think got him?"

"I don't know. I didn't hear anything. When I came to everything was gone, even my car, and I stumbled over Bud. I—I'm afraid he'll bleed to death."

"Go back and finish that bandage, and no false moves. You know that Tom Ryder and Bill Dillon were in the Swamp to-night. They're probably still in it, and the money with them. Who is this fellow? I don't know him."

"Bud Jordan."

"Another of your hand-picked friends. He's probably the one that gave me the crack on the head; and he's also probably the one who gave you the crack on yours and tried to get away with the money."

"The dirty, double-crossing louse!"

"There seem to be several bright and shining examples of 'honour among thieves' around here to-night. Well, Fred, pick up your little playmate and carry him down that path ahead of me. I want to get him where I can throw some water in his face and make him talk."

"I can't see."

"What you can't see I'll tell you about. I'll carry this lantern. Go ahead, and I warn you again, don't try any tricks. You got away from me once to-night, and you're not going to do it again—not and live."

They made the journey to the Duncan cabin in silence. It was well past midnight when Sarah Duncan was roused from her sleep by a gust of cool air from the open door. She gave one look, and screamed.

"It's all right, Sarah. Don't be afraid. I've got Fred covered, and the other one is helpless."

"You don't need to worry about me," said Fred. "I'm in enough trouble now. I'm not anxious to get in any deeper."

"Well, I'm not taking any chances. Lay Bud down on that couch, and then sit down on the edge of it beside him. I have to keep you both covered with one gun. Sarah, you pour some water on his face."

Sarah went to the kitchen and returned with a pan of water in one hand and a flat iron in the other. The Angel laughed.

"What's the iron for, Sarah?"

"The men took all the guns, and I can throw better than I can shoot, anyway."

So Dick found them when he opened the door a few minutes later and rushed into the room, followed by his squad of men. He had heard the shot, and his first thought had been for the Angel. After all, she was more important than anything or anybody.

"Come on, men!" he had shouted. "I have a hunch that we are needed at the cabin." He turned and ran, the men following.

Bud opened his eyes and struggled to sit up.

"Sam," said Dick, "you hold him. And, Slim, you hold Fred. Where will I find some rope, Mrs. Duncan?"

"Go out the back door and take down the clothes line."

While Fred and Bud were being securely bound, the Angel explained to Dick what had happened. She stepped over to the couch.

"Bud, do you know where the money is?"

Bud hesitated.

Dick picked up his gun. "You better talk, and talk quick!"

Bud was very white and he was writhing from the pain in his leg.

"Not for sure. But it was Bill Dillon's voice told me to put up my hands."

"And did you put them up?"

"No—I shot in the direction of his voice."

"Know whether you hit him or not?"

"No."

"What was the money in?"

"A brown grip."

"Know whether anybody was with Bill or not?"

"Tom Ryder was with him when we left, earlier this evenin'."

Fred spoke.

"Tom's a terrible coward. Chances are, if there was any shooting he'd run."

"Maybe—maybe not. It would depend on how good the chances were for getting away with the money."

"Dick," said the Angel, "we must get word to the men to surround the Swamp and watch all the trains at the tank. Let's go!"

"You must not go, dear. You've done enough to-night."

"Let's not argue that any more. Three of you men stay here with Mrs. Duncan and guard Fred and Bud. The others locate all they can of Duncan's and McLean's men, and pass the word along. I want you to come with me. That satchel might be somewhere around the room, and men never can find anything. Have you another lantern, Sarah?"

Sarah brought another lantern and they started.

It was not difficult to locate the men. All of them had heard the shot and were coming in the direction of the path. Dick and the Angel gave directions, and this time the men scattered to surround the Swamp. A small number went toward the tank to watch the trains as they stopped for water. McLean chose three men and went with Dick and the Angel.

Bill Dillon had not lain along the limb many minutes before he felt a strange weakness creeping over him, and then drowsiness. He decided he had better climb down. As he tried to move his arms he discovered they were very numb, and one hand came in contact with something warm and sticky. Blood! He had been hit by one of Bud's bullets and had not known it! Again he struggled to move. He felt himself slipping, and then everything went black.

The Angel, with Dick, McLean, and the three others, nearing Freckles' room, heard a crash, and then silence. They all ran, holding their lights ahead of them. They came to a dark heap—a man's crumpled body, the head twisted grotesquely underneath the chest. McLean rolled it over and straightened it out. No pulse and no heart beats, and the head rolled sideways.

"Stay back, Angel. It's Bill Dillon, and his neck's broken. He has fallen out of this tree."

"That accounts for every one but Tom," said the Angel in a businesslike manner, "and the money."

"You men," McLean directed, "carry the body out and put it in one of the delivery wagons. Take it into town to the undertaker's. Angel, what kind of a car did Fred drive?"

"A Buick roadster."

"Let's look for it."

They went out to the road, but Fred's car was not there.

"That settles it," said McLean. "Tom is gone with the money, in Fred's car. One of you boys drive to town and tell the operator to wire descriptions to all the small towns around here. I guess that's the best we can do to-night."

"I suppose it's silly," said the Angel, "but I have a queer feeling that the money is in the Swamp."

"What about Tom?"

"He may be here, too. Someone else may have taken Fred's car."

"Yes, that's so."

"Let's go back to Duncan's until daylight; it won't be long. No one can get in or out of the Swamp to-night, and we can make a more thorough search when we can see."

"All right, Angel, just as you say."

When they reached the cabin a messenger arrived from Duncan to say that the night trains were gone, and that no one had attempted to board either of them; and Duncan wanted instructions.

"Tell him to keep the men in the Swamp and arcund it. There is still one man not accounted for, and the money has not been found. Tell him the men will be relieved at daylight."

The man departed.

"I'll take Fred and Bud to town and turn them over to the sheriff. And I'll have a fresh crew of men here at daylight to replace those who have hunted all night. What about you, Angel? Haven't you had enough excitement for one night?"

The Angel was tired but smiling. A pang shot suddenly through McLean's heart as he realized that Dick had an arm around her and she was leaning her head on his shoulder.

"Yes, I'm ready for some sleep. I'm going right into Sarah's spare bed, so I'll be here at daylight. I want to look for that satchel myself. And you'd better arrange to have Fred and Bud brought out here in the morning. I want to know the exact spot where Fred was hit, and where Bud was standing when he shot, the direction he fired, et cetera."

"That's another brilliant idea, Angel. I'll do it."

"And send a wire to Mr. Finch at the county seat to send currency here on the morning train. Tell him it's a case of emergency and not to fail. Sign my name. It will get here before time for the bank to open. Then you open the bank on time, and if anyone comes in for their money, pay them."

"Yes. And what will I say about your dad?"

"Say he is on his way home."

"All right. And you, Dick?"

"I'm staying here, too. You can't keep me away from Dorothy. I think Mrs. Duncan will let me nap for a couple of hours on her couch."

The Angel and Dick waved good-bye to McLean as he started out with Fred and Bud, the latter weak from loss of blood, and a couple of extra men as guards. But McLean had a dull ache in his heart all the way into town. He almost forgot the fire, and the dead man, and the money. All he could see was the Angel's bright head on Dick's shoulder.

CHAPTER XIV

Wherein McLean Runs the Bank, and the Money Is Found

NEXT morning everyone in the Duncan cabin was stirring at daybreak. Mrs. Duncan and the children were in the kitchen preparing the usual country breakfast of ham and eggs, fried potatoes, hot biscuits, maple syrup, and pie. The table was spread with a red cloth and in the centre was a bouquet of vivid wild flowers. Young Sarah and Mary were arranging huge platters of steaming food, and Mrs. Duncan was pouring enormous cups of clear, golden-brown coffee from a gallon coffee pot.

"My! how good that smells, Sarah. No percolator or drip-pot in the world could make better coffee than that!"

Sarah laughed. If there was anything she thoroughly enjoyed it was having her cooking praised and eaten.

"I still make coffee as my mother taught me—beat a whole egg in the dry coffee; then pour cold water on it and let it stand a few hours; then let it come to a boil slowly and boil for two minutes; clear it with a dash of cold water——"

"——and behold! nectar fit for the gods!"

The men from town had arrived, and Duncan had been out telling them where to go and asking them to send back all the men who had remained on duty the entire night. Most of them went to town, but he invited a few of his and McLean's friends to stay for breakfast.

Duncan seated himself and poured a generous share of rich yellow cream into his cup. He looked proudly at Sarah.

"No one cooks better food than my Sarah," and he smiled at her fondly as she went about the table serving the men, who were eating like famished wolves. She ran a hand through his hair as she passed him on her way to the kitchen.

Dick had seated himself by the Angel. They seemed none the worse for their experiences of the night before, excepting for the bump on the Angel's head and the long scratch across her cheek, and they were not painful. Dick put an arm around her.

"Sleep all right, honey girl?"

"Like a log, until the birds wakened me at dawn. This is the first sunrise I've seen in a long time. Glorious morning, isn't it?"

"Couldn't be finer."

"I just feel in my bones that we are going to have good luck to-day."

"Sure we are!"

"More coffee, Mr. Dick?" Sarah was still plying the men with food.

"Yes, please. I shouldn't, but I can't resist. It's a good thing I don't eat here often. I'd weigh two hundred!"

Sarah beamed.

"Me, too!" The men began straying away from the table and lighting their pipes. They seemed in no hurry to leave, wandering out in the yard, enjoying the fragrance and the fresh sweetness of the air such as one finds nowhere but in the country in the early morning.

Sarah came and sat beside the Angel.

"Now, Sarah, it's time someone served you. Allow me!" and the Angel rose and began passing food. Dick rushed to the kitchen for the coffee pot. Sarah enjoyed the attention, and their talk and laughter, but every time she looked at the Angel, she could see Freckles and the hurt there would be in his eyes if he could see his beloved Angel with another man's arm around her.

"Dick," the Angel asked, "did you see Mr. Snyder or Mr. Logan out here last night? In the excitement I forgot to look for them."

"Yes, dear, they were both here. I saw them several times. I think they went into town with McLean."

"I wonder what they will do this morning."

"There isn't much they can do. Fred is in jail, and he is the man whose confession clears your father of any suspicion anyone might have had."

"Dear old Dad! Wonder what will happen at the bank this morning."

"Don't worry about the bank, McLean will take care of that; and he will take care of the examiners and the customers."

"That he will," agreed Sarah, "he's Scotch, like Duncan."

The Angel laughed.

"Dick, let's go out to the room and have a look around, while we wait for the marshal to bring Fred and Bud."

"All right, dear."

They went out arm in arm, and Sarah stood at the window with a troubled heart and watched them out of sight into the Swamp.

The town was buzzing with excitement. McLean met the early morning train, with Snyder and Logan. The currency and silver came, four sacks of it. They took it to the bank and set things to rights as best they could. Carpenters had removed the jagged glass from the window and were busy cross-barring it with pine strips, and covering it with wire screening to serve as a makeshift until a new plate glass could come from Chicago.

As the time drew near for the bank to open, many farmers drove in from the country, and both sides of the main street were well lined with Fords and horses and buggies. Many men in little groups stood about the street. The farmers had put everything they had in the bank. If they were alarmed and made a run on the bank, there would not be enough cash for everyone. McLean was worried; but if he could convince the business men, he could hold the others in line, too.

"Boys," he said to Snyder and Logan, "we may have a tough job, and we may not. Kingsley has the confidence of these men. I don't know whether I have or not; but I intend to do a tall job of talking, and I expect you fellows to back me up in anything I say. The idea is to keep them from drawing money—if they see we have it, they are not so likely to want it. Now, you boys help me."

They went into the vault and opened the bags, placing a generous array of cash in the drawer by the cashier's window. Then they took empty bags, put silver in the bottom and stuffed papers in the top, so that when the bank opened there were at least a dozen money bags sitting conspicuously on the floor of the vault.

"We will leave the revolvers out of sight. Kingsley

always kept one at each window, but I think it would be a bad idea to have them in evidence this morning. Looks too much as if we expected trouble. We must keep serene and calm, no matter what happens. No violence."

"I think you're right, McLean. Well, it's nine o'clock." Snyder went to the front door, swung it open, and unhooked the screen.

Several of the most excitable customers entered first. There are always a few "doubting Thomases." Except for the front window, the interior of the bank looked as usual. No guards—no guns—vault open—money in the cash drawer as usual—a calm face at each of the three windows. They asked many questions, and received lucid, reasonable answers; there was no hesitancy or quibbling.

"Certainly we have the money, gentlemen," McLean was saying, "but why draw it out? You have no place as safe as this to put it. Having just been robbed, this bank probably is the safest one in the country—it won't be robbed again for a long time, if ever."

They could see the truth in that. They were accustomed to seeing Dorothy in the bank when her father was gone. They asked about her.

"She stayed at Duncan's. She says she is going to conduct personally the search for the money. She says men never can find anything."

There was a general laugh at that.

They heard a commotion and loud voices in the street. and looked out. It was the sheriff and his deputies escorting Fred and Bud to the Swamp. Many of the men followed them. A few customers drew small amounts of cash for immediate needs, but there was no stampede and no cause for alarm. McLean did most of the talking; there was something about his face and quiet, deep voice that inspired confidence. Men came in, asked their questions, were satisfied with the answers, and went out again. So it went on for several hours. McLean wiped his perspiring face.

"Gosh! boys, that's the most talking I ever did in my life! We're sitting pretty now, unless that mob that went to the Swamp decides to lynch those two."

"I never thought of that."

"Well, after all, Bill is dead and Bud shot him—and Fred stole the money. Lord knows, they're guilty enough."

Just then the telegraph operator came in the door with a telegram in his hand.

"Tom has been caught driving Fred's car, Mr. McLean. But he hasn't the money. He says the last he saw of the satchel it was in Bud's hand when he started shooting. He says he ran when the firing began."

"Who sent the message?"

"The sheriff in Watertown; he says he is bringing Tom over here this afternoon."

"Send that message to the Swamp at once. It looks as if the girl were right. She said last night she had a hunch that the money was in the Swamp. And tell her, too, please, that things here at the bank are in fine shape."

"What a bunch those three are! Murder—bank robbers—bootleggers—stolen car: they have plenty hanging over their heads. Glad I'm not in their shoes."

"And none of them ever intended to get into such a mess. It's just what happens when a kid gets a wrong start."

A boy came in with a second telegram. It was addressed to the Angel, but McLean opened it. As he suspected, it was from Mr. Kingsley, from Chicago.

We will be home this afternoon at one-forty. Read about the fire. Too bad, but don't worry. Love. MOTHER AND DAD.

McLean sighed. "That's a relief, too. Things seem to be working out at last. Don't say anything about this —we don't want a mob at the train."

Dick and the Angel reached Freckles' room and began examining footprints and looking for anything that might be a clue. Dick watched the Angel go to the case and look at things carefully. He saw a few bottles, some dried moths and butterflies, several books, candles, a lantern, a flashlight, cotton, gauze, bandages, a large knife, and a magnifying glass before she closed the door.

"Who put that case there, Dot? Who uses it?"

"The—the Bird Woman—I mean—my mother. She comes here often to make photographs. She—she keeps some of her things in it for convenience."

But the Angel avoided Dick's eyes as she spoke, and that was not like the Angel.

"This looks like a real room—it couldn't have just grown this way all by itself. Must have been here a long time, too. It's sure pretty. Who's idea was it?"

"Mr.—Mr. McLean's, I guess—he owns the lease on the whole Swamp. Duncan keeps this particular spot in order. Mr. McLean comes here a lot, you know." Again she avoided his eyes.

"Yes; he says you do, too."

"Yes, I do. I come—to—see Mrs. Duncan and the children."

"Oh-h—I see."

Dick felt that she was evading him, that she was not being quite honest; but he could not just put his finger on what was wrong.

"I notice Mrs. Duncan and Mr. McLean calling you 'Angel.' Gee, that's a great name for you! Where did you get it?"

"An old—friend—of the family named me that years ago."

As the Angel spoke she looked over at the log on which Freckles had been sitting the day she first parted the bushes and looked in at him—the day he had named her the "Swamp Angel." Almost unconsciously her hand closed over the letter in her pocket. What a sunny-faced, light-hearted boy he was then; and what a bitter, taciturn man he was now! Dick's voice roused her.

"Well, it's a great name for you. Wish you'd tell me all about it."

"It's a long story. I might tell you some time, but not —not now."

"Just as you say. But would you mind if I called you that, too?"

"Oh, no—you must not—not ever! I couldn't bear it from you."

The Angel realized too late that she had said too much. Dick looked distinctly hurt.

"All right, dear, but you needn't be so vehement about it. I wouldn't for the world, if you'd rather I didn't."

"I'm sorry. I didn't mean to be nasty. Forgive me, Dick, dear?"

"Surest thing you know! Forget it."

They heard cars and voices, for which the Angel was devoutly thankful. They went out to meet Murray. Bud's leg was bandaged and he was using crutches.

"Murray, is Bud's leg broken?"

"No, only a bad wound in the fleshy part of his calf—not serious."

The Angel spoke to the men.

"Now, Fred, will you and Bud go to the exact spots you were on when Bud struck you on the head?"

They did.

"Fred had the satchel?"

"Yes."

"Then what happened?"

Bud spoke: "I struck him on the head with the handle of my revolver. He fell. I took the satchel an' had just taken two or three steps back toward the car when I heard Bill's voice say, 'Pretty work, sonny. Too bad you can't get away with it. Drop that satchel an' put 'em up!' I whirled an' fired several shots in the direction of his voice, an' he fired at me. A bullet hit me in the leg an' I fell. He was on me before I could fire again. He grabbed my revolver an' struck me on the head. That's all I remember."

"Did Fred have a revolver?"

"Yes, in his pocket."

"Neither Fred's gun nor Bud's has been found. The only revolver in Bill's clothes was his own. Is that all?"

"All that's important," said Fred. "I came to first and saw Bud was hurt. I hadn't heard the shots, and didn't know what had happened. Then I heard voices, so I dragged Bud over there in the high grass."

"Can you find the spot?"

"Yes, right over there where the grass is broken off."

"Then what did you do?"

"Lay there until the dizziness in my head was gone and I didn't hear the men any more. Then I carried Bud in the room there and broke open the door of the case and took out some bandages. I was fixing Bud's leg when you came."

"That sounds like a straight story. Thanks, Fred. That's all, Mr. Murray. You can take them back now."

"Yes, Miss Kingsley."

Mr. Murray left with his prisoners and deputies. Several men had arrived from the cabin.

"Now, Dick, that satchel can't be far from a line drawn from here to that highest tree over there from which Bill fell. He was wounded, so he couldn't have wandered about for very long."

The Angel went to Freckles' case and took from it a ball of twine. She tied one end to a bush near where Bud had fallen and, taking up the ball, she motioned Dick to follow her. She walked in as direct a line as possible to the tree, trailing string behind her, a distance of perhaps a third of a mile. She tied the string around the tree and went back to the men.

"Now, boys, we will use that string as a sort of guiding line. We will search quite a distance on either side of it. Bill may have thrown the satchel when he heard us coming; it may have sunk in the mire, or landed in a pool. I think it would be a good idea for one of you men to go back to the cabin and borrow Duncan's high boots; it may be necessary to wade."

Bob Brown volunteered.

"I'll go, miss," and he started off on a run.

"As you search, look closely for spots of blood; he may

have been bleeding. Now let's start, and look carefully, boys."

They looked for a long time with no result. Bob came back with the boots on and began a systematic exploration through the patch of swamp grass. After several hours the messenger from town arrived with McLean's message.

"Thanks very much. Please go back and ask Mr. Murray to bring Tom out here as soon as they get in to town with him."

Then the Angel called the men to come to her. When they were gathered around her she said: "I've just had word that Tom is found, but he has not the satchel and says he never did have it. I have sent word to Mr. Murray to bring him out here when they bring him into town. Now, boys, that means the little old brown satchel is here somewhere, and surely it can't be far away. I'm expecting my dad to arrive almost any day now, and it would be grand if we could have that money before he arrives. Mr. McLean has sent word that everything is fine at the bank. That means that Dad's friends still trust him, and that they did not draw out their money. It makes me feel like a million dollars! What a consolation good friends are, and what a relief to have McLean at the bank while I'm here! And it's been wonderful the way all of you men have stuck by me and worked. You are all fine, and I appreciate it more than I can say. But I didn't start out to make a speech. Let's get to work again—harder than ever. We've *got* to find it!"

And they *did* go back to work "harder than ever," but no luck. They forgot all about lunch time, until Mrs. Duncan and the children arrived with baskets of sandwiches, apples, and coffee. As she sat on a log and munched her sandwich, the Angel told Sarah the news she had from McLean.

"The children and I will stay and help, Angel. Children have pretty sharp eyes."

"Tad," said the Angel, "do you know where your father is?"

"Yes, ma'am."

"Would you ask him to send me five or six men? Maybe somebody fresh on the job would help."

"Yes, ma'am," and Tad was off.

In an hour six more men arrived, and again the Angel explained her plan as she passed the sandwiches and coffee.

"Now if any of you men have an idea, for goodness' sake, don't be afraid to spring it! We're working more or less in the dark, and one man's opinion is as good as another's. Anybody have anything to suggest?"

The men shook their heads.

"Well, if anyone thinks of anything that has the earmarks of a bright idea, speak up!"

The men grinned.

"I don't feel a bit funny," she explained to Dick, "but we've got to keep the men good-natured; they'll work better."

Dick nodded. "Come on, boys, let's do our level best!"

In the bank, McLean looked at his watch.

"It's twelve-thirty, boys. I think I'll let you hold the fort while I grab a bite of lunch. I'll have some lunch sent in here for you. Then I'll go get Kingsley's car and meet the train."

At one-forty the bride and groom stepped from the

train. They were shocked at the desolation of the half-burned town. They greeted McLean warmly, but their first words, almost in unison, were, "Where's the Angel?"

McLean swallowed. A crowd was beginning to gather.

"If you'll just get into the car, I'll take you up to the bank and explain."

They rode in silence. When McLean stopped, Kingsley saw the window closed with boards and screening.

"There's been trouble—bank robbed?"

McLean nodded.

"Let's get inside."

Kingsley shook hands with Mr. Snyder and Mr. Logan, but his eyes roamed the room in a quick search for the Angel.

"For God's sake!—the Angel—she isn't hurt, is she?"

"No, she is all right. If you and Mrs. Kingsley will step into your office, I'll tell you everything."

They seated themselves and McLean told the story. The Bird Woman listened silently. She was one of those rare women who know when and how to keep quiet.

The word spread rapidly about the town that Mr. and Mrs. Kingsley were returned. When McLean and the Kingsleys stepped out of the office, a group of men had collected in and about the bank. Mr. Kingsley stood near the door where all of them could hear him. The Bird Woman was beside him, her hand on his arm. She was nodding and smiling to everyone.

"Men, you have all been great! Not one of you will lose a dollar, whether the money is found or not. You can pass that word along as official." Mr. Kingsley's eyes filled with tears. "But now, boys, I'm going to the Swamp to see my girl——" His voice broke and he could not finish.

McLean spoke. "I'm going to drive them. We will be back here in an hour."

The crowd broke into a cheer as they climbed into the car and started away. During the ride McLean gave them more details, so that by the time they reached the Swamp Mr. and Mrs. Kingsley knew as much as he did. McLean honked the horn, but there was no response. The Swamp seemed strangely quiet. They stepped out of the car and went to Freckles' room, calling Dick and the Angel at every step.

The Angel and Dick were on their knees prying frantically at the wood blocking the hole in the hollow log at the foot of the big tree. A couple of the men were standing back of them. The others went back to the room to see what the honking and calls meant.

"That's my dad's voice, Dick! Work fast!" She smiled as she heard the Bird Woman's familiar and inquiring, "Who—hoo-oo?"

"I know they're anxious, but they'll have to wait a few seconds longer—don't answer yet. Oh, Dick! if only that satchel is in here——"

The rotten wood loosened, and Dick pulled it out. The Angel pushed him away, lay flat on her stomach, and stretched her arm far back into the opening. There it was! She pulled it out triumphantly—the brown satchel at last! She stood up, and cupping her hands around her mouth, she gave the answering call, "You-hoo-oo!" Then she caught up the grip and ran, Dick and the others following. Tired, dishevelled, and dirty, she ran straight into her dad's arms.

"Here it is, Dad! Here it is! Oh, I'm *so* glad to see you."

From him she turned to the Bird Woman. "*Mother*, I've needed you so! I'm so—so tired," and she buried her head in the Bird Woman's neck.

Mr. Kingsley's eyes twinkled.

"This bag seems pretty important. Anything in it?"

The Angel's face went a perfect blank. "I never thought to look in it—I didn't even ask Fred for the key."

Mr. Kingsley pulled out his knife and cut a slit in the side of the bag.

"It's here all right, but we won't count it now." He looked long at the ugly scab across the Angel's cheek. "Where did you get that cut, dear?"

"Someone threw a brick through the bank window, and a piece of falling glass hit me."

"*Who* threw a brick?"

"I don't know, Dad, I don't want to know. I didn't even try to find out."

"No, *you* wouldn't."

"Whoever did it was all excited, Dad, and I'm sure he had no intention of hurting me. Let's forget it."

"All right, but I think he should be punished. It's dangerous business—throwing bricks."

Bob Brown stepped forward. "I threw the brick, sir. You are right, and I'm sorry. I ought to be punished."

Before Mr. Kingsley could speak, the Angel went over and held out her hand.

"Shake hands, Bob. You've worked hard enough to pay for all the damage you did. Now run along home, and forget it, and good luck!"

"Well, that shows how much influence I have in my

own family," and Mr. Kingsley smiled as he said good-bye to the men.

Sarah Duncan was weeping openly.

"Never mind, Sarah, it's all over now and everything's all right. Don't cry," and the Bird Woman patted Sarah's shoulder affectionately. But Sarah was not so easily reconciled.

"The money's found, and the thieves are caught; but what about the Angel and this young man? What about Freckles?"

"That's the next thing on the programme, Sarah. As soon as the Angel has time to rest and recover from this experience, we are going to get to the bottom of the Irish question."

Sarah wiped her eyes and smiled.

The Angel turned to the men.

"Our work's over. I can't tell you how much I thank you. You may all go now." She called the Duncan children. "You kiddies can tell your father to let all the men go."

"Young lady, you can stop giving orders now, and climb into that car. You and your mother are going home, and McLean and I are going back to the bank."

"'Bye, dear, I'll see you to-night."

"Won't you ride with us, Dick?"

"My car is at Duncan's—I think I'll drive it back to town."

The Angel kissed Sarah and left with her father and mother.

CHAPTER XV

Wherein Dick Proposes and the Angel Accepts

THE next few days were busy ones, but everything was running smoothly now, and the excitement had cooled. Except for the ruins left by the fire and the smashed bank window, there was no evidence remaining of anything that might have stirred the tranquillity of the little town. The shortage on the books amounted to only twenty-five hundred dollars, and that Mr. Kingsley agreed to replace, on condition that Fred was to be allowed to work in prison to repay it. Mr. Logan and Mr. Snyder went back to Indianapolis; Mr. Kingsley was once more in charge with a new bookkeeper.

The Bird Woman had kept the Angel in bed as long as she could—which was not very long. Though she seemed rested, the Angel was not herself at all. Mr. Kingsley apparently did not notice any change, but the new mother noted at once the too-brilliant eyes, the unnatural colour, the constant rapid conversation, and the quick, nervous movements. She decided to question the Angel and see if Freckles was the difficulty.

"What's on your mind, girlie?" she asked, as she drew the Angel down beside her on the divan and kissed her.

The Angel took Freckles' letter out of the front of her

dress and silently handed it to her mother. She read it through once; and then she read it again.

"Why, what have they done to our boy? It doesn't sound like him at all."

"No, it doesn't. Oh, Mother, how could he have changed like that? I'm sure I couldn't; neither could you."

"You must remember that Freckles is abnormally sensitive, my dear; also, that he has their blood in his veins; some of it may have cropped out."

"Yes, but he said he loved me. This doesn't sound much like it."

"Oh, yes, it does—that's exactly what it does sound like. This time, Angel, you will have to rescue him from something worse than death."

"From what?"

"From the depths of despair and discouragement into which he has allowed himself to fall."

"I have *some* pride. I can't keep chasing him and arguing with him forever."

"Quite right, my dear. There must be some other way. This is a case where the woman must be the stronger."

"I thought I had all this foolishness out of his head once; I thought it was out to stay. Guess I overestimated my ability a bit."

"Well, there is no need to decide in a hurry. We will think it over for a few days, and perhaps a way will suggest itself."

"Yes, I have a mental picture of a bright little suggestion rushing up and knocking on the door!"

Her mother smiled. "It doesn't sound like you, my dear, to be so easily discouraged. Try not to worry. *All* of us can't be wrong about Freckles."

The Angel was restless and unsatisfied. She took the letter and started out.

"Where are you going, dear?"

"I'm going down to the bank to see if Dad will have any brilliant ideas on the subject of red-haired, freckle-faced, stubborn Irishmen," and the Angel kissed her mother as she departed.

"Hello, Dad," she said a few minutes later, walking into her dad's office. "Busy?"

"Never too busy to talk to you, my dear. What is it?"

She handed him Freckles' letter.

"Hmm-mm-mm—how long have you had this?"

"About a week."

"Boy's sure down in the mouth, isn't he?"

"Worse than that. You know, he's twenty-four now; it must be more than a childish peeve."

"You're right; it sounds like the result of considerable deliberation. He evidently has decided that his life is ruined, and that the only remedy is to ruin yours, too."

He was a wise father. He saw that his daughter was hurt and disgusted; the only cure was to make some disparaging remarks about Frenckles that would make her defend him. If he agreed with her, it would only make her worse. He guessed right. The Angel looked at him quickly, but he was puffing his cigar unconcernedly, while painstakingly he drew intricate designs on his desk blotter with a pencil.

"Oh, I don't think he wants to ruin my life."

"Well, it sounds like it: he knows you, so he also knows that you don't change your mind with every puff of wind, as he seems to have done."

The Angel's dad, watching her, saw that she was

getting pretty cross with him, and that was just what he wanted. He went on: "Yes, I'm surely surprised and disappointed with that young man; isn't made of the stuff I thought he was."

"It's no sign he isn't made of good stuff just because he's changed his mind."

"There are some things men don't change their minds about."

"Am I one of them?"

"Exactly."

"You aren't much of a comfort to-day, Dad. Think I'll run along."

All the way home she thought of her mother's words and of her dad's. Then she reread her letter. She thought she understood something of how he felt and why—something of how they had managed him—something of its effect on him. Their system was all wrong. The Angel knew that the one thing essential to his happiness was for him to be wholly independent. She guessed, and correctly, that all they had done to him and for him had tended toward making him wholly dependent. Her problem, then, was how to combat this false viewpoint of his; how to stand him solidly on his own feet. He needed a job; something to interest him; something for which to strive; a goal to reach. Her parents seemed able to offer no adequate suggestion. Well, she would find a way alone.

That evening, as the Angel dressed for a party, she thought of Freckles and his unanswered letter. By this time he must have gotten the one she wrote on the day her dad was married. The two must have passed on the way. She thought, and thought; and the more she thought, the more ridiculous the whole situation became. She had thrashed out all the circumstances with him once: his birth, his family, his education, his work, his missing hand. Why should she go through it all again? What *was* the matter with him? Had he no faith in her? Of what stuff did he think she was made? He should know she would not change. Despite her love, her pride was hurt. If he would go back over it all every time he got a fit of the blues, what was the use trying to convince him again? She would only be wasting time. When she heard Dick's whistle, she had left off being sorry for Freckles, and had begun to feel sorry for herself. That was a dangerous stage.

As she stood framed in the light of the open doorway, Dick caught his breath. Never had she looked so lovely. She was wearing drapes and folds and layers of pale green chiffon, an imported creation her mother had brought her from the city.

"Don't I look like Mrs. Astor—anyone bring my plush horse?" she demanded as she pirouetted before them. "Hello, Dickie, why so solemn?"

Dick, recovering from his momentary lapse, smiled. "Hello, dear! Not solemn, just momentarily lost in admiration. You look like a water lily, all yellow and white and green!"

"Yellow hair; white face; green dress. What an eye the boy has for colour!" Lolly chimed in. "If you'd just go out and float on a pool in the Limberlost, the picture would be complete. You other girls may as well choose your seats against the wall now; line forms on the left!"

"Oh, Lolly, do be quiet! I'll get my coat and join you in a jiff——"

"Well, don't be a week!"

"You know I'm always on time." She kissed her dad and mother, who had followed her out on the porch.

"Take good care of her, Dick, and come home early."

The irrepressible Lolly burst forth again. "Yes, she'll be home early, but not in time to see you put out the cat."

They went back in the house, and as he lighted his pipe the Angel's dad asked, "Has she said anything to you about Freckles lately?"

"Yes, to-day. Has she said anything to you?"

"She gave me a letter from him to read."

"I read it, too."

"How does she seem to you?"

"Sometimes all right; sometimes not herself—listless, disinterested, distraught; sometimes an unnatural lot of colour; sometimes pale. I believe she is worried."

"She seems in good spirits to-night."

"Pride, my dear. Pride will do anything for a woman."

"Has she answered the letter?"

"I don't know. She did not say, and I have not asked, but I think not. I hesitate to broach the subject again until I can offer some helpful advice. I confess, I'm baffled."

"He would come if she sent for him. Any man would; you know that."

"Certainly, and she knows it, too. But she is too proud to send for him. The understanding was that he was to come for her when his education was finished. I won't advise her to send for him: I'm sure I wouldn't do it myself."

"You women are too darned fussy about trifles."

"It isn't a trifle to her: it's quite an important crisis

in her life. I'd like to *shake* Freckles! You men are always leaving the important decisions to us, 'passing the buck,' I believe you call it."

"Maybe that's because we think you know what we want better than we know ourselves."

"We may not know what you want, but we know what's good for you."

"Practically one and the same thing, my dear," and the Angel's dad smiled knowingly.

"Oh, I'm not so sure; but I must say *you* stand up well under punishment."

"That's because I want whatever you say is good for me."

"Important if true. This may all be enlightening and entertaining conversation for us, but it isn't helping the children. What can we do to make them both happy? It's a large order."

"The Angel is pretty young, but she is also pretty self-sufficient. I'm willing to gamble she'll settle her own difficulties in her own way," and her dad puffed contentedly.

"I agree; but it does seem as if our years of experience ought to count for something."

"Let's sleep on it, my dear, and see what the morning brings forth. You might have one of your well-known 'hunches' by that time," and the Angel's dad wound his father's old Seth Thomas and put out the cat.

At the dance, the Angel and her friends were having a marvellous time. Dick was entranced. He was particularly attentive, scarcely allowing her out of his sight.

The Angel was watching Dick as she had never watched him before. Never had he seemed so satisfying:

handsome; nice manners; dressed in good taste. Well, why not be nice to him? He was a peach, and she was terribly lonely and blue.

"Oh, gee, what a crush our Richard has! Looks like a dying calf," and Lolly sighed and stared off into space.

"Yes, he does make it rather apparent."

"*Apparent!* He tells the world every time he looks at her. It's devotion de luxe."

"Let's have another round of this painless punch and go home. A small dose of moonlight and roses, and Dickie will be sunk."

Lolly was right. When Dick and the Angel reached home, they strolled over in the corner of the yard where there were three huge trees, and under them rugs, comfy chairs, settees, cushions, a hammock; flowers along the stone fence; moonlight filtering through the trees. The stage was perfectly set.

When Dick proposed, the Angel accepted him. Freckles' letter remained unanswered.

The Angel was having a gay little dinner party. Not that she wanted it, but her mother had suggested it because the Angel was unhappy and worried. She had told no one of her engagement to Dick; she was not quite happy about it. Dick had readily agreed that they keep it secret; in his blissful state he would have consented to anything she suggested.

"Who hung the meaningless appendage 'Lolly' on you?" asked Ted as Lolly took his place.

"My charming and thoughtful sister; she called me 'lolly-pop' when I was a kid. I suppose I was round and fat——"

"—and *sweet*," someone added.

Jean picked up Lolly's placecard on which was written "Lolly Gookins."

"Well, if you ask me," she said, "your last name is funnier than your first; sounds like some kind of a pet name for the baby."

"Can't be bothered with such trifles; I'm just a little dandruff trying to get a head."

"While you are quibbling in this silly fashion, I'm waiting for someone to get big-hearted and pass me the rolls."

Jack broke a roll, and scattered crumbs over the cloth in the process.

"My! what a breeze!"

"What time is it, dearie?"

"Time for you to shut up and give some other guy a chance to express himself."

"Do you mean to assert that you have any gems of wisdom to express?"

"My head's crowded with 'em."

"What a surprise! But before you shoot, give us time to prepare for the momentous occasion."

"Excuse me for living!"

"O. K. this time, but don't let it happen again."

"I wish you'd get rid of that summer cold pretty soon; your nose looks like the first green at the country club."

"What do you mean?"

"Easy to see. If you weren't all so dumb I wouldn't have to explain every little witticism of mine!"

"Have some olives?"

"No, thanks, don't like 'em."

"Well, eat 'em anyway and show your broughtens-ups."

"Really, the sweetness of your respective tempers completely overwhelms one."

"I beg your pardon."

"You should."

The Angel could not help smiling, but she was quiet and preoccupied. Her thoughts were miles away. Dick, with the usual egotism of the male, supposed she was thinking of him.

Lolly noticed her silence and, rising, he said: "Now, children, let's all give a rising vote of thanks to our hostess for knowing enough to keep her emotions under control! We could wave our handkerchiefs three times!" Lolly gave a prefect imitation of a Ladies' Club saluting a temperance speaker. They all roared.

Dinner over, they strolled into the music room, rolled up the rug, and danced. Dick was devouring the Angel with his eyes, and the others were greatly amused. A few of them knew something of Freckles, but they liked the Angel and, with the loyalty of youngsters, they would not doublecross her, even in fun. She had not spoken of him. That was their cue; neither would they.

A group had gathered, Lolly the centre of it as customary.

"Right this way, ladies and gentlemen! Choose your ponies for the race. Prize, offered by Mr. Richard Summerfield, will be four flies fed to the winner by Mr. Summerfield, himself—in person—with his own hand—at the victor's usual breakfast hour in the morning, which same hour I am officially advised is five o'clock. Will we all be present at the presentation? In spirit only, friends, in spirit *only*. Place your bets!"

As Lolly talked he took out of his pocket the five diminutive turtles he had taken from the goldfish bowl, and was lining them up for a race. The guests shrieked with laughter.

"How dare you abuse my pets like this?" The Angel gathered them up and dropped them back in the bowl, where they swam contentedly, none the worse for their experience.

"I wasn't abusing them; they *wanted* to race; I *asked* them!"

Dick drew the Angel aside.

"Darling, I wish they would go home; I want you all to myself. I can't stand their foolishness. They act like *children*."

"You're not so terribly ancient yourself."

"Well, I *feel* grown up. I've a lot of responsibility now; I've got to do something big for you."

"Don't take yourself so seriously, dear."

"I have a good job. My father says I am making good, and if I am I'll be advanced. Just let them watch my smoke now; that promotion is as good as cinched already. I hope a raise goes with it! I hadn't thought of that; I'll have to ask Father."

The Angel smiled.

"You *are* practical, aren't you?"

"I have to be, with you to take care of. Oh, I'm so happy!"

"We must go back to the others; we have to be polite at any cost."

As they strolled in Lolly was saying, "Come on, gang, romance is abroad. The gallant knight chooses to be alone with his lady. Let us away to ''Tomaine Tommy's' and see if he has any food for reflection—I mean, digestion."

When they had gone, Dick drew the Angel to him.

"Kiss me good-night, sweet?"

They were engaged. She could not refuse. She kissed him, but there was nothing ardent about it.

Going upstairs, the Angel was thoughtful. Being engaged to Dick was all right, but she was doubtful about his kisses; she was not sure she liked them; they were disturbing. Freckles had said she was "free," but was she? That kiss burned her lips. Freckles' kisses had not been like that. Freckles! What was he doing now? If only he had not written that dreadful letter, she would not be in such an awful predicament now. It was all his fault! But what a horrible environment he must be in to have killed all his fine enthusiasms and high resolves. What a relentless, unsympathetic person Lord O'More was; he did not try to understand anyone's else opinion. Lady O'More was some better, but her husband had dominated her so long that she had ceased to struggle; she did not know her soul was her own. She might rebel momentarily, but in the end she bent to his will like the tide running to the sea.

The Angel could not imagine Freckles being afraid of any person or condition. Freckles, who had braved the terrors of the Limberlost alone and unprotected; who killed rattlesnakes; who fought timber thieves; who conquered the fear in his soul by his own strength of will; who saved her life at the risk of his own. Freckles subdued—conquered—crushed. How pitiful! It was unbelievable. She thought of him swinging along the Limberlost trail, his feet in high boots, his revolver in his belt, his cap set jauntily on his stubborn hair, his eyes sparkling and unafraid, always whistling as his cudgel fell at regular intervals, testing the wires that ran around McLean's lease. Lines of the old song he sang to the big Dutch timber thief he had thrashed soundly ran through her head:

> It was the Dutch—it was the Dutch—
> Do you think it was the Irish hollered help?
> Not much! It was the Dutch . . .

Singing! His voice! At last she had it! It dawned upon her suddenly. His music! Why had she not thought of it before? That glorious, mellow tenor voice of his, that set the echoes ringing in the old Swamp. He could do wonders with his voice, and he probably had done nothing. At least, he had never mentioned it, and she had not suggested it to him, thinking it best to let him work out his career in his own way. But now it was apparent that he needed help. Maybe he did not want her, or need her any more; but he should have a chance at a life of his own making, a chance to earn his own money, a chance to make a place for himself in the world. She would try it: it seemed the only hope.

Then the Angel had a brilliant idea, and she went to sleep with a little smile playing around her lips.

Next morning the Angel seemed her old self again. She laughed and chatted and ate her breakfast with real relish. Her dad and mother noticed the change and flashed pleased glances. They wondered what had happened. But they asked no questions; the Angel would tell them in her own time and way. Just as they were leaving the table they heard a little thud. The Angel ran to the big plate-glass window in the living room and looked out; on the porch floor lay a tiny humming bird.

"Oh Mother, look! What happened?"

"The reflection of the light on the glass looks like

water to the birds, and they fly toward it. When they strike it with their beaks, it stuns them."

They ran out, picked up the bird, and the Angel's mother examined him carefully.

"He is still breathing, and I don't believe he is seriously hurt. I think he will be all right in a minute. I'll give him a little bracer. He'd love a drop of whisky, if this wasn't a dry country."

She walked to the breakfast table, took a drop of honey in a teaspoon, diluted it with two drops of water, and stuck the end of the long, slender bill in it. Soon they saw a tiny black tongue darting back and forth into the honey, and the bird opened its eyes. At first he was a little wobbly on his legs, but he finally sat on the Angel's finger and made a feeble attempt to straighten his ruffled feathers.

"Take him out and let him go, dear. He's as good as new now."

After the little fellow flashed away, the Angel went upstairs, made her bed, and tidied her room. She waited until she saw her dad go to the bank, and her mother go out to give her invalid birds their breakfast. The supply of sick and wounded birds seemed inexhaustible. She no sooner cured one bunch and set them free than the youngsters began arriving with others. The same day she reached home from her trip, a small boy came to her with a baby bird that had fallen into a pool of crude oil. That was too much even for the Bird Woman, and despite her greasing and soaking, the little fellow died.

Finally the Angel tiptoed up the attic stairs and hunted among the trunks and boxes until she found her banjo. She had not touched it since Freckles left. The dark red case was covered with dust and cobwebs, but she carried it to her room cleaned it, and hid it carefully under the bed before she went out.

She called to her mother, "I'm going down town on an errand. Want anything?"

"Thank you, no, dear."

The Angel went to the drug store and came home with a bulgy envelope. She looked for her mother and finally located her in the wild flower garden.

"She will work there for hours; no danger of her hearing me," thought the Angel.

She went to her room, took the banjo from its case and examined it thoroughly. She took the key and tightened the drum, set the bridge, and taking a new set of strings from the little envelope, she restrung it. It seemed to be all right. She had a little difficulty tuning it, and finally had to take it down to the piano before it pleased her. Back in her room, she closed the door and windows, sat down, and let her fingers ramble idly over the strings as she hummed a little tune. Gradually it came back to her, and her cheeks were red with excitement as the familiar chords sounded through the little room. After a half hour's practice—yes, she was sure she could do it.

The Angel sat down to think over things quietly. She must make her plans sensibly and with no mistakes. After considering her problem from every angle, she decided she needed help from someone older; who better than her mother? She went out to the wild garden where she found her mother seated under a tree in profound thought.

"What deep, dark plot are you hatching now?" queried the Angel.

"Only planning some late summer planting. I want

to move in some plants in full bloom now, so that the seed can fall naturally and be blown about by the wind just as it is in the woods. It seems more careless; I hate studied effects in wild gardens."

"Or tame gardens, you might add."

"Yes, you're right. But tell me, to what am I indebted for this unexpected visit? I thought you had gone down town for the morning."

"If I may interrupt you for a few minutes, I'd like to tell you about a plan of mine, and see what you think of it."

"Most assuredly. Come and sit beside me, dear."

For a long time they sat in conversation. Then the Bird Woman rose.

"It sounds feasible. At any rate, it's worth trying. I'll go with you, and we'll catch the four o'clock train. But we'll have to hurry: it's lunch time now."

"Promise me not to tell Dad. If my plan fails, no one must know it but us two."

"I promise."

The Angel excused herself and left the lunch table early. She went to her room and began to pack. When she had gone, her mother said to her dad: "I want to go away for a couple of days with the Angel."

"Rather sudden, isn't it? Where?"

"To Chicago."

"That's a bad place to go in August. If it's just for a change for her, why not farther north, where it's cooler?"

"Yes, I know that, but it's not 'just for a change' for the Angel. However, it is an idea of hers, and it sounds like a good one. It's about Freckles, but I promised her faithfully I would not tell; not even you, dear."

"Of course, go right along. I'd trust either of you a long way: together you should be invincible!"

"You're a darling. We are off at four. We will stop in the bank to say good-bye; also for some spare change."

"I thought that would be next on the programme. And I suppose neither of you has a thing to wear!"

She laughed. "As we are leaving at four, we have no time to shop, and I don't fancy shopping in Chicago in August, so your finances won't suffer this time."

"I was only joking. I'd do anything to make the Angel happy. If you agree with her, it must be all right."

Two hectic days in Chicago; sights and sounds that neither of them liked; the heat and smoke of the city; the rumble of elevated trains; crowded streets; traffic congestion; hotels; taxicabs; stifling offices; elevators; interviews. They emerged tired but triumphant, and before they took the train home, a package was started on its way to Freckles.

CHAPTER XVI

Wherein a Package Arrives in Ireland; Kathleen Hides It; Barlow Fights for It

FOR several weeks Terence had improved but slightly. His condition and his behaviour were neither one satisfactory to his physicians. In fact, he did not behave at all; he acted more like a balky, spoiled child than like a man. He would not read, write, talk, or show the slightest interest in anything; they even had great difficulty in making him eat. He stared at the ceiling for hours. Kathleen really tried to entertain him and to help care for him. She brought him bouquets of wild flowers, but she got no more response than a perfunctory "Thank you. Don't trouble about me."

"It's no trouble, Terence, dear. They make your room more cheerful."

"Well, they don't make me more cheerful; they only make me think——" His voice trailed off into silence.

"Think of what?"

"Of something I'm trying to forget."

"Can't you tell me about it, dear? Maybe it would do you good. I'd love to understand you better, and sympathize with you, if you really have troubles."

"Oh, I don't want to talk!" and he would throw himself on the bed like a peevish child, tossing around until they became frightened and had to ask him to be quiet.

When Kathleen tried to read to him, he pretended to go to sleep; and as soon as she tiptoed out of the room his eyes flew open, and he began staring at the ceiling again. Even Rags exerted himself in an effort to be entertaining, and he succeeded in gaining more response and more attention than the family, it must be admitted in all fairness to the dog. Anything more ridiculous than huge, ungraceful Rags cavorting around in one of his lighter moods, it would be difficult to imagine. He would act as kittenish as was possible for such a heavy, awkward animal, and he looked too silly for words, lying on his back, pawing the air, rolling over and rubbing his nose, and merrily swinging the revolving tail at an unusually rapid rate. And then he would look at Terence just as if he had accomplished a great feat and expected to be rewarded. Terence had to laugh; he could not help it. The only smiles the boy had were for the dog.

"Good boy, Rags!" he would say as he patted Rags' head. "You're a three-ring circus all by yourself, aren't you?"

Aunt Ellen spent hours with the cook, trying to think of tasty dishes to tempt him. He would smile half-heartedly and thank her, but more often than not the food remained untouched. Uncle Maxwell was impossible; the boy was worse after each visit from him, so he ceased coming into the room at all. He was only a pathetic old man as he stepped quietly to the door once or twice each day to inquire for "my nephew." Uncle Maxwell was having time and opportunity for much thought. Secretly, Aunt Ellen was glad of it, and was hoping it would do him some good. If only something would happen to soften him, just a little, it would be so much easier for all of them.

Terence was terribly grouchy with the nurses, and seeing how they annoyed him, Barlow offered to take their places. So the nurses were dismissed and Barlow undertook the entire care of him. Terence was conscious all the time now, but sometimes in intense pain. The doctor said he was out of danger; his brain was not injured; there was no reason why he should not recuperate rapidly if he would only try. But he would not. He was a mystery to all of them but Barlow.

Barlow *knew*, and his heart was racked. Such exceptionally fine stuff there was in the boy, lying dormant: nothing to rouse him or bring to the surface all the inherently splendid elements in his nature. He had all the romance and gentle sweetness which St. Patrick must have found in the Irish people when he first went among them. Coming from a race which believed in fairies with all the charm and simplicity of childlike faith, Terence had the whimsicality of his ancestors, imbued as they were with the spirit of tradition and legend, the sentiment and caprice of an enchanted folk living in a visionary world.

But there was nothing now, and there never had been anything, about the O'More household to arouse any emotions in one save those of stern reality. Terence had long ago learned to restrain his natural impulses and "come down to earth," so to speak. It was no atmosphere for a dreamer who wanted his fancies to roam among the heights, and the poetic dreams and imaginary visions died within his soul before they were born. The boy was wasting away; something fundamental and necessary to his physical and mental well-being was dying within him. Something must rouse him from this killing lethargy. But what?

Barlow had pondered the situation much and could arrive at no solution. He was delighted that Terence was determined to leave. Away from the formal indifference of this house, he might blossom forth and be his old self again. Barlow remembered with a pang the spontaneity and sparkling, contagious smile of the boy when he first arrived. How the boy had pled with them to call him "Freckles," the friendly, affectionate nickname which he had been accustomed to hearing in the Limberlost; how he had fought at first to retain his natural joy and youthful whims; and then how he had given up despairingly, and gradually succumbed to the older, colder precepts of age and dignity. Apparently there was none of the old fire left: it had been extinguished ruthlessly and unregretfully by those too indifferent or ignorant of its existence to feel any remorse at its departure. But Barlow was sure, in his own shrewd mind, that sparks of it were left: sparks perhaps only smouldering and almost smothered by ashes of coldness and unconcern, but sparks that could be brought to life and blown into flames by a little warmth and affectionate solicitude.

There was nothing Barlow would not do for "his boy." He had even thought of writing to the Angel, but he knew Terence would never forgive him for such interference as that, although he was sure the Angel would understand. He had read and reread the Angel's letter to the boy until the pages were nearly worn out. It was the only thing in which Terence seemed interested; the only thing that helped.

"You see, sir, she loves you and is waiting for you. You need not worry," Barlow said by way of solace.

"I know that, old man, but I did a cowardly thing,

and I *do* worry. Instead of leaving here, whether my uncle wanted me to or not, and going to work so that I would have gotten my self-respect back, I wrote her that contemptible letter I told you about. She got it a day or two after she wrote this one: they must have passed on the way."

"But you can answer this letter, sir."

"No, I can't; not until I get an answer to mine. Anyway, what would I say? Things are worse now than they were then. But you did not let me finish. The worst thing I did was to accuse her of changing, too. I had a right to say what I chose about myself, but I had no right to assume anything about her. What a perfect ass I am!"

"Don't worry, sir. Things have a way of coming out right. Life isn't so bad if you give it a chance. You think about getting well, sir; that is the most important thing just now."

"I guess you're right. I suppose you unpacked our bags?"

"Yes, I did. I thought it best after you were hurt. But I did it quickly and quietly and said nothing about it. No one knows they were packed."

"That's fine, Barlow. We can't leave until I am better. If I ever get out of this damned bed, there is going to be a ruction around here. I don't care what they want; and they can have their money, too. I'll make something of myself, by myself, or I'll beg in the street—one or the other."

Barlow saw that the boy was excited now. He must calm down; it was no time to argue. There was a soft tap at the door.

"Sounds like Aunt Ellen's thunderous approach, Barlow. Open the door."

"Yes, but you must not excite yourself, my boy. It's time for your broth: I'll fetch it myself."

"You're very thoughtful and kind, Barlow. You must be tired out. I'm afraid I'm not a model patient, but I don't know what I'd do without you."

Barlow opened the door, bowed to Lady O'More, and stepped out into the hall. Lady O'More went to the bed and kissed Terence lightly on the forehead. Rags approached, somewhat timidly, wagging his revolving tail.

"How do you do, Rags?"

It always amused Terence to hear Lady O'More speak to Rags as formally as she would have addressed a perfect stranger.

"You look splendid to-day, Terence, dear. Would you like a cup of tea with me?"

"Thank you, no, Aunt Ellen. No doubt it's terrible, but after four years I am still not sufficiently British to crave tea."

"Anything I can do for you?"

"No, thanks."

"We have a lovely dinner, planned especially for you."

"Thanks a lot, but I'm not hungry."

"No, you never are. Pretty soon I think we can wheel you out into the sunshine, and then you'll get an appetite."

"I'm afraid it will take more than sunshine to give me an appetite."

"Whatever it takes we will get it."

Terence reached for her hand.

"I'm really sorry that I'm such an unsatisfactory

patient. It isn't your fault. Everything has been done for me. But I am discontented and unhappy, Aunt Ellen, that's the whole trouble, and I get worse instead of better."

"I've talked to your uncle and I've tried to make him see your viewpoint; but I'm afraid he doesn't see it."

"No, and he never will. But you're great to intercede for me and I appreciate it. I think *you* understand, Aunt Ellen."

"I'd do anything for your happiness, dear."

"Yes, I believe you would. Now don't feel badly, and go and have your tea with Uncle Maxwell. He'd be a peach of a scout, if he wasn't so narrow-minded."

They heard Uncle Maxwell's familiar tread coming up the stairs, and then his imperative knock.

"Come in," called Terence. "We were just talking about you when we heard you coming."

"Indeed. I am flattered."

"Perhaps. Anyway, I was just telling Aunt Ellen what a good fellow you'd be if you didn't sputter so much, and weren't so positive about everything you think."

"It is a great thing to have an opinion, my boy, and to stand by it."

"Yes, *if* you're right."

"Who is to be the judge of that?"

"*Anyone* who knows more about the subject under discussion, whatever it may be."

"Very interesting, I am sure. Who is there to tell me whether I am right or wrong?"

"Well, *I* can, when you're talking about *me*."

Uncle Maxwell began to get pretty red in the face, always a danger signal.

"I don't say you are wrong *all* the time; only part of the time."

"Very generous of you, I'm sure."

Aunt Ellen was beginning to get nervous. Terence was not well enough for one of their volcanic eruptions.

"Come, dear," she said, putting her arm through her husband's, "let's go down and get our tea."

Uncle Maxwell allowed himself to be led away, not because he wanted to end the argument, but because he wanted his tea.

As Barlow stepped into the hall, Kathleen came out of her room, and both of them saw the butler coming upstairs with the mail. Kathleen ran past Barlow and took the mail; but Barlow, stepping quickly behind her, saw that there was a package addressed to his master in the Angel's writing. Kathleen took the mail into her room. Barlow, pausing halfway down the steps, saw that when she came out and entered his master's room, the letters and papers were in her hand, but the package was not. Barlow quietly came back and stepped to the door. Distinctly he heard the boy's question, "Any mail for me?" and Kathleen's answer, "No, dear, nothing to-day."

Barlow was furious, but when he entered the room with the broth a few minutes later, there was no sign that he had seen or heard anything.

Terence drank the broth, and Kathleen seated herself beside the bed with a magazine. This was Barlow's opportunity. He went out, ostensibly to take the empty cup downstairs; but in the hall, he set the cup on a table, went quickly into Kathleen's room, and closed the door.

"Terence, dear, what shall I read this afternoon? Here's an article on sports, one on the latest books——"

"Better read the one on sports; I'm such a marvellous sportsman. Maybe it would tell me how to dive without cracking my head on a rock."

"You must be getting better; the sarcasm has begun again."

"It's never stopped. When I grow up, I'm going to be just like Uncle Maxwell. If that doesn't scare you, nothing will."

"I don't want to be scared, and you're grown up now."

"Oh, *am* I? How did you guess it? For a man, I'm a good example of a baby. You don't know the half of it!"

"It must be you never heard those two lines:

> "Men are only boys grown tall,
> Hearts don't change much, after all."

"Piffle! Everything changes—that's what makes the world go round." But the last line rang in his ears:

> Hearts don't change much, after all.

"Terence, you are impossible!"

"That's your first piece of real news, provided anyone is interested."

"Terence," impatiently, "we would like to be interested if you would only let us. *I'm* going to be interested in spite of you, but you are such an icicle. I only came in here to be nice to you; you're such a dear underneath. Why don't you be your real self? I think your sarcasm and cynicism are just a pose."

"Is that so? I'm sure I don't know how you're

going to tell whether you're right or wrong, and that's a calamity. Women, I'm advised on reliable authority, like to be right always."

"Yes, and they usually *are!* That's what makes the men so provoked with us sometimes, having to admit we are right and they are wrong."

Terence almost smiled.

Provoked, Kathleen left, much to his relief.

Barlow had hunted carefully, but he had not found the package in Kathleen's room. He decided he would wait for her; someway he would make her give it to him. It was an unheard-of thing, and might mean dismissal; but he did not mind that if it helped Freckles.

Imagine Kathleen's surprise when she opened her door and saw Barlow sitting calmly on a chair waiting for her. He stood up and faced her.

"Barlow, what is the meaning of this? Such insolence I have never known!"

"I want Mr. Terence's mail. You know he has been allowed his mail for several days now. I think you were the one who wanted the doctor's orders obeyed."

"Mr. Terence got no mail."

"Oh, yes, he did, miss. I saw the parcel addressed to him. I did not see the letters; but I know there is a package."

"Do you mean to call me a liar?"

"I did not call you anything. I am merely stating facts when I say I saw the parcel. I saw you bring it into this room, and you have not taken it out."

"So you watched me, did you?"

"I did, and I'll continue watching you until I get the package."

"You are frank, to say the least."

"I've always found frankness an advantage."

"How dare you do a thing like this? It's—it's inexcusable! I will have you discharged."

"Very well, miss, but first you will give the parcel to me."

"And if I refuse?"

"I will tell Mr. Terence you have it."

She decided to try different tactics. Somehow she must bluff her way out of her predicament.

"Suppose I scream?"

"What you do is for you to decide; use your own judgment, but I advise you to do as I say with as little commotion as possible.

"Why not give it to Mr. Terence? It's his. Why do you want it?

"You know that he asks me to open all his mail. I never see you reading any of his letters to him."

The sting in Barlow's words was unmistakable, and it only made Kathleen more furious. She was trapped and she knew it.

"Wait until to-morrow. If you give it to him now he will know it came with the other mail."

Perhaps she could put him off; anything to gain time. She needed time to think. Barlow was imperturbable; he answered her firmly and convincingly.

"I will not wait a minute; you should have thought of that before. It's a rather serious offense to take mail which does not belong to you."

Kathleen was thoroughly frightened now. The fact that she had done a serious thing was just beginning to occur to her. She was in an embarrassing position, and all because she had not been smart enough to outwit a valet. It was maddening. She saw that Barlow was determined. There was one last resort; she would try tears. Most men, she knew, hated to have women cry. She would stop commanding and try pleading. She took out her handkerchief and began to sob. For some reason, to Barlow, they were not very convincing sobs, although she did squeeze out a few tears.

"Barlow," she coaxed, "don't be horrid. You put me in a very embarrassing situation."

"Pardon me, miss, you put yourself there."

"Yes, I suppose I did. But it's only a package; it can't be very important. Really, there was no letter."

"The package is from America, and you don't know whether it is important or not."

"Neither do you."

"No, but I intend to find out, and then I will be in a position to let you know."

"Thanks, but you haven't got it yet."

"I don't wish to talk any longer. It's beneath your dignity to argue with a servant, anyway. Suppose Lady O'More should come in here now, what would she think? How could you explain? *I* wish she would come in, and Lord O'More with her."

This made Kathleen realize just how serious her position was.

"You must decide what you are going to do quickly. Either you give me the parcel *now*, or I am going straight to Lord O'More and tell him the whole story."

Reluctantly, Kathleen took the package from its hiding place in her desk and handed it to Barlow.

"Thank you, miss. If I were you, I would not mention having me dismissed. This will not make a pretty story: I do not believe Mr. Terence would see your side of this little affair."

"On, get out of here, and let me alone!" said Kathleen—a woman's last retort when she knows she is wrong and beaten.

Barlow took the precious package to his room and opened it: he intended to be quite sure whether the contents would make the boy better or worse. He examined it carefully, a puzzled frown between his eyes. Then he locked it in his trunk. He looked out his door. No one in sight. Good! He went into Terence's room. Terence lay there, his eyes closed, one hand on Rags' head. He seemed to be asleep.

Quickly Barlow put on his coat and hat, went downstairs, and let himself out into the dusk.

CHAPTER XVII

Wherein McLean Goes on a Journey and the Angel Breaks Her Engagement

WHEN the Angel reached home from Chicago, she found herself confronted with an exceedingly unpleasant task. She must break her engagement to Dick. On the train she had thought it all over. She was convinced that she loved no one but Freckles, and that she must tell Dick all about him at once. She went to the telephone.

"Dick," she asked, when she heard his voice, "will you come to see me right away? I have something to tell you."

"Sure, darling, I'll be right there. It's great to hear your voice. You've been gone *ages!*"

His voice sounded so exuberant, so happy. She hated to hurt him. What a dreadful mistake she had made! It was all her own fault. The best she could do to right the wrong she had done was to tell the truth.

She watched for his car, and went to the gate to meet him. He rushed at her like a hungry bear, put both arms around her, and gave her a kiss squarely on the mouth.

"You are lovelier than ever! I've been so lonesome, dear, you've no idea how glad I am to see you! Have a nice trip?"

"It was hot in Chicago. I—I went on business with Mother."

"I wondered why the two of you dashed off in such a hurry. Business successful?"

"We don't—know yet."

The Angel took Dick's hand and led him over to the nook under the trees.

"Dick," she began when they were seated, "I've done a terrible thing. I can only hope that you will forgive me."

"Why, yes, dear, of course. I'd forgive you anything, anything at all. But I can't believe you have done anything so awful, especially to me."

"Oh, yes, I have, Dick. I've done a really terrible thing to you."

"I can't bear to see you look so troubled. Don't worry, darling—I'll forgive you."

"I know you will; you always play such a square game. I am the one who did not play fair this time."

"Dorothy, for goodness' sake, what *is* the matter?"

"I engaged myself to you when I loved another man."

Dick looked stunned. His face paled and his body tensed. His teeth were biting into his lower lip, and his finger nails were cutting the palms of his clenched hands. He did not answer; only his hurt eyes stared at her, as if seeing her for the first time.

"Oh, Dick, *don't* look at me like that! I'm *so* sorry. Really, I thought I was being honest; I didn't think I loved him when I did it, but I know now that I did. I've loved him always; I've never loved anyone else; I never will. And you are the best friend I've ever had! To think it had to be you whom I should hurt so dreadfully."

Still Dick said nothing: just looked at her in a baffled, confused sort of way, as if he did not understand what she said.

The Angel's eyes were full of tears, but she forced herself to continue.

"I was so lonely, and so worried. I haven't seen him for four years. You *are* such a peach, Dick! You were kind and attentive and sweet to me just when I needed a friend. And I took advantage of it. I'm *so* ashamed. You are just like the Rock of Gibraltar, Dick; always there, always safe, something substantial to lean against. But I must not make excuses. There is no excuse for me. I took advantage of your love because it soothed me, made things easier for me. It was a selfish and wicked thing to do. Can you imagine what my dad and mother are going to say to me for this? You should *hate* me, Dick. You should never speak to me again."

The Angel was sobbing. Dick took her hand.

"Don't, dear. I'm here, and I will be here always for you to lean on. You did not realize what you were doing; you are not the kind to do things like that deliberately or purposely. But who is this other man?"

"You are a perfect darling to understand. You would say just the right thing to comfort poor me. Do you remember asking me who gave me the name 'Angel'?"

"Yes, dear."

"Well, 'Angel' isn't all of it. Really, it's 'Swamp Angel.'" Then she began at the beginning and told him all about Freckles; she felt she owed him a candid explanation after her inexcusable behaviour. She painted a lively, colourful picture of Freckles, tinged with just the right shade of loneliness and sensitiveness, and brightened by just the effective degree of wistful humour to be appealing. Despite the fact that the lad was his rival, Dick began to like him.

"So he has been away four years: his education is finished," the Angel ended her story.

"And he will be home soon. Is that the reason you told me about him now, so that I could do a graceful fade-out?"

The Angel shook her head.

"No, Dick, I told you because I have discovered that I love him. I thought I didn't, but I do. I was hurt and disappointed. I was sincere when I engaged myself to you, but it can't last any longer. You see that, don't you?"

"But is he coming soon? I should think he would be breaking all speed records to get here."

Again the Angel shook her head.

"I thought so, too, but I don't know now," and she handed Freckles' letter to Dick. "Maybe I shouldn't show you this, but it will explain better than I can."

In silence Dick read the letter.

"So you see, Dick, maybe I can't have him after all, maybe he doesn't love me; but no matter: loving him I cannot marry you. As soon as I realized it I came to you. I'm dreadfully sorry, but it's better for you to know it now than after it's too late."

"Don't think any more about me; it's your happiness that counts. It's a pretty stiff jolt, and it rather shakes my faith in womanhood, but I do not intend to let it ruin my life. I'll pick up the stray ends and start over," and he managed a sickly smile through set teeth. "Any-one who would write a letter like this to you ought to be shot. I've no sympathy for him. He must be crazy."

"Yes, it *is* an awful letter, but I'm sure he doesn't

mean it. It's a state of mind that will pass. I'm sure he loves me way down deep: perhaps I'm wrong. Anyway, I'm afraid I'll go on loving him, so I couldn't possibly marry you. I've done a wicked, unjust thing, but I couldn't be as bad as that."

"No, I cannot imagine you being 'bad'; it's a word that doesn't fit you. I am going to run along now; I have a feeling I'd like to be alone. Later I've a meeting with Dad and the directors; it's about my promotion; it won't mean so much now, but it will mean more work, so I can't think about myself. Good-bye, dear."

"Good-bye, Dick. *Please* forgive me, and come to see me soon."

How unjust some things in life seem! Here was Dick, full of ambition and energy, working to his full capacity and willing and eager to take on more because of her, and all for nothing: she could not love him or make him happy. And in a far country there was a boy unable to get hold of himself or accomplish anything even with her love as an incentive. Blue, discouraged, and hopeless, and unable to rise above it; making both of them unhappy because of a silly, sensitive attitude entirely incompatible with any genuine sincerity of purpose or action. But life is like that.

As the gate closed after Dick, the Angel heard her dad's voice calling her. She went into his study.

"My dear, Mr. McLean is coming to see me this afternoon. He is anxious about Freckles; says he has had no letter from him for two months. If you think it's all right, I'd like to have Freckles' letter to show to him."

The Angel took the letter from her sweater pocket and handed it to him.

"Of course, Dad. Mr. McLean should know everything about it. He will be hurt; he did everything for Freckles, and he seems so ungrateful. If he doesn't come back here as we all planned, Mr. McLean will never get over it."

"Well, it won't hurt McLean any more than it has hurt us. When are you going to tell me about that secret trip to Chicago?"

"Pretty soon, Dad. You'll have to trust us a little longer. You see—we—we—we tried an experiment. We can't talk until we see how it works."

"You know best. But what a muddle!"

At the bank McLean was waiting for the Man of Affairs. He took the letter from his pocket and silently handed it to McLean, who read it hurriedly, and then read it again.

"Great heavens, man! What hell that boy has been through! This letter is certainly the product of a distorted, perverted viewpoint, totally unlike Freckles."

"Yes, and what hell my girl has been through, too, don't forget that! This thing is not one-sided, not by a long shot. Maybe you don't know it, but there's something else to think about. Dick Summerfield is hard hit; you know how attractive the Angel is. Dick is a splendid chap; I'd hate to see him get a rotten deal."

"I don't think you need worry on that score. The Angel is not that kind."

"Not intentionally, of course. But she is very young and thoughtless at times; wholly inexperienced. We are all human, and the best of us make mistakes. She has been lonely and blue and hurt for a long time, and Freckles has not been what you would call a comfort lately. I couldn't ask her to sit at home alone, and Dick has been taking her everywhere. Lord knows, stranger things than that have happened. That's a *fine* letter!"

McLean could not ignore the sarcasm in the banker's voice, and he could not bear to have Freckles criticized. But he knew it was true. His own cheery, fun-loving boy, whom he loved as a son; the same boy, who, at nineteen, had fought fear within himself and fear of the great swamp, and conquered both alone. Now he was licked—and by whom and for what? What a pity!

"It's my fault," he said. "I should not have let them take him away from us. I *could* have kept him, and I'm sorry I didn't. He did not want to go, but they had so much more to offer him than I had; at least, I *thought* they had——"

"Yes, I thought so, too; we were a couple of old idiots. We should have let the youngsters alone. We were wrong. Four years in the open spoiled the boy for confinement, idleness, and society. What a mistake we made! We're a pair of blundering fools!"

"It was my fault more than yours; Freckles would have done whatever I said. Well, I got him into this mess, it's up to me to get him out. The question is, how?"

"It's a real question. My wife and the Angel and myself have been working on it for some time. Any suggestions will be more than welcome."

McLean did not answer. He picked up his hat, walked to his hotel, packed his bags, and boarded a train at five o'clock.

After Mr. McLean left the bank, the Man of Affairs sat in deep thought for a long time. He felt sorry for McLean; he was so honest; so straightforward; he worked so diligently, and had so little of joy or pleasure in his life. After a strenuous day's work, to go to dinner and a small suite of rooms in a country hotel alone was not exactly an enviable lot. It was a life that would make an ordinary man taciturn and reticent; but McLean was always approachable, even-tempered, and kind.

He had showered all the love of his pent-up soul on Freckles; had delighted in the boy's development and the good stuff that was in him. He had watched him grow tall and strong, and as he developed a bravery and honesty equal to his own, McLean had actually beamed. He had not spoiled the lad. He had paid him a fair salary for his work, and it was a job many strong men would have liked. As the boy had conquered his fear of the Swamp, McLean had watched him with keen, understanding eyes, delighted in his spunk, and had learned to love him as he would have loved a son of his own.

For a time it had meant companionship for both of them and McLean had made many plans for the boy's future. Then the Swamp Angel had appeared on the scene and given Freckles new courage and ambition. How he had worshipped her! And how McLean had worried about the boy: worried about the attitude the girl's father might take toward the homeless, nameless orphan boy with the crippled arm. But on that score he might have saved his anxiety. There was no littleness in the soul of the banker. The infirmity was never mentioned, and the boy had proved himself clean and fine in every respect. When he had saved the Angel's life at the risk of his own by throwing her from the path of a falling tree, and for weeks had lain hovering between life and death with a crushed chest, McLean had been dumb with misery. When the boy was better and the O'Mores had arrived and claimed him, McLean had let him go without a murmur, thinking it would be a great opportunity for the lad. No one knew just what it had cost him, nor how empty his life had been for the four years of Freckles' absence.

As the Angel's dad walked home, he was still pondering. He found the Angel and his wife awaiting him. He kissed them both and handed Freckles' letter back to the Angel. She took it a bit wearily.

"What did Mr. McLean say, Dad?"

"A great many things, but the only important one was that he felt Freckles' present predicament was his fault. He said he got him into it, and it was up to him to get him out."

The Angel and her mother exchanged glances.

"What is he going to do?"

"I don't know. He is not a man to reveal his plans. I feel very sorry for him. He is all wrapped up in the boy, and now he is dreadfully worried. I guess I did not give him much consolation. I'm pretty disgusted with the young gentleman, although I'm fond of him. McLean left my office like a man walking in his sleep."

"Let's ask him to dinner, Mother. It will be better for him than spending the evening alone."

The Bird Woman went to the telephone and called McLean's hotel. In a few minutes she was back.

"Now what do you think has happened? The clerk

at the hotel says Mr. McLean is not there; that he left in a hurry on the five o'clock train."

"Where did he go?"

"The clerk said he left no forwarding address—just said he was going to Chicago."

"Hmm-mm-mm, Chicago seems to be a favourite haunt of my family and friends lately—wonder what the attraction is. First you two; now McLean; think I'll go next," and he smiled at the expressions of his wife and daughter.

"I wonder why he went there," mused the Bird Woman.

"Well, whatever he does, I don't believe it will interfere with what we did: still you never can tell; it's a funny proposition."

"Isn't it strange that what we do in this life never affects us alone? Always, always some of our family or friends must suffer or rejoice with us; we never laugh alone, or cry alone. Just because Freckles has a fit of temporary aberration, Mr. McLean is frantic, you and Dad are worried, I am all upset, and poor Dick ——" She paused.

"What about Dick?" asked her dad quickly.

"Well, I may as well own up first as last that I played him a dirty trick. Just when I felt deserted and abused, Dick proposed to me. He seemed so lovable and so reliable, and I—I—accepted him."

"Why, Angel, how *could* you?"

"I don't know, I'm sure. My pride, I guess. I have no excuses to offer. It was just when I was feeling sorriest for myself, and most disgusted with Freckles. I suppose my idea was to 'get even' with him. It was common and cheap. Dick is splendid; I'll never forgive myself."

"How unworthy of you, Angel!" said her mother. But before the Angel could answer, her dad spoke.

"Perhaps. But it strikes me that young man deserves whatever he gets. If Freckles loses you, he has no one to blame but himself. He will have to come to his senses pretty soon, or he won't have any friends left. But I'm sorry for Dick; darned sorry! Freckles deserves a couple of stiff jolts, but Dick doesn't."

"Yes, I agree," said her mother. "It was not fair to Dick; he cares for you tremendously, anyone can see that."

"Oh, please don't rub it in! No one knows that quite so well as I do. When he kept kissing me, I knew I could not go through with it—that's all."

"You must tell him at once, and make what amends you can," advised her dad.

"I have already told him, and I told him all about Freckles. I felt that I owed him a full explanation. He was a peach about it, but it hurt him terribly; he won't get over it for a long time, and neither will I. Talk about dragging one's pride in the dust! Mine is completely smothered in dust. I doubt if I'll ever be able to find it again."

"I can't believe it."

"Neither can I. I said I was sorry and I apologized the best I knew how. I told him to forget me, and never speak to me again; but he can't do that any more than I could forget Freckles. Freckles! I wonder what he would think of me now."

"Well, no matter what he thought, he couldn't say much, since he is the cause of the whole affair," said the Angel's dad.

"Oh, no, he wasn't! Nothing he did was any excuse

for me. Because one person does wrong is no reason that another one should. I'm to blame; no one else; get that straight now."

"What did Dick say?"

"Dick was sensible about it. That is my one comfort. He didn't throw one of those ruined-for-life, never-get-over-it fits. He said he had a fine father, and his work; that he would make the best of it. He said that he wanted to stay friends with me, and that if I needed him for anything, I would find him standing by."

"That is more than you deserve. What a muddle it all is! I wonder who will untangle the threads."

"Well, Freckles tangled them, and he will have to untangle them," said the Angel's dad.

"But Mr. McLean said he was to blame, and *he* had to straighten things out."

"And Mother and I have a finger in the pie, too. We have one hope left," and the Angel sighed and twisted her wet handkerchief.

"Well, that lets me out," said her dad. "When a couple of women get their heads together, look out!"

"Especially when one of them is the Angel's."

"It was my idea, but I could not have carried it out without you," and the Angel crossed to her mother and put an arm around her.

"When are you two going to let me in on that mysterious trip to Chicago?"

"It ought not to be very long now: be patient a little while longer."

Dinner was a quiet affair, each being absorbed in his own thoughts. The Bird Woman was thinking of the Angel. She was only twenty, and she had an unusually level head on her shoulders. True, she had made a mistake with Dick, but she had admitted it, and said she was sorry, which is more than most of us will do. When she discovered her wrong, she righted it as best she could. Trying to analyze the situation, the paths all led to Freckles. She was furious at him, but with all a woman's motherly instincts, she felt sorry for him. She must not love him less because he, like the Angel, had made a mistake. There were mitigating circumstances, surely, and until she knew all the details, she must give him the benefit of the doubt.

CHAPTER XVIII

Wherein Barlow Goes into the City and Makes a Purchase

THE shadows were lengthening on the grass and a few early stars were peeking through the twilight as Barlow let himself out of the door. He looked around cautiously; there was no one in sight. He hoped no one would miss him until he got back, but if anyone did, it was just too bad. If he had not thought his errand important he might have felt guilty, for it was four years since he had left the house without telling "his boy" where he was going and just how long he would be gone. No matter how Barlow addressed the lad before the family and friends (it might be "His Lordship," or "Mr. Terence," or "Lord O'More"), in his heart it was always "my boy." He had been "my boy" ever since he had first arrived and Barlow grew to understand the lonely, sensitive, heart-hungry lad. He did not think the boy realized the love he had for him; but lately Terence had shown a decided affection for the old man which made him very happy. After the few intimate talks, they understood each other perfectly: each knew on what footing he stood with the other. When Terence had asked Barlow to leave with him, the old man's heart was filled with happiness. He was more than ever determined that things should work out right for the boy.

Terence did not talk much, but he liked to know Barlow was near. Of late he had taken very little time off; the boy seemed to miss him more and more. If he stayed away for a half day, he came back to find Terence in a fit of "blues," although he always said, "So long, Barlow. Don't spend all your money in one place, and don't forget to come back." Sometimes it sounded as if he thought Barlow really might not return.

"He need not worry," thought the faithful soul, "I'll come back to him as long as I'm alive—that deceitful, scheming girl can't drive me away. She is trying to vamp the boy, but he is too smart. She hasn't a chance beside the Angel." Barlow chuckled. How he hated Kathleen!

He hastened to the stables and there he found only Terence's groom. That fitted with his plan beautifully. The fewer people that knew where he went, the better. One's secrets always leak out when more than one person knows them.

"Thomas," Barlow explained, "I'm going on an errand for Mr. Terence. If anyone asks for me, *you have not seen me*. Understand?"

Thomas nodded.

"That's another lie to my credit—but I *am* going on an errand for him, only he doesn't know it," Barlow defended himself under his breath.

"I'd like Butter Ball hitched to the light phaëton," he continued aloud. "I'm in a hurry, I'll help."

As Thomas ran the phaëton out of the stables he asked: "How is Mr. Terence?"

"He is getting better slowly." Then Barlow thought of the package in his trunk and added, "But I *think* he is going to get well rapidly now."

"The young gentleman is not happy here, is he?"

"Do you see that, too?"

"Sure I see it! Everyone sees it but the two who should see it."

"Don't worry, Thomas. I think things are going to be brighter for our boy."

Thomas came over and laid a hand confidentially on Barlow's arm.

"Is there a girl in it, Barlow?"

"There usually is, isn't there?"

"I thought so. This young lady here hates to let him out of her sight, but she only worries him."

Thomas led the beautiful, glossy little Butter Ball out of the stable. Just the colour of old honey she was, and too fat; but she was so friendly it was impossible not to feed her.

"This mare misses Terence very much, but his own Lady Bird is hard to handle. She is cross: some days she won't eat; and she won't take any sugar from any of us; all of us have tried it."

"I'll tell the lad about her. It will please him. Maybe he will hurry down to feed her." Barlow climbed into the phaëton and Thomas handed the reins to him.

"Tell Mr. Terence I said 'good luck,' and we are all anxious to see him."

"I will, Thomas. I'll be back in a few hours, and don't forget what I told you."

"All right. I'll wait and put up the mare."

Barlow picked the whip out of the socket and touched Butter Ball. "Sorry, old girl, but we are in a hurry." Butter Ball took the road at a brisk pace.

In her room, Kathleen rapidly recovered her composure. It would not do to acknowledge defeat at the hands of a valet. Her eyes and nose must not be red; she bathed them quickly in cold water. She arranged her hair with unusual care, brushing it until it looked sleek as cat's fur. Then she selected her most becoming frock; she must look her very nicest. But her mind was in a turmoil. What could be in that package? What would that meddling old fool of a valet do? She must face it, whatever happened; he was only a servant, after all. But Terence was fond of him, she knew that; and Barlow would stop at nothing if he thought it was for the good of his master. She was in a decidedly uncomfortable state of mind as she opened her door.

She listened, but she heard no voices and saw no one. Terence's door was open. Cautiously, she peeked in. Terence was petting Rags. She walked in. Barlow was not in sight, and there was no trace of the package. What a relief!

She decided she would greet Terence in the breezy American way which he seemed to like. She would not be dignified or formal: and, if he was sarcastic with her, she would not fold her tent like the Arabs, and silently steal away, but she would come back at him. He seemed to enjoy an argument. Kathleen was just beginning to understand Irishmen!

"Hello," she said airily, "gloomy as ever? That's great!"

Terence grinned.

"Oh, no, I'm always happy at meal time, I have such a marvellous appetite!"

Kathleen knew that he ate scarcely anything. Here it was, just what she expected; but she hadn't been looking for it quite so soon.

"Why don't you try liver pills? They are great for the digestion."

"There's nothing wrong with my liver or my digestion either one."

"Oh, yes, there is. I insist. There's only one excuse for such a filthy disposition as you have, and that's a bad liver. Yours must be the world's worst liver."

In spite of himself, Terence grinned again. By George! the girl did have some spunk, after all! If she could be amusing, why hadn't she tried it before? He was infernally tired of lowered voices, smothered laughter, soft footfalls, everybody saying Yes and afraid to disagree with him. He was tired of being asked fifty times a day if there was anything he wanted, and how he wanted it, or why he didn't want it. A man got tired being eternally petted and babied.

Men never get tired of being petted and babied, but Terence was young. He really had a lot of things to learn, and whether he liked it or not, some of them he had to learn from girls. One does that sort of thing in spite of one's self.

Kathleen noticed the grins, and they encouraged her considerably. At last she was on the right track. It was too late, but she did not know that.

"If you have any of your much-touted pills, I'll take one, just to oblige." He spoke banteringly; it was much better than the usual bitterness.

"Thanks for the confidence in my suggestion, old dear, but I don't keep a supply. I don't *need* them."

"You win!"

They laughed.

"Really, Kathleen, you are quite delightful in this mood. You should have them more often."

"Thanks for the tip, I'll try."

She did not want him to know that it was just another case of the little boy whistling to keep up his courage. Underneath she was all of a dither about Barlow and the mysterious package. She could not stand the suspense any longer.

"Terence, dear, did Barlow come in here with a package?"

"No; what package? Did one come by mail?"

"I—I don't know. I just thought I saw him have a package in his hands."

"You brought the mail in here yourself. He left the room a minute or two before you came in. I haven't seen him since."

Kathleen felt her face reddening; she was getting in deeper and deeper. She turned toward the window so that he could not see her. She should not have mentioned the package; she ought to have known better. Perhaps she could change the subject.

"Where is Barlow? He usually interrupts every conversation we have."

Kathleen went over and knelt down beside Rags. She began scratching him under his lower jaw. Rags adored it, and he stretched on his side and rolled his head toward her, so that she could reach him more easily. Quite some time ago she had learned that with Terence and Rags it was a case of "love me, love my dog." You could not be friends with Terence without being friendly to his dog.

"I don't know where he is. He has stuck around here like a leech, bless his heart! I'm glad he's gone; a change will do him good. But what were you saying about a package?"

"I just thought I saw one. Maybe—I was wrong."

"You are a queer one; first you see it, and then you don't. You ought to make up your mind and stick to it."

Just in time, Aunt Ellen came in with a tray.

"Good-evening, dear. Barlow did not come after your tray, so I brought it myself."

"You should not have done that, Aunt Ellen. I'm afraid it was too heavy for you."

Aunt Ellen set the tray on a low table beside the bed.

"I quite enjoyed doing it, dear. But it is the first time Barlow has not appeared on the minute to fetch your dinner. Where is he?"

"Probably my sweet disposition got too much for him and he went out for air."

Aunt Ellen looked distressed.

"Now none of that, young man, or we might open the window and give you the air," said Kathleen. "Never mind him," soothingly to Aunt Ellen, "he has a perpetual grouch. Pathetic in one so young, isn't it?"

"I'm sure he does not mean to have one, dear."

"Oh, yes, he does; he dotes on it!"

Aunt Ellen spread the napkin.

"Now you tell me what to do, and I'll manage everything just like Barlow."

But Terence did not want to tell her what to do, or how to do it. He did not want to tell her to cut his chop, as if for a baby. He hated to be waited upon when anyone was around. Confound it! where was Barlow? What did he mean, leaving him to the mercy of two women? So he only said: "I don't want any dinner, thank you." He picked up the glass of milk and drank it.

"Not *any*, dear?" Aunt Ellen sighed.

"Not any. I'm a milk-fed baby, you know."

"Terence, dear, you *are* so difficult."

Terence picked up a magazine and began to turn the pages restlessly.

"I'm sorry, Aunt Ellen, but I can't eat when I'm not hungry."

"I'll take the tray down for you," and Kathleen picked it up and departed.

"You cannot get strong unless you eat, dear. I think I will ask the doctor for a tonic for you."

"The only tonic I want is work; something to do; *anything* to do. Aunt Ellen, when I get well, I'm going to leave here. I'm going to hunt until I find a job, no matter how long it takes. I'm going to make good at one thing or another; it doesn't make much difference to me what it is."

"Do you have to leave us to do that, dear?"

"It will be better if I do. Uncle Maxwell has definitely refused his consent. In fact, he said I would do as he said as long as I stayed under his roof."

"Half of this roof is mine, my dear, and you may stay under it as long as you like."

It was so unexpected that Terence burst out laughing.

"Bravo, Aunt Ellen! But I think it's best if I go. Uncle Maxwell would only make things unpleasant for both of us. Barlow will go along to look after me. He is a very good friend of mine, Aunt Ellen. A splendid fellow!"

"Yes, dear, I know he is, and I know also that he loves you. I will not feel uneasy about you as long as he is with you. But, my dear, I love you, too; I shall miss you dreadfully. But I want you to know that I think you are right. Young men need to be occupied. Maxwell is entirely wrong. If I can help you now, or at any future time, I will be happy. Just devote yourself now to getting strong, and don't worry about anything."

Aunt Ellen brushed away a couple of stray tears. Terence squeezed her hand.

"You're a peach, Aunt Ellen. I always did think you understood; I told Barlow so. Just because I go to the city to find a job is no sign that I'll never see you again. I will, often. I promise."

"You are a brilliant man, Terence. It is right that you should work. You should be a great man some day, and you will be. I know you will."

"Thank you, Aunt Ellen. Your confidence means a lot. You are the only one who believes in me; you and Barlow."

"Terence, forgive me for mentioning her, but what about the young lady in America?"

"I am not sure about her; but I am very sure about myself. I love her now more than I ever did."

"And you want to establish yourself here, and then go to America?"

"Yes."

"And Kathleen only annoys you?"

"Kathleen only annoys me. Are you disappointed?"

"I am not sure. I have great confidence in your judgment. The American girl gave every evidence of beauty, education, and careful training."

They heard Uncle Maxwell's step on the stairs, then his imperative knock.

"Good-evening, Terence. How are you this evening?"

"Better, thank you. In fact, I feel the best I have since my stupid accident."

"That's great; hope you will be out of this bed soon."

Terence and Aunt Ellen stared at each other, amazed at his cordiality.

"Ellen, I've been waiting for you. I thought we were going for a moonlight ride. Kathleen is ready, too."

"I'm coming right away, dear," and she stooped to kiss Terence. "You won't be lonely?"

"No, of course not. I think Barlow will be here soon. Good-bye, and have a nice ride."

"Good-bye, dear. I wish you could come along; it's a gorgeous night. We will come up and say good-night when we return. We will not be gone long."

As they were leaving, Terence called out, "Uncle Maxwell, would you send Thomas up here? I want to talk to him about Lady Bird. And, Aunt Ellen, I'm hungry. If you'll send that tray back up here, I'll eat my dinner!"

Aunt Ellen went for her ride with a lighter heart than she had carried for many weeks. The boy was better. It was the first time he had been hungry. He wanted to talk about his horse; it was the first interest he had shown in anything.

It was a glorious, moon-bathed night. The horses were prancing and impatient. They were gone longer than they had planned. So brilliant were the moon and stars that it was almost as if they were driving in daylight. They could see plainly, and the silvery sheen flooded everything, giving an added charm. Aunt Ellen remarked about the coziness of the small, thatched-roof cottages, covered with masses of pink climbing roses, and the tiny fenced-in gardens. More often than not the beds of vegetables were bordered with blooming flowers. A few hives of bees were set at intervals, with blooming shrubs between them so that the bees did not have to go far for their sweets. They even encouraged the bees to be lazy, as Uncle Maxwell put it.

"The Irish farmers," said Aunt Ellen, "have a quaint and friendly custom. An empty chair is always kept in the garden for any guest who happens in. He is seated among the flowers and asked to have a glass of milk. The habit became so much a part of them that one day an old grandmother escorted her guest to the garden and started to give him the seat before she remembered that it was raining."

"They are slow and indolent; ought to be ashamed of themselves." Uncle Maxwell spoke sharply.

Aunt Ellen shook her head. "They would like to do better if they could, but they have no money. There are not enough schools to educate them. They haven't even clothes lines—they hang their clothes on thorn bushes, so that the wind cannot blow them away. The children go to America, and the fathers and mothers have no one left at home to help them. It is a shame and a disgrace that our children have to be driven from home for education and advantages. Their country needs them."

Kathleen, absorbed in her own turbulent thoughts, answered her absent-mindedly.

"They are a lazy lot," Uncle Maxwell snapped.

"Not lazy, just ignorant as to the possibilities of their land. There is no market for their produce, and no one interested in creating one. They need direction and encouragement. They have health and energy, but no one to guide them. They would work honestly and sincerely, had they anything tangible for which to labour. There seems no goal for them to reach beyond providing food and clothing for their families. They would do big things if they had any incentive."

"Piffle!" snorted Uncle Maxwell.

Uncle Maxwell drove his own horses. Now he sat, straight and silent, his only enjoyment watching the horses as they fell into different gaits when he loosened or tightened the reins. He missed the fuchsias growing inside the hedges; the white-washed gates and fences; the masses of larkspur, lupin, and foxglove; the huge Irish oaks, beeches, and feathered elms, the whole flooded with the gleaming moonlight. He followed the narrow road at will; there were no signs to guide one. Unless you knew the country, you could only stop at the cottages and ask for information. But Uncle Maxwell, not caring for scenery, always took one road—the one which led into the city. He seemed to enjoy the lights as he pranced his horses down the main street.

There were few travellers on the road at this hour and the O'Mores were surprised when they saw a horse coming toward them rapidly, and making clouds of dust. They recognized Butter Ball, and then Barlow. Only Kathleen's keen eyes noticed the large bundle beside him, and the care with which he was keeping one hand on it while he drove with the other.

So it was that when Barlow reached home, no one was there. As he drove up to the stables, Thomas met him.

"I've talked to Mr. Terence, Barlow. He sent for me

and talked about the horses for a long time. He's going to talk to Lady Bird through the window to-morrow, and then I'm going to try her on the sugar again. He seems in pretty good shape; he ate a good dinner."

"That's fine! I passed the family on the road. Do you know where they are going?"

"No, but into town, I suppose. That's where Lord O'More always goes."

Barlow nodded.

"Better give Butter Ball a rub-down, Thomas. I drove fast; she's pretty warm. Good-night."

Barlow lifted the heavy bundle off the seat and carried it carefully to his room, where he unwrapped it with great care. He unlocked his trunk and took out the Angel's precious package. For the next half hour he was very busy.

CHAPTER XIX

Wherein McLean Crosses the Ocean and Discovers a New Interest in Life

WHEN James Ross McLean left the Limberlost, he had but one clear idea in his head, and that was to go to Freckles as quickly as possible. He was sure Freckles needed him. The boy was in the dumps; it would not do to allow him to go on any longer in that mood. He must be gotten out of it.

McLean hated cities; accustomed to the solitude of forests and the life in a small town, the noises and turmoil of a city confused him. If he had not felt that in this case the cause justified the means, he never would have had the courage to make the trip alone. After several long, dirty, dusty train rides, he found himself in New York, tired and nervous, too agitated to eat. Almost before he realized it, he was on a huge boat bound for England. He found the ocean soothing to his frayed nerves. As he sat stretched in his deck chair, a lovely Scotch rug, the plaid of his grandfather's clan, thrown over him, he took off his hat and ran a hand through his hair. Peace and quiet at last! Such a relief after the last few days of hectic travelling. The salty tang of the sea air seemed to imbue him with new courage and vigour; it seemed to blow the cobwebs from his brain. Gradually, his thoughts became lucid and took definite shape. Freckles belonged to him first. He would take the boy away; just how, he did not know—or care. Some way he would do it. True, there might be fewer advantages, but there would be sympathy and understanding. Where love is things are sure to be all right. Unselfish, great-hearted McLean, with a philosophy of life as simple and sweet as himself. And he a bachelor!

McLean did not know what the irascible Lord O'More would do, but he was no longer in awe of him. No one mattered now but the boy. He hoped there would not be a scene; but if there was, he was all set for it. Freckles' system was being poisoned slowly; little suggestions dropped here and there were taking root, and were growing and developing like an insidious disease. It had to stop.

Lady O'More was a negligible quantity so far as any difficulty was concerned. She was far too mouselike to be any sort of match for her husband. Her naturally sweet disposition and attractive personality had been crushed instead of being allowed to flourish. Lord O'More, unless he changed his ways, had much for which to answer. Such was McLean's decision. That disposed of Lord and Lady O'More, enemies not too formidable.

Then there was the Angel to consider. McLean felt reasonably certain that her father and mother would agree to whatever arrangement suited her. She was beautiful, and she had all the inherent pride and independence of youth. But if there was love—ah!—that was the answer. For a supposedly unsentimental bachelor McLean was fairly good at analyzing the youthful victims who wander aimlessly through the amorous mazes of romance. When he considered every angle of the situation, and untangled all the threads to the best of his knowledge and ability, it boiled down to Freckles and the Angel. They were the two whose lives must not be wrecked by the stupidity of their elders. Age cannot judge youth by the standards of age; youth must be judged by the standards of youth. That is the reason the advice of the elders is so often disregarded by youngsters, who respect their elder advisors only in proportion to the measure in which they understand and respect youthful opinions. For youth is not dumb; not by any means; perhaps impulsive and ill advised at times, but almost always tractable if approached in an unantagonistic and sensible manner.

Next to Freckles, McLean loved the Angel. If they were happy no one else mattered.

"Even I don't count," he mused. "I'll do anything, or make any sacrifice, for the kids."

In truth, Lord O'More's castle of tyranny was tottering on its foundations. People who are wrong cannot remain wrong forever, any more than wrong things can endure forever; eventually they are discovered and made right. People cannot be unfair and unjust always; they must see the light before it is too late, and have time to make reparation for their mistakes, whether intentional or otherwise.

Gradually, as McLean's turbulent thoughts formed into a definite shape and he decided absolutely what he was going to do, he became calm and quiet; his old self again. He began to enjoy himself, and to take note of his fellow passengers. In the deck chair next to him sat a most attractive woman. The stray locks of hair that blew across her mobile face were white and softly curling. McLean looked at her eyes; they were wide-open, understanding eyes, with much of kindness and gentleness in their depths, and there were tiny wrinkles at the corners. McLean smiled. He remembered his mother's advice to him when he was a young man.

"My boy," she had said, "never marry a girl unless she has little wrinkles at the corners of her eyes. They are the 'laughing wrinkles' and they always indicate a sweet, happy disposition. Those who have them laugh much."

McLean kept watching her over his paper. He did not exactly mean to do it, but some way he did. He saw a handsome, stalwart young man come up and speak to her. They seemed to be very good friends. Then actual pain stabbed McLean's heart. The right coat sleeve was tucked neatly in the coat pocket. McLean passed his hand across his eyes and looked again. Yes, he was right. The right hand was gone, and at almost exactly the same place as Freckles'. McLean seemed fascinated; he could scarcely take his eyes from the boy, and he could not help comparing the two boys, his own with the stranger. This lad was not sad or morose; one could see that at a glance. He was alert, and his eyes snapped. He was interested in everything about him, and he was enjoying life tremendously. There was an eagerness on his face, and as he sat chatting with the woman, an impetuous, cheery laugh rang out again and again.

McLean felt that there was a bond between them because of Freckles. He sat watching, with tears in his eyes, this man who loved boys, this man who would have made such a wonderful father for a houseful of kiddies, and who, for some inexplicable reason, life had cheated of fatherhood.

McLean made up his mind. He would speak to them. He felt that he must because of the boy; and then, she *was* a most alluring woman. He read a few pages more and when the boy had left he folded his paper and made the plunge. He was not adroit nor adept in making advances to strange women; he had had no experience, and he had no idea of how to make a pretty speech. So he made no apologies or excuses, or haven't-I-met-you-before alibis. He went at this as he would tackle a business proposition, straight from the shoulder. And, if the truth were known, that is what most women prefer. McLean leaned toward the woman and took off his cap.

"My name is James Ross McLean," he said. "I am without anyone to talk with; would you take pity on a lonely man?"

She looked at him with an unembarrassed smile, and came back with an equally straightforward answer.

"My name is Elizabeth Anderson, and I should be delighted to be friends."

One could not look at McLean and fail to trust him; Mrs. Anderson was a very discriminating and particular person. As she smiled, all the wrinkles around her eyes deepened; the corners of her mouth puckered up; and there was an enticing dimple in one pale pink cheek. Her mouth was not of the rosebud variety; it was comfortably large, and her full red lips parted over even white teeth. Her voice was low and even-toned. Instantly, McLean liked her; he liked her very much. Their conversation drifted around among commonplaces, as first conversations will. But McLean kept thinking of the boy. Finally, he could not stand the suspense any longer.

"Pardon me, if I seem personal, but this fine-looking chap who talks to you, is he your son?"

Instantly her face changed, and she shook her head.

"No, he isn't. I lost my boy in an airplane crash.

But I am not sorry I let him fly," she defended herself fiercely. "He loved it most of anything in the world, and he had a wonderful time. I believe it is better to live a short, happy life than a long one filled with regrets and discontent."

"I'm sorry. You have a great theory for rearing boys. It's sad that you lost your son. Boys should be given a sound general education for a foundation, and by that time they should be capable of choosing their own professions, and should be allowed to do so. But this boy?"

McLean *had* to know about him; he seemed a link between Freckles and himself; sort of a kindred spirit.

"This boy is Paul Stewart, the son of friends of mine. They are splendid people with two daughters younger than Paul. He developed blood poison in his right hand from a small cut, and had to have it taken off halfway between his wrist and elbow. He needed both hands to continue his work. We were told that there is a place in Germany where one may have an artificial hand made just the size and shape of the other hand, with jointed fingers which may be moved and placed in different positions. They are really very useful. His father investigated thoroughly and found that it was true. You may also have a hand of hard rubber which is pliable. They strap on quite painlessly and inconspicuously. Then you may have a flesh-coloured glove, matched to the shade of the other hand, or a black one, to slip over it when it isn't being used. If it is held in the pocket during social events, or on the street, people need never know it is an artificial hand. It is a great idea, and Paul has gone through the pain and shock of it all, carried along by the thought that he need not give up his life work after all. His spirit and courage are wonderful; it is a joy to be around him."

"And you?"

For a staid and unemotional Scotsman, McLean had reached what might almost be called excitement. He could scarcely sit still. Now he could go to Freckles with a real idea; something tangible; something that would be of genuine service to him.

"It is necessary for the person who wants the hand to go to the factory himself. Paul's people had large bills in connection with his illness and operation; there was no money for Paul to go. Mr. Stewart, rather than make Paul wait, decided to borrow the money, but I thought it was too bad for him to assume the burden of a debt. I was living a very useless life. My husband has been dead for years; I have plenty of money, and I live alone."

It was only when she made this statement that McLean was suddenly brought to the realization that although his first concern was the boy, he really had been attracted to the woman before the boy appeared on the scene, and that all the time, underneath, he had been tremendously interested in her and her own situation in life. She was a widow, and lived alone! McLean pulled his chair closer.

"Am I boring you?"

"I've never been so interested in my life." And it was true.

"My time was taken up with clubs, bridge, teas, luncheons, clothes—anything to pass the days. The only real good I've done for years has been some charity work. Aside from that, I've done nothing that was the slightest good to me or to anyone else. This was a chance for me to be of some real use. I could have lent Paul the money to come, but his mother and I could not bear the thought of sending him away alone. So here we are! Paul is all 'hopped-up,' as he says, and I am the happiest I've been in years. You know, Mr. McLean, the most we get out of life is what we do for other people."

That was a thought, too. McLean was beginning to think he might be able to do quite a lot for other people. Maybe he could make Freckles and the Angel happy; maybe he could bring Lord O'More to his senses, and that would make him and Lady O'More both happy; maybe he could bring a new interest into the life of Elizabeth Anderson and make her happier; maybe he could bring a wife and a home into his own too-drab existence; maybe——

"You cannot guess how happy you have made me. If you will allow me, I'm going to tell you all about my boy now; my boy, who really isn't mine."

Something seemed to tell McLean that she would understand and respect his confidence. He told her everything, beginning at the lumber camp in the Limberlost, and omitting nothing. It was a dramatic story, and it lost none of its value in the telling, as McLean's deep voice rumbled on and on, his eyes seeming to see it all as he talked.

It might have been noted, by anyone with an observing eye, that Mrs. Anderson was not displeased when she learned, during the course of McLean's recital, that he was a bachelor, and unattached. She was a perfect listener—she responded to his every mood. When Freckles was the lonely, hungry boy, she wept; when he was happy and singing about his work, she smiled; and now, she sighed.

"He must be a remarkable boy to feel so many vastly

different emotions, and to react to them all so sincerely. But there are no two ways about it, youth *does* forget, and forgive, thank God! The thought of a hand will be something new to think about; it will take him out of his present depression, and that is just what he needs. He will respond to this modern idea; it will put new life into him to know that his arm need not remain either useless or unsightly. Three fourths of his sensitiveness has been due to that. The cause for it once removed, he will be a different boy. You just wait and see if I am not right!"

"I believe you are right, and I know you are a great comfort to a blundering old bachelor, struggling to do what is best, and not knowing what to do."

But as Mrs. Anderson looked at him, he seemed neither "blundering" nor "old." He was a big man, emanating health; his face was bronzed from sun and wind; thick, iron-gray hair was brushed straight back from a high forehead; keen gray eyes, splotched with brown, looked directly into hers. To be sure, the jaw and chin were a bit square, but that was not an unsurmountable obstacle. It would be possible to overcome that by tactful handling.

"I am glad if I am any help to you; but you are not 'old' and you are not 'blundering.' Even if you *think* so, it's a bad idea to say it; you might come to *believe* it."

McLean laughed.

Paul, coming along the deck, was surprised to see Mrs. Anderson in such an interested, animated conversation with what had been, just a couple of hours before, a perfect stranger. He was not sure he liked it; but after he was introduced, McLean broke through the boy's reserve in a very short time, as was his habit.

Paul liked him instantly. He was treated as a man, not as a boy; at once they were on common ground. They were very congenial, and dinner that evening was a decided success. The three became fast friends. In fact, McLean and Mrs. Anderson seemed to be developing more than friendship. When they reached the "James" and "Elizabeth" stage, Paul began drifting away and leaving the two together.

"It will be great if they make a go of it," he thought. "They seem to suit each other perfectly; and they are both lonely."

Strange as it may seem, both McLean and Mrs. Anderson had begun to think the same thing, each in his own little private brain corners reserved for secrets. They were together almost constantly; it was amazing, the number of things they liked doing together. McLean had not danced for years, but with a few lessons from Mrs. Anderson, he picked it up very quickly. Both were good swimmers, and they were in the pool every day. They played some cards, enjoyed the same things to read and the same kind of music. They ate their meals together, and walked for miles around the deck.

After a couple of days, when they reached the "Jim" and "Betty dear" stage, Paul faded almost entirely out of the picture. He loved watching them; and he was content to amuse himself with the other young people aboard the boat.

One evening after dinner they came out on deck to find one of those black nights at sea; no moon and no stars, which young lovers think so conducive to romance. A thick blackness enveloped them. "Jim" took "Betty dear's" arm, and she snuggled closer; they leaned on the rail and looked at nothing. They could not even see each other, but—it happened. James Ross McLean, who never in his life had been known as anything faintly resembling a "fast worker," found himself engaged. And he was pleased with himself as the cat who swallowed the canary.

Paul was delighted. He had grown to love McLean as all young people did; his even temper, his keen insight, his instant understanding. Rapidly they made their plans, and by the time the boat docked, the schedule was complete. Mrs. Anderson and Paul were going to proceed at once to Berlin, locate themselves comfortably in a hotel, and have the work on Paul's hand started. McLean would go to Ireland, make all necessary explanations to Freckles, and bring him to Berlin. The boys could become acquainted while their hands were being made. "Jimmy darling" and "Betty dearest" could amuse themselves sightseeing.

CHAPTER XX

Wherein Freckles and McLean Make Plans and Lord O'More Approves

IT WAS only a few minutes after the O'Mores and Kathleen departed for their drive until the butler came into Terence's room carrying a second steaming hot dinner. As he looked at it, the boy felt a bit guilty for being so childish.

"I'm sorry to trouble you, Benton, I—I wasn't hungry before. Thank you."

He ate the food with relish. It was the first time anything had tasted good to him. Just as he finished Thomas came. He was embarrassed, as he had never been inside the house before.

"Hello, Thomas, I'm glad to see you," and Terence held out his hand. Thomas shook it awkwardly.

"Good-evening, sir, I'm pleased to see you. Feeling better, sir?"

"Yes, I think I am. Sit down, Thomas. How is Lady Bird?"

"She is lonesome for you, sir. How are you, Rags? You haven't been to see me for a long time." Rags went over to welcome Thomas. Rags, and his windmill tail.

"Tell me all about the horses, Thomas." They

launched a discussion of horses and dogs which lasted a couple of hours.

After Thomas left, the house seemed very quiet. The talk had refreshed Terence, but it had also made him a little tired. He picked up a magazine and read a story or two—felt drowsy—the magazine slipped from his fingers—his gaze drifted across the room to the two feathers——

His thoughts, waking or sleeping, were always of the Angel. No word of any kind had come from her since she had gotten his letter. How he hated himself for that letter! What a cad she must think him! And her parents and his beloved Boss! How cowardly he had been to allow himself to be defeated, and then acknowledge it to his dearest friends! He *must* prove himself worthy of their belief in him; he *would* break loose from this confounded narrow, idle existence, and make a man of himself. That was all—just a *man*. Then he would go to them and tell them what he had done. If the Angel had waited for him, he would be unbelievably happy. If she had not, he was to blame, and it would serve him darned well right. But the least he could do was to let her, and his other dear ones, see that at last their faith in him had not been in vain.

He was walking through the Limberlost now, as he had walked years ago. The sun-flecked path leading to his room stretched ahead of him; fleecy, feathery clouds drifted across the sky; the perfume of countless wild flowers was in his nostrils; birds sang love songs to one another; gorgeously hued butterflies hovered above gaily coloured blossoms; and when he reached his room—the Angel seated there! The Angel, with the sun playing hide-and-seek through her gleaming curls—her cheeks flushed—her eager eyes sparkling with excitement. She was twanging her banjo in accompaniment to his voice as he sang:

"Three little leaves of Irish green
United on one stem;
Love, truth, and valour do they mean,
They form——"

Then the Angel's voice:

"Oh, do you love,
Oh, say you love,
You love the Shamrock green——"

Terence's body tensed, and his hand clenched suddenly. God! he *did* hear her voice! It was coming through his half-open door. He childishly bit his finger to see if he was awake, and he *was*. He raised himself slightly on one elbow and listened. She was saying, "Freckles, shame on you! You're not trying! Look me in the eye! Now you square your shoulders; throw out your chest; lift up your head; and *sing*. You know you can do it. Come now, once more. Sing as if you were proud of the Shamrock—it's the emblem of a great race. My father says the Irish have lots of things to make them proud as peacocks."

Terence sat up suddenly, and sang. He had not tried his voice in years. He stretched his arms toward the door, as if he expected the Angel to walk through it. There was a divine light on his face; his thought flew back to that other day, long go, when she had said those very words to him. When the chorus was ended, he stopped. Again her voice penetrated his bewildered brain:

"Good boy. Freckles, I'm proud of you; you will be a great singer, and when you are, please do not forget your friends in the Limberlost. We love you, we miss you, we are waiting for you." And once more came the lilting melody; the soft, sweet voice, accompanied by the strumming banjo.

Again his thoughts wandered to that day long ago. The Angel had kissed his forehead in her pride and enthusiasm. Even now he put up a cautious hand, as if to see if he could feel it. He remembered how his heart had nearly burst on his way home to supper, and how he had been afraid to wash until he asked Sarah Duncan if kisses washed off. He smiled as her confident reply came to him, "No, laddie, they do not——"

Barlow was watching through the door, happy tears streaming unheeded down his cheeks and dropping on his coat. His purchase in the city had been a portable Victrola; the contents of the Angel's package had been a record made during her two days' stay in Chicago with her mother. Barlow had practised in his own room until he knew how to adjust it. Then he had carried it into Freckles' sitting room and left the door open. Freckles was apparently sleeping. Good enough. The music would waken him. He turned the little lever and waited. Here was his reward for the two lies, his fight with Kathleen, his trip into the city, the money he had spent. Just one look at the boy's transfigured face made up for everything. He wound up the machine, set the needle, started it again, and went softly into the room.

"Barlow!" gasped the boy, "what is it? Am I delirious again? Is it a miracle, or am I just hearing things? Is it really my darling Angel's voice?"

"It's a record, sir. The Angel sent it. I went to the

city and bought the machine so we could play it. I wasn't sure, at first, just what it was. Such a voice as you have, sir! Why do you never sing? Some music in this old house would be a blessing for us all."

"I couldn't bear the thought of singing after I'd left the only home and friends I'd ever had. I have not sung since I sang for the Angel, four years ago. She discovered my voice, and made me sing for her, playing accompaniments for me on her banjo. I decided I would never sing again unless it was for her. But tell me, when did this record come? Wasn't it addressed to me? Why didn't I get it?"

Again Barlow explained.

"I can't imagine why Kathleen should want to do a thing like that."

"She is jealous of the American young lady, my boy. She did not want you to have anything that would remind you of her."

"But it's a serious offense to interfere with the mail."

"She did not stop to think of that. But she did think of it before I finished persuading her to give it to me."

Terence smiled.

"Why, *Barlow*, I hope you weren't actually *severe* with the young lady."

"Well, I convinced her that I meant what I said."

"I wish I could have heard that conversation. I have a couple of things to say to that young lady myself, and I am reasonably sure that she will be convinced that I mean what I say, too."

"Don't fret yourself about Miss Kathleen, sir. Just think about the Angel, and be happy. Could you sing again, my boy?"

"I don't know, Barlow, but I feel inspired to try,

if you'll move that machine in here and start that record again."

With his eyes on the two feathers, he began once more.

When the O'Mores and Kathleen came in, they heard a rich tenor voice ringing through the house. What could it mean? Who was it? It came from upstairs. Following the sound, they rushed into Terence's room. He was sitting up, singing. In a corner of the room the Victrola was doing its utmost, and Barlow was standing triumphantly beside it. For a moment they were speechless. At the end of the song Terence stopped, and the Angel's voice went on alone. At her command, "Come, now, once more," he began again, and sang through the chorus. Barlow shut off the machine, but he did not go.

"What a heavenly voice!"

"My dear, why have you never sung for us before?"

And Uncle Maxwell's harsh, decisive tones, "What blasted idiocy is this? Where did that damned thing come from? Terence, you'll kill yourself! Lie down!"

Terence lay back on his pillows, tired but happy. His voice was not gone; he had it. Practice and instruction were all he needed. Something to work for at last! Again the Angel was his incentive to live and his inspiration to sing. Only the Angel could have thought of awakening him by that method—so much better than a long harangue in a letter. You could always depend on the Angel to do something different and original.

"Undoubtedly for the first time in your life you are wrong. I will not kill myself. On the contrary, my dear uncle, I feel like living for the first time since I came into your home. 'That damned thing,' as you so graphically describe it, is my Angel's voice, calling me; the only person in the world who believes I can do something, and who really wants me to do it; and also perhaps the only living soul who has the temerity to defy you in your own home—you and your hide-bound ideas. It's a great idea—think I'll follow suit. That Victrola is one thing you can't talk down, or make shut up," and Terence laughed for the first time in weeks.

Aunt Ellen gasped and turned pale. Kathleen, feeling weak in the knees, sank into a chair.

"Barlow," snapped Uncle Maxwell, "leave the room."

"Excuse me, Uncle, Barlow happens to be taking orders from me at present. Barlow, stay where you are."

"Yes, sir." Barlow stayed.

"Very well, if you care to discuss family affairs before a servant."

"Barlow happens to know all about my business, and he is no longer a servant. He was discharged this afternoon. He is just an affectionate, devoted friend who is staying with me. I wish to introduce him—this is *Mr.* Warren Barlow."

The family were so stunned they did not know what to do, and they could not think of anything quickly enough; so they bowed stiffly.

"Also, Barlow is trustworthy and honourable. The only person I care to excuse from this discussion is Miss Strathern, who is neither trustworthy nor honourable."

"Terence, have you gone mad?"

"No, I have not. Barlow, will you kindly relate the story of the package from America?"

Barlow began rather hesitatingly. Kathleen sat like a statue, immensely interested in the toes of her shoes.

Uncle Maxwell interrupted.

"Terence, I'm sure you have lost your senses!"

"No, I've found them. This record came for me in the mail this afternoon. Before she goes, I'd like Miss Strathern to explain why she did not bring it in here with the other mail, and why, when I asked her if there was any mail for me, she answered, 'No.'"

All turned inquiring eyes toward Kathleen. She was very pale, but it would not do to weaken before them all. There was no wriggling out of it now; she must face it.

"I did not mean to do anything wrong; I'm not a criminal. I did what I thought was best, and I do not see any occasion for making such a fuss about it. I only meant to wait a few days, until you were stronger, to give it to you. I thought it might upset you, and I—I—think it has."

The family looked unconvinced.

"Yes, thank heaven, it has, but we won't discuss it any further. One excuse is as good as another for that trick, young lady. You are not a competent judge of how important it was, or of how much 'fuss' should be made about it. You may go now, and you need not trouble yourself to come into my room again."

"Oh, very well, but you are unjust and sarcastic as usual. You never did appreciate——"

Aunt Ellen interrupted.

"You had best go now, my dear. Terence has had enough excitement for one evening; he should be quiet now. I'll come into your room later."

Having thus peremptorily dismissed Kathleen, Freckles turned to Uncle Maxwell. He had not the slightest intention of being quiet.

"We may just as well settle things now as any other

time. As soon as I am out of this bed (and you'll be surprised how soon that will be) I am going into the city and get a man's job."

It was a queer picture the four of them made, there in the darkened room. The frenzied old man, purple with rage; the tiny, dignified old lady, her hands clasped rigidly; Barlow, silent, standing like a sentinel beside the bed; the pale, thin patient, cheeks flushed and eyes blazing with anger and excitement; Rags beside him, eyes shining and tail whirling so fast it was almost invisible.

"I brought you over here and took you into my own home thinking——" But he got no farther. The knocker on the front door boomed; there were decisive voices and footfalls on the stairs.

The English Channel was very rough, as usual, and when McLean landed, he was headachy and his legs swayed under him. But he would not stop for anything, his one idea was to get to Freckles as quickly as possible. He bought a small motor car in Liverpool and had it shipped to Dublin. At a garage there he hired a man who knew the country to drive him to the O'More estate. Primarily, McLean was a business man, and as they drove along he was struck by the undeveloped possibilities of the country. Everything was primitive and old-fashioned; large stretches of fertile soil were uncultivated and covered with weeds. There were no cultivators, no tractors, no reapers; there seemed to be no machinery, either antiquated or modern, with which to work. But he knew that English and German money was not easily available for investment in Ireland. The

Irish must save their own country, backed by American money.

It was very dark by the time he reached the country place of the O'Mores, and he could see little of the house or its surroundings. He asked his driver to wait and, locating the old-fashioned knocker on the door, he gave it several resounding bangs. The sleepy butler opened the door and at first refused to admit him. There was some argument, but McLean, seeing lights upstairs, and hearing Lord O'More's voice, brushed past the butler and went upstairs without being announced. He followed the sound of the voices, and was aghast when he looked in Freckles' room—Freckles in bed, pale and wan; Lord O'More red-faced and raving; Barlow standing "at attention"; and Lady O'More speechless in her chair.

"Oh, it's my beloved Boss!"

Freckles held out his arms, and McLean rushed into them. After the excitement of the greetings was over, they explained Freckles' accident. McLean looked thoughtful for a minute, and then said, "There seemed to be some sort of argument going on as I came in. What was it all about, Freckles?"

"That's easy, Boss. Barlow, just play that record again."

They listened in silence.

"Leave it to the Angel to think of something different. Lord, what a girl she is; one in a million!"

Lord O'More spoke first.

"We were discussing my nephew's future. I was just telling him what was best for him when you came in."

Freckles interrupted.

"I am going to get a job. Goodness knows, there are plenty of them lying around loose."

"Just what, for instance?" asked Uncle Maxwell.

"The people of your country, my dear uncle, need help and encouragement. They have no industries, no factories, no place for men and boys to work. The farmers need advice. Half the children go to America because there is nothing to keep them here. It is all the fault of men such as you, who have brains and money, who could teach them and advise them if they were not too lazy and selfish. Land lies wasted because they have no machinery. I told one farmer that Ireland should supply itself and the whole of England with potatoes, and he answered me drearily, 'Oh, there are so many weeds!'"

"That's it, they are lazy——"

"No, that is *not* it. They need direction; they are not educated to their possibilities. Why, enough water runs idle to the sea to supply power for many large industries."

"It takes money——"

"Certainly it does, and you, and many others like you, have plenty to help. Other countries find money to develop their resources. Why not use your brains and money to help your fellow men? It would all revert to you in the end; and you might forget your grouch if you were busy. But, at that, I think you're too shortsighted and too damnably selfish."

Lord O'More was raging, but he had to control himself because of McLean. The latter gentleman was keeping in the background. He wanted to get the lay of the land and sort of feel his way. What he had to say could wait.

"Are you going to play Santa Claus to my poor,

ignorant country?" Uncle Maxwell inquired sarcastically.

"I'd like nothing better than to try it, as far as one man can go. I'd love to hire a crew of men and put them to drilling wells and setting windmills for the farmer. A farmer's wife spends a half day's time with a donkey cart, hauling water. Look what she could do about the house and garden in that time."

Uncle Maxwell only sneered.

"Your farmers try to be thrifty. They have learned that goats give more milk than cows, comparatively speaking, and that goats find their own living. Yet cattle would thrive in this country, and huge creameries could be established. You tell me there is nothing I can do. Why, if I did nothing but ride a horse over this country and give farmers a bit of advice about what to do, and how to do it, it would be invaluable to them. And yet you, and a lot more of your blue-blooded aristocracy, sit back and let your country rot: you're a fine lot of slackers, and you ought to be ashamed of yourselves!"

By this time Uncle Maxwell was pacing the floor, his face purple.

"How dare you call me a slacker, you insolent young puppy?"

"I suppose because you are one. Any man who stands on the side lines and watches his country decay without lifting a hand in protest is equally as guilty as the man who refuses to fight. In fact, I think he's worse!"

McLean grinned as the old man grew more enraged. Freckles started to speak again, but McLean interrupted him and addressed his remarks to Uncle Maxwell.

"I think Freckles is too weak to talk any more. I recall a day in a Chicago hospital when you did a great deal of talking, and I listened. Now *I* will do the talking, and *you* will listen!" Strangely enough, McLean's tone carried the same air of finality as he continued: "For four years Freckles has been completely dominated by your wishes. He has been allowed to develop no personality or individuality. He is idle, restless, and useless. It is time for him to decide what he wants to do, and do it, without interference from anyone. All I ask for him is a chance, and I am here to see that he gets it. Needless to state, I will stay until he does. That's final; no argument necessary. You've had your turn; now I'll take mine. At the moment, I am not sure just what Freckles wants, but I have some potent suggestions to make. My business needs a manager while I take a vacation; I haven't had one in years."

For the first time in his life Lord O'More was silenced. Every time he tried to speak, McLean shut him up with some cutting remark. Finally he managed to say, "I've done my best for him."

"No, you've done nothing of the kind; you've done your worst. Here he is, a man licked; beaten by your infernal petting and coddling and bossing. It's a crime! He wants to get out and fight his own way in the world, and, by heaven, he's going to do it!"

Freckles was openly enjoying O'More's discomfiture. Barlow kept his face under control by keeping his hand over his mouth. Even Aunt Ellen was smiling into her handkerchief. She spoke, for the first time.

"Mr. McLean, you and Terence are right. I have tried to tell Maxwell these things, but he has never paid the slightest attention to me."

"No, he wouldn't. Any one with so little understanding of human nature ought never to have any authority over others."

Uncle Maxwell saw that he was beaten, and determined to take it gracefully.

"There's one thing more: let's forget this Lordship business as far as Freckles is concerned. Essentially, he is an American; he will never be happy here. Lords aren't so much in America; besides, I don't think Freckles' Swamp and my lumberjacks would like it," and McLean winked at the boy. "So let's all say 'Freckles' from now on; it will make the boy feel more at home. And now," he continued, "Freckles seems tired. If you would all be kind enough, I'd like a few words alone with him before I go to my hotel."

"Barlow," said Lord O'More, "get the room down the hall ready for Mr. McLean. Did you bring any luggage?"

"One bag is in my car below. My driver is down there waiting for me."

"Very well. Barlow, tell Thomas to find a place in the stables for Mr. McLean's car and to put up his driver."

"You forget that I told you Barlow is no longer a servant, Uncle Maxwell."

Barlow crossed to the bed.

"S-sh-sh. Never mind, my boy. Don't say anything more to him to-night. I'm glad to get the room ready and to serve you and Mr. McLean."

"Just as you say, Barlow."

"That is kind of you," said McLean. "I don't want to intrude, but I *will* enjoy being near the boy."

"Good-night, Mr. McLean."

Uncle Maxwell held out his hand, much to the surprise of everyone, and McLean took it.

"I guess you are right, Mr. McLean, whatever Ter—er—Freckles decides will be right with me."

"Atta boy, Uncle Maxwell. Don't choke on it!" and Freckles smiled.

At last Freckles and McLean were alone.

"It's time for you to be quiet and go to sleep."

"Oh, dear Boss, I can't sleep—I'm too happy. I'll promise to be quiet, if you'll stay and talk to me for a while."

Freckles' questions were of the Angel. McLean was cautious. He said nothing of Dick; he did not want to worry Freckles now.

"She still loves me, Boss?"

"I believe she does. Knowing her as you do, what made you think she would change? You've done her a terrible injustice, and hurt her feelings besides. If you were small, I'd spank you!"

"I've been in an awful mood due to the hostile environment here; my plans and my desires balked at every turn. I wasn't getting anywhere."

"Nothing is an excuse for doubting the Angel."

"I know it, and I'll spend the remainder of my life making it up to her."

They talked for a little while, and then Freckles dropped to sleep, his eyes on the feathers, and the Angel's voice singing in his ears.

CHAPTER XXI

Wherein Freckles Comes Home

THE next few days were busy ones. Freckles, with an incentive at last, grew strong rapidly. The contrast was remarkable; no trace now of the listless, wan, indifferent boy who refused to eat or take any interest in life. He ate like a farmer; they wondered where he put all the food he consumed and all the milk he drank. The doctors were delighted.

The whole atmosphere of the house was changed. Freckles' exuberance was contagious. Surprising as it may seem, Uncle Maxwell caught something of the spirit of the boy; and he was a different man. The household seemed to hinge on him. As he grew more agreeable, Aunt Ellen blossomed and expanded like a rose in June. She tripped about the house humming little tunes—almost forgotten verses she had known in her girlhood. Even the servants grew gay and light-hearted. For, believe it or not, the dispositions of servants in a house make a lot of difference. If they are willing and eager to please, they emanate that sort of atmosphere; if they are crabbed, grouchy, and discontented, you feel it immediately. And it usually depends on how they are treated. Too many employers forget that their servants are human beings, and as such are entitled to a little pleasure and just consideration in life. A smile and a cheerful "Good-morning" changes the whole day for a servant, and take only a few minutes. A happy cook makes all the difference with the meals.

Uncle Maxwell and Aunt Ellen even made friends with Rags, and he was so happy he went dashing about the house, madly swishing his tail, like a baby cyclone. He bumped into everyone and knocked over small tables and chairs and mussed up all the rugs, but no one seemed to mind. On the day they brought Freckles out among the flowers in an invalid chair for the first time, Rags nearly wrecked the garden. He rushed through everything, chasing bees and barking; there was no stopping him. Thomas brought Lady Bird out to see Terence, and she pranced and whinnied as she ate her sugar. There was no more difficulty about feeding her.

Kathleen came out rather timidly.

"This seems to be quite a celebration—I'd like to join it if I may. Would you forgive me, and be friends?"

Freckles held out his hand.

"I am too full of happiness to hold any grudges. Of course I forgive you. Forget it, and just sit down and see what an amiable fellow I am."

"I always knew you could be, if you wanted to."

"Yes, you ladies always know a lot after the last card is played. But never mind; sit down and talk; I'm going to have my lunch out here, isn't that great! Gee, I'm happy to be outdoors again!"

Kathleen nodded.

"I may as well tell you that my rotten temper the last few months has been due to Uncle Maxwell's refusing to let me work, and—and—well, I had a sort of misunderstanding with the girl I love, and that always puts a man in a vile humour, even though it's his own fault. But I think things are going to be all right now, hence the grand and glorious feeling."

Kathleen gave no sign, but it really hurt. So she had no chance at all. He did love the American girl.

"That's fine. I'm very happy for both of you. How about congratulations?"

"Not yet. I'll let the lady make her own announcement, if there is one."

They saw McLean strolling toward them. Kathleen rose.

"I think I'll go in now and see if I can do anything for Aunt Ellen. Mr. McLean may want to talk to you alone."

Kathleen was right; that was just what McLean did want.

"I have a couple of things to tell you, my boy. I have waited a few days until you were stronger."

"I'm O. K. now, Boss. I feel strong as a lion. You can shoot the works, and it won't faze me a bit."

McLean laughed.

"To begin with, I'm engaged."

"Engaged? Engaged to what?"

"Engaged to be married, what do you suppose?"

It was Freckles' turn to laugh.

"Jerusalem crickets! I never thought of that! But I'm for it—I think it's great. But who is she? The most wonderful woman in the world, I suppose."

"Absolutely! You are right the first time."

McLean went into great detail about Mrs. Anderson.

"Now for the other surprise, my boy. How would you like an artificial hand—one that strapped on without showing—one that had jointed fingers and a glove to cover it, matched to the colour of your skin?"

Freckles' joy was pathetic.

"I'm going to sing, Boss. I promised the Angel long ago I would. That is what she wants me to do. I think that is what she wanted the record to tell me."

"Yes, I think so, too. She felt you needed something to wake you up."

"Then with gloves they would never miss the hand!"

"Exactly."

McLean told him of Paul and their plans.

"It's perfect, Boss. I didn't know anything in this old world *could* be so perfect. I'm so happy I can hardly stand it. But you—will you be married here?"

"I am not sure, but I have a notion that if Elizabeth will marry me when we get to Berlin, we can have a little honeymoon about Europe, while you and Paul get acquainted and have your hands made. I think Paul is going to be very good medicine for you; his philosophy of life is so totally different."

"What do you mean?"

"Instead of taking the loss of his hand as an insurmountable calamity, he takes it as an unavoidable accident; it's too bad, but it's gone, and now he must make the best of it. He is light-hearted and debonair; there is none of this super-sensitiveness in his make-up."

"How old is he?"

"Twenty-five. Just one year more ancient than you. And his hand has been gone less than a year. Having always had it, it must be very difficult for him to get along without it. And he has no money for a valet. He tips porters and bellboys to help him when he travels. You see, Freckles, there *are* folks in the world worse off than you."

"You're not by any chance scolding me, are you?"

"I'm afraid I am. You seem pretty good since I came, but before that——"

"I know, you're thinking of that filthy letter I wrote the Angel."

"I am."

"Did you read it?"

"I did; her father showed it to me."

"I was never so ashamed of anything in my life as I am of that."

"You should be."

"Don't let's talk about it. I'm ready to do *anything* by way of apology. Do you think I should write to her?"

"No. I have written to her and explained everything. The thing for you to do is concentrate on getting strong as quickly as possible. Then as soon as the hands are finished, we will go to her as fast as trains and boats will carry us."

"What have you said to Mrs. Anderson?"

"I've explained that you are ill, and that we will be delayed. She has replied. She says that they are having a glorious time; that Paul is more enthusiastic than ever over the possibilities of his hand; that they will wait for us."

"Boss, why don't you go to them now? I can come later."

"No, thank you. I wait for you. I'm not taking any chances."

"Then why can't we go now? The doctor does not want me to walk yet, but Barlow would go with us, and I would go in a wheel chair; it would save a lot of time and I'm sure it wouldn't hurt me a bit."

"The doctor is coming to-morrow; I'll talk to him."

The next morning Freckles called Barlow and McLean to him.

"Barlow, you've been a great friend to me. I'd like to show my appreciation and gratitude. What are your plans for the future?"

"To stay with you as long as you want me."

"That's great, but I can't be as selfish as that. I want you to be independent and live your own life. Do you think you'd like America?"

"I think I'd like my own country best, sir. I've been thinking about the things you say this country needs. I've worked all my life, and I've saved a tidy sum; I'd like to buy a farm and develop it along the lines you suggest. I would make a model of it for other farmers to come and see. I'd have a well, and a windmill, and modern machinery. Advice would be free, and if I made it pay, I'd like to loan money at small interest to other farmers to help them get a start."

"That's a great idea. I'd like nothing better than to contribute a substantial sum toward seed and machinery."

Lord O'More had entered and was listening. He spoke before Barlow could reply.

"F—Freckles, you were right about me. I am going to try to be less selfish. I need something to interest me, and to take up my time. I will take my money and I will interest my wealthy friends. I think we had better see about building some dams and conserving water power for electricity. Also, we need to create a market for produce."

"That's it, Uncle Maxwell! I knew there was good stuff in you if we ever found a way to break through the crust and pry it out! There are a thousand things to be done: all you have to do is take your choice."

Barlow's eyes shone. He was really showing some emotion.

"I love this country, Lord O'More. All these things, they would be wonderful!"

"I am just coming to a realizing sense of what a great country this would be if it were properly developed and exploited. It's a beautiful country for tourists, but the roads are in bad condition. Strange, I never saw it before this."

"The important thing is that you see it now. Your idea of improving roads is a dandy. People won't fall for scenery, no matter how gorgeous, if they have to have a chiropractic treatment while they are trying to enjoy themselves. Tourists these days are spoiled; they are accustomed to every luxury. They will not go places where there is no convenience or comfort."

As they talked, their enthusiasm grew. Ideas and suggestions came so fast they tumbled over each other. Aunt Ellen, hearing their eager voices, went to see what it was all about.

"My, my, if there was not so much difference between the masculine and feminine voice, I would say you sounded like a group of ladies chatting over their tea."

The men laughed, but as she listened Aunt Ellen added her suggestions, for she had long been distressed by the condition of the farms and the farmers' families.

"Don't forget the wives and children, my dears. The houses need conveniences; and there must be schools for the children. There are so many such darling laughing-eyed babies," and Aunt Ellen's eyes grew misty.

"Aunt Ellen, there is plenty of work for you among the women: just get busy. I think there are a few of your friends who would eat up work like that. I know you would," and Freckles winked at Uncle Maxwell.

"Yes, my dear, go as far as you like among the wives and babies; we will gladly leave that to you."

Uncle Maxwell chuckled.

"You'll be surprised at how far she'll go, too, Uncle Maxwell."

Aunt Ellen gave him a grateful smile and withdrew. She was thinking seriously; she had plans of her own to make.

The doctor heard the voices. First, he thought it was a quarrel, but when he realized the voices were friendly, he smiled.

"Good-morning, gentlemen! Such an animated conference—it does one's heart good! Do tell me what it is all about."

Freckles could not wait to ask about leaving for Berlin. After he had explained everything, the doctor spoke.

"All you have needed to get well has been the proper impetus. Now that you have acquired it, you should recover rapidly. I should say you might undertake the trip in three days with perfect safety. Just go slowly, and do not tire yourself."

"I will see to that, sir," Barlow promised. "I am going with you to Berlin, and I will stay until you sail for America. Then I come back to Ireland and work with Lord O'More."

The specified three days were extremely full. McLean spent hours driving in his car with Lady O'More, suggesting to her ways in which she might be of the most help to wives and mothers. It was something of a proposition for a bachelor, but he did know something of the work done in America by women and women's clubs.

Lord O'More's interest knew no bounds, as he began thinking of others for the first time in his life; and as his interest grew, his disposition improved. He actually became kind and thoughtful of others: one heard Lady O'More laugh.

It was a queer little party that started happily for Berlin. The red-haired Irish lad in the invalid chair; the brawny, grizzled Scotsman, who seemed to be general manager; the devoted, British Barlow, struggling to prevent Rags, tugging at his leash, from knocking over some innocent bystander, or throwing a wobbly baby off its balance with his ever-whirling tail. There had been some discussion about bringing Rags, but Freckles had settled it quickly.

"Wherever I go, Rags goes," he had said, and the argument had ended there.

Lord and Lady O'More were sad on their way home from the station; but they had a real interest in life at last; something for which to work; something that would bring peace and happiness into the evening of life. Lord O'More reached for Lady O'More's hand: Ellen took it, and smiled into Maxwell's eyes.

Autumn had crept into the heart of the Limberlost. The air was cooler; the delicate spring flowers were gone, and the pale green of early foliage was replaced by the deep, rich red, bronze, and gold of fall leaves. Now one saw the bright yellow of goldenrod; the dark cerise of ironwort; the intense orange of butterfly flower; the strong rose of joe-pye weed; and the blues of wild asters and chicory. In the fields the grain was cut; great yellow pumpkins dotted the ground between the shocks of corn, and at twilight the fireflies lighted their tiny lanterns over the golden sheaves of wheat and oats. The air was heavy with the perfume of drying clover hay and alfalfa. Many of the smaller birds had gone south for the winter, so that their dainty songs were replaced by the harsh calls of greedy blackbirds and ravens as they salvaged what grain and corn they could from the stubble. The air was filled with the chattering of squirrels as they busily carried nuts and grain into winter quarters in hollow trees.

For the Angel, the summer was more or less of a nightmare. It was very hot through July and August; a scorching sun beat down with little cessation; shallow-rooted vegetation was literally cooked. The Angel grew pale and listless, but she steadfastly refused to go north with her mother, as Mr. Kingsley wanted them to do. There was much activity in the little town. Burned buildings were being replaced as rapidly as possible, and Mr. Kingsley was constantly overseeing and advising. The Angel decided her place was beside her parents; besides, she was waiting . . . For just what she was waiting, she did not know. She had received McLean's letter; it was the brief, brusque letter of a business man, yet whenever the blue fog became too thick for the Angel, she read it, and from it derived some measure of solace.

Dear Girl:

I am with Freckles, at the O'More home in Ireland. The boy has been terribly ill, and recuperation has been slow, due to his mental condition. He is fighting with himself, trying to get back his equilibrium; trying to decide what is best for him: all the time filled with remorse because of his insane letter to you.

Lord O'More has passed out of the picture so far as Freckles is concerned; the reason I will explain later.

Personally, I am fine. The trip has done wonders for me; and I have a big surprise for you. Just now I am merely "standing by," to see that Freckles is allowed to follow his own inclinations, freely and fully, whenever he decides just what they are.

Meantime, my dear, be patient with us—we are just a couple of blundering males; but we mean well, and we will be coming along to you one of these days. You know Freckles' character, its depth and its weakness; and I am sure you understand.

I can assure you, our hearts are in the right place, and that place is with you, your father and mother, and the Limberlost.

Ever faithfully and affectionately,
JAMES R. MCLEAN.

Everyone was kind to the Angel, and her parents were especially considerate. She tried to join in the sports and gaiety of her crowd, but it was difficult. Someway, the summer passed.

It was dusk on an evening in mid-October. The Angel had gotten through one of her difficult days—one of those days when everything goes wrong. She took her banjo and went to the Limberlost. Freckles' room was in perfect shape. She had kept the vines trimmed, the fallen leaves cleared away, and the mosses watered, so that they did not die during the prolonged dry spell. There had been refreshing fall rains: now it was cool and restful, the autumn flowers were in their glory, the vines and shrubs were washed clean of dust, the mosses were green, and brown and gold leaves were fluttering over the old Swamp like myriads of Yellow Emperor moths.

She was sitting in Freckles' room, playing and singing

their little Irish melody, her eyes droopy and dreamy, when from somewhere—surely she could not be wrong—from somewhere behind her—Freckles' voice joined her in the chorus! Stupefied, she looked. Sure enough—there he was—taller, broader, and older, but the same Freckles, with the laughing eyes and bright, rebellious hair! Freckles came toward her and held out his arms—*both* arms—and without a word she rushed into them. Then an age-old scene followed, but one ever new to lovers who have been parted for a long time. When they recovered from their state of breathless ecstasy, Freckles explained everything, satisfactorily, of course, the while he put a gorgeous ruby ring on her finger—"Red, just like the heart of you, Angel."

"I've a surprise for you, dear heart. Mr. McLean is married to a lovely woman he met on the boat. They are at your home now, waiting for us. When we arrived, and you were not there, I *knew* you were here."

"Why didn't you let us know you were coming? *Nothing* could have kept me from the train."

"Someway, I couldn't bear the thought of seeing you first in a railroad station. This is perfect—just as I would have had it."

"How did you get here?"

"Your mother drove me. When we saw your car, she let me out and went back."

"I'm unspeakably happy for McLean."

"He says I am to manage his business. Meanwhile, I'm to go to Chicago for music lessons every week, and then——"

"— and then?"

"And then, you and I are to go abroad on our honeymoon, and we are to stay a year, and I am to study music some more"—and they passed into oblivion again.

"Angel, you've never said a word about my new hand. I have two, one wood and one hard rubber, jointed different ways, and gloves of all colours," and he told her about Paul, who had left them and gone to his own mother.

"It's great if you're pleased, dear, but, personally, your hand was never the slightest concern: I never even thought about it."

Again she was almost smothered in kisses.

"But we should go, darling, it isn't fair to the others. And besides, there is another member of our family whom you have not met. I want you to like him *very* much."

Freckles laughed at her disconcerted expression.

"Don't worry, sweet, it's only Rags—best and ugliest dog in the world!"

So they strolled along the little path leading out of the shades and shadows of the Limberlost, to the open road of life stretching before them, lighted by the golden glow of an enormous harvest moon.

THE END